BENEATH THE MOCKINGBIRD'S WINGS

★★★

BOOKS BY GILBERT MORRIS

Through a Glass Darkly

THE HOUSE OF WINSLOW SERIES

1. *The Honorable Imposter*
2. *The Captive Bride*
3. *The Indentured Heart*
4. *The Gentle Rebel*
5. *The Saintly Buccaneer*
6. *The Holy Warrior*
7. *The Reluctant Bridegroom*
8. *The Last Confederate*
9. *The Dixie Widow*
10. *The Wounded Yankee*
11. *The Union Belle*
12. *The Final Adversary*
13. *The Crossed Sabres*
14. *The Valiant Gunman*
15. *The Gallant Outlaw*
16. *The Jeweled Spur*
17. *The Yukon Queen*
18. *The Rough Rider*
19. *The Iron Lady*
20. *The Silver Star*
21. *The Shadow Portrait*
22. *The White Hunter*
23. *The Flying Cavalier*

THE LIBERTY BELL

1. *Sound the Trumpet*
2. *Song in a Strange Land*
3. *Tread Upon the Lion*
4. *Arrow of the Almighty*
5. *Wind From the Wilderness*
6. *The Right Hand of God*
7. *Command the Sun*

CHENEY DUVALL, M.D.
(with Lynn Morris)

1. *The Stars for a Light*
2. *Shadow of the Mountains*
3. *A City Not Forsaken*
4. *Toward the Sunrising*
5. *Secret Place of Thunder*
6. *In the Twilight, in the Evening*
7. *Island of the Innocent*
8. *Driven With the Wind*

THE SPIRIT OF APPALACHIA
(with Aaron McCarver)

1. *Over the Misty Mountains*
2. *Beyond the Quiet Hills*
3. *Among the King's Soldiers*
4. *Beneath the Mockingbird's Wings*

TIME NAVIGATORS
(for Young Teens)

1. *Dangerous Voyage*
2. *Vanishing Clues*
3. *Race Against Time*

00A

BENEATH THE MOCKINGBIRD'S WINGS

★★★

GILBERT MORRIS &
AARON McCARVER

BETHANY HOUSE PUBLISHERS
MINNEAPOLIS, MINNESOTA 55438

Cover by Dan Thornberg

Published by Bethany House Publishers
A Ministry of Bethany Fellowship International
11400 Hampshire Avenue South
Minneapolis, Minnesota 55438
www.bethanyhouse.com

Printed in the United States of America by
Bethany Press International, Minneapolis, Minnesota 55438

Library of Congress Cataloging-in-Publication Data

Beneath the mockingbird's wings / by Gilbert Morris & Aaron McCarver.
p. cm. — (The spirit of Appalachia ; 4)
ISBN 1-55661-888-3
1. Frontier and pioneer life—Appalachian Region—Fiction. 2. Indians of North America—Appalachian Region—Fiction. 3. Appalachian Region—History—Fiction. 4. Cherokee Indians—Fiction. I. McCarver, Aaron. II. Title.
PS3563.O8742 B46 2000
813'.54—dc21 99-050633
CIP

1/02
Gift

Dedication

This book is dedicated to my two brothers-in-law,
Danny Bradford and Kenny Slatton.

Danny, I have never heard you say a word in anger to my sister or to your children. You may not always say a lot, but your actions speak volumes to all around you.

Kenny, you brought love back to my sister's life after circumstances seemed to take it away. I can only pray I am able to do the same for anyone God brings across my path.

You are both so special to me. Thank you for making sure that my nieces and nephews are being raised in Christian homes. Thank you for taking care of my sisters and becoming a part of our family. But mostly, thank you for accepting me, not just as a brother-in-law, but as a true brother!

GILBERT MORRIS spent ten years as a pastor before becoming Professor of English at Ouachita Baptist University of Arkansas. During the summers of 1984 and 1985, he did postgraduate work at the University of London. A prolific writer, he has had over twenty-five scholarly articles and two hundred poems published in various periodicals, and he and his wife live on the Gulf Coast of Alabama.

AARON McCARVER is the Dean of Students at Wesley College in Florence, Mississippi, where he also teaches drama and Christian literature. His deep interest in Christian fiction and broad knowledge of the CBA market have given him the background for editorial consultation with all the "writing Morrises" as well as other novelists. It was through his editorial relationship with Gilbert that this book series came to life.

Contents

PART IV: A Home With Christ

Character List

Now that freedom has been won, the Watauga settlers labor to make their homes a part of the new nation. As new settlers pour into the rich land to stake out their own homesteads, the Cherokee fight to hold on to their way of life. While Hawk and Elizabeth Spencer find themselves torn between their Cherokee friends and those who work to make their settlement into the state of Franklin, they must also help the next generation find their place over the Misty Mountains.

Hannah Spencer—The youngest daughter of Hawk and Elizabeth finds her heart torn between two young men. When one seems to lose his way, she must rely on her faith in God to show him the way home.

Nathanael "Fox" Carter—After losing his father and fleeing in fear from the only home he has ever known, he must travel over the mountains with his mother to rejoin her family. Here he finds himself torn between two heritages, not seeming to belong to either. As loneliness and anger push him toward a violent future, his only hope lies in the faith of a young heart.

Ethan Cagle—Love seems sure to be his until a young man of mixed heritage arrives in Franklin. Only a secret love can stop him from following jealousy down a dangerous path.

Eve Martin—Her quiet spirit and shy nature hide a sensitive and loving heart. In order to help the one she loves, she must put aside her own dreams and risk losing him forever.

Awinita—She must return to the land of her people to save her son, but a dangerous love from her past could destroy them both.

Sequatchie—He must summon every ounce of his faith to help his nephew find his way. But all he holds dear is threatened when an old enemy returns seeking vengeance.

Akando—Hatred and bitterness have always been his tools in trying to drive the white man back over the mountains. When a past love spurns him again, he sets in motion actions that could ignite the flames of war.

Naaman Carter—He wants what rightfully belongs to his nephew. And greed and jealousy will lead him into getting what he wants, no matter the cost.

Beneath the Mockingbird's Wings

James Spencer
b. February 10, 1710
d. August 7, 1782

m. July 6, 1732

Esther Whitman
b. April 29, 1712

— **Jehoshaphat "Hawk" Spencer**
b. May 24, 1735

Faith Hancock
b. August 4, 1735
d. November 25, 1755

m. June 12, 1753

Jehoshaphat "Hawk" Spencer

— **Jacob Spencer**
b. November 25, 1755

Amanda Taylor
b. October 12, 1758

m. June 14, 1778

Jacob Spencer

Jehoshaphat "Hawk" Spencer

m. November 3, 1771

Elizabeth Martin

— **Hannah Spencer**
b. August 6, 1772

— **Joshua Spencer**
b. January 27, 1774

William Martin, Sr.
b. July 28, 1707
d. July 28, 1777

m. May 4, 1735

Anne Hardwick
b. October 11, 1715

— **Elizabeth Martin**
b. February 18, 1737

— **William Martin, Jr.**
b. December 2, 1745

Elizabeth Martin

m. March 4, 1756

Patrick MacNeal
b. September 9, 1736
d. September 17, 1770

— **Andrew MacNeal**
b. March 15, 1757

m. July 4, 1777

Abigail Stevens
b. June 17, 1757

— **Sarah MacNeal**
b. April 28, 1760

m. November 14, 1780

Seth Donovan
b. June 1, 1756

William Martin, Jr.

m. August 1, 1771

Rebekah Edwards
b. February 28, 1750

— **Eve Martin**
b. April 16, 1773

— **David Martin**
b. July 1, 1774

Prologue

Late October 1781

Moving around the table and replenishing the food as it was consumed, Hulda was conscious, as always, of the antagonism that existed at the dining table of Havenwood Plantation. Meals were not pleasant occasions, for the most part, and as Hulda set a plate of ham down in front of Noah Carter, she scanned his face guardedly. *Mr. Carter, he looks old. . . .* She knew for a fact that he was sixty-nine and was not in good health. A wave of sadness swept over Hulda as she studied his lined face. He had been a good master to her, as he had been to all his slaves. Now as he sat at the table, still tall but stooped with age, she had a sad premonition that he would not be long on this earth. She stepped over beside Naomi Carter, Noah's wife, and knew that the mistress of Havenwood was also well aware that her husband's place at the end of the table would soon be empty.

Hulda lifted her eyes, and her lips drew tight as she looked across the table at Naaman Carter and his wife, Julia Mayhew Carter. Naaman, at the age of forty-one, was the younger of Noah and Naomi's two sons. Naaman and Julia were the parents of Linus and Lydia, and of the four, Hulda had warm affections only for Lydia. The old servant woman had worried about Naaman, even when he was a small boy. He had been greatly spoiled by his mother and had grown up into a selfish man. He was fine looking, slim and nearly six feet tall with auburn hair and green eyes, but his good looks meant nothing to the slaves who had often tasted his harshness with the whip. His wife, Julia, had come from a wealthy family and, like her husband, cared only for her own comfort. Their son Linus was much like them, and only in Lydia did Hulda see traces of the goodness of the older Carters.

Hulda moved along filling the tea glasses and listening as the conversation went around the table. The Carters were her family, and she was jealous of anyone who threatened them.

"Where are the children?" Naomi spoke of her three grandchildren, Nathanael, Linus, and Lydia.

"They ate earlier. They are outside playing now," Julia answered her mother-in-law's query.

"Well, I'm glad the war seems to be finally over," Noah said. His faded eyes grew bright for a moment, and he said, "It has been a long, hard struggle for freedom."

Naaman glanced at his father and shook his head with a stubborn motion. "It's only a matter of time until this new government collapses, Father."

"That's true," Julia said quickly. "You'll see the day that the Colonies will *beg* England to take them back under her banner."

It was Naomi, not Noah, who answered these comments. She was always defensive of her husband and regretted that Naaman and his wife were so strongly opposed to the Revolution. She and Noah had both been proud of their older son, Titus, who had enlisted at the beginning of the struggle for freedom from the British crown. They had also come to approve of Titus's marriage to a full-blooded Cherokee woman, Awinita, and both of them loved their grandson Nathanael, perhaps more than they loved their other grandchildren.

"This is going to be a free country!" Naomi said sternly. "We're not going to be under the heels of the British anymore."

Awinita, who was sitting next to her mother-in-law, smiled and put her hand on the older woman's arm. "And Titus will be coming home soon." She was a proud woman with a striking appearance. Her complexion was much fairer than most other Cherokee women, and her features were finely and beautifully formed. Her eyes were soft, a golden brown, and her hair a glossy ebony.

"Yes, daughter, I'm looking forward to that day," Noah said heartily.

Hulda, replenishing the tea in Awinita's glass, caught a glimpse of Naaman's and Julia's faces. *They won't be glad—not them two! They's for that ol' king and always was!*

An awkward silence fell over the table, and a tall black man appeared at the dining room door, saying, "They's a gentleman to see you, Mr. Noah."

"A gentleman! Who is it, Holder?"

"I don't know, sah. He be a soldier."

"Maybe it's news about Titus," Awinita sighed.

"Show him in at once," Noah said, and every eye turned to the door.

The soldier who entered was a slight man of some fifty years. He stopped abruptly, glancing nervously around the table. "My name is Lieutenant Johnston," he said. "I'm looking for Mr. Noah Carter."

"I'm Noah Carter. What can I do for you, Lieutenant Johnston?"

The soldier licked his lips nervously. "I-I'd rather have a meeting with you in private."

Instantly everyone in the room knew something was wrong. Hulda looked around the table and saw fear in the faces of Titus's parents.

"What does it concern, Lieutenant?" Naomi Carter asked quietly.

Lieutenant Johnston hesitated. "I . . . I have very bad news," he said.

Awinita said quietly, "Is it about my husband, Titus Carter?"

Lieutenant Johnston turned to face her. He hesitated again, then shrugged his shoulders. "I'm sorry to be the bearer of such terrible news, but I must tell you, Mrs. Carter . . . that your husband was killed at Yorktown—just before the British surrendered."

A single cry escaped Naomi's lips, and she reached out and took her husband's hand. Noah stared at the officer, devastated. Not only was his son dead, but he had planned on having Titus take over the plantation—and now that could not be.

"Come in and tell us all you can, Lieutenant," Noah said.

Lieutenant Johnston hated this duty but knew that it must be done. He took a seat and awkwardly related what he knew about the death of the man who had filled the lives of these people. When he was through, he took his leave awkwardly, making his apologies. As he left the room, he turned once quickly, saying, "I'm very sorry," then left without another word.

Noah had scarcely moved during the officer's recitation, and now he said, "Hulda, the children are playing outside. Go bring Nathanael in. Don't tell him about any of this."

"Yes, sah," Hulda said and left the room.

"Julia, you come with me," Naaman said quickly. "Send the children upstairs. We'll tell them the news." Turning to his parents, he said, "I know you'll want to talk to Nathanael alone."

"I think that . . . that would be best, Naaman," Naomi said as the tears coursed down her cheeks.

As Naaman and Julia left the room, Julia whispered, "Why did you want to get away, Naaman?"

"I won't stay and pretend to mourn a brother I hate. You hate him, too."

"But you can't say things like that!" Julia protested. "We'll show the proper amount of mourning, but this place will be ours now, Naaman."

"No, it won't."

"But you're Noah's only living son!"

"You're forgetting the settlement."

Julia's hope to inherit Havenwood quickly faded, and now a scowl replaced her smile. "But things are—well, they're different now!"

The settlement Naaman referred to had taken place a few years earlier. Naaman hated the life of a planter. He longed to move to Williamsburg and go into business. He had finally persuaded his father to split the estate, give the land and the house to Titus and the equivalent value in cash to him. Noah had opposed it but in the end had given in.

However, Naaman's business ventures had not worked out well for him. He had speculated in risky enterprises, and most of the money he'd received was now gone. The humiliation of those losses had caused anger and bitterness to grow in Naaman and his wife, and now they both felt they *deserved* a share of Havenwood. This envy had festered in them, and they had developed a vitriolic hatred for Titus—and for his Cherokee wife and son.

Julia's eyes narrowed. "Can't we do *something*?"

"I've got a plan," Naaman said. "If it works, we'll send that Indian woman and her son back to where they belong—if they don't meet some tragedy before then."

Julia cast a quick glance at her husband's face. She had no idea what he was talking about, but she did know that he hated his brother and his sister-in-law and his nephew with every fiber of his being. She herself did not feel so strongly, but the idea of being in control of Havenwood pleased her immensely. "We'll have to show proper respect," she whispered.

"For a while," Naaman said grimly, and the two went up the stairs.

"Look! There's something at the edge of the woods!" said Nathanael Carter, a lean boy of eleven with a coppery complexion. He turned to his two cousins, his eyes gleaming. "I think it's a fox!" His coal black hair caught the light of the late October sun, and his deep-set brown eyes twinkled with pleasure.

"I don't see anything, Nate," said Linus, a short, stocky boy the same age as Nathanael.

"Neither do I. You're always seeing things," six-year-old Lydia said.

The three cousins were so different that it was often impossible for them to spend time together, but on Havenwood Plantation there were no other children for them to play with, so they were forced into one another's company.

"Come on. I'm going to see what it is." Nathanael sprinted for the woods that bordered Havenwood on the west. It was a favorite place for the young boy.

"Come on, Linus!" Lydia cried. She started after her cousin, and Linus followed reluctantly. By the time the two reached the edge of the woods, Nathanael was standing very still looking down at what was lying in a tuft of field grass.

"What is it, Nate?" Lydia cried.

Nathanael did not move his head. "Look," he said simply and pointed.

Lydia moved in closer and then her eyes flew open. "Why, it's a baby fox!"

"Yes. And he's hurt."

"What's wrong with him?" Linus asked, crowding in to stare at the small animal.

"I don't know." Nathanael bent closer and studied the sharp-featured face of the tiny animal. He himself had been named Fox by his Cherokee mother, Awinita. The first time she had held her newborn son, she had seen something in the infant's face that reminded her of an alert young fox. Now leaning forward, Nathanael murmured, "He's too young to be out by himself. I wonder where his mother is."

Lydia, who loved small animals, said in a worried tone, "Do you think he'll live?"

"Don't know. Young animals and birds don't usually make it."

Linus Carter, who usually took the opposite opinion of his cousin Nathanael, said abruptly, "Let's kill it!"

"Kill it!" Nathanael whirled around, his eyes glowing with anger. "What do you mean *kill it*?"

Linus puffed his lips out, glad at having made his cousin angry. He was often bested by Nathanael at physical games, for he himself was overweight and not good at such things. "I say let's kill it. It'll only grow up to be a killer. That's all foxes do—kill things." He laughed suddenly and pointed at his cousin. "He's a savage—just like everything named Fox."

The bronzed features of Nathanael seemed to grow even darker. A flush came up into his cheeks, and he stepped forward, crying out, "You take that back, Linus!"

"Won't!"

"You better or I'll bash you!"

"You better not! Grandfather Noah will cane you for it!"

"You take back what you said about me! I'm not a savage!"

Lydia cried out, "Take it back, Linus! You didn't mean it."

"I did, too! He's just a savage. That's all Indians are—savages!"

Without another word Nathanael threw himself forward and bowled Linus over in the dust at the edge of the field. Linus yelled and screamed, but Nathanael maintained a silence as he pummeled his cousin.

Lydia began to cry and ran over to pull at them helplessly. "Stop it!" she said. "You know you're not supposed to fight!"

Her words had no effect on Nathanael. Indeed, he was acting more like a wolf than a fox as he mauled his cousin. Only vaguely did he hear an adult voice calling him, and not until a hand seized his arm and jerked him off did he stop hitting Linus. The anger that had rushed through him was one he rarely felt, but being called a savage and having his Cherokee ancestry made fun of had infuriated him. He knew some sort of punishment would be forthcoming, but he did not care. He turned to face the black woman Hulda, the house servant, who was holding his arm.

Nathanael stepped back from Linus, who was sprawled on the ground, and looked up at Hulda.

"What you two fighting about?" she demanded to know.

"Nothing," the boy said.

Hulda knew that hot pinchers would not pull it out of him, and a great sorrow filled her heart as she said, "Come inside now. Your grandpa and your grandma, they wanna see you."

"I'm going to tell Grandpa what he did. He's nothin' but a savage!" Linus cried as he got up.

"You hush your mouth, Linus, and don't say nothin'. You and Lydia go on up to your parents' room. They wanna talk to you, too."

All three children were mystified. Nathanael assumed it was something to do with the fight—that they had been seen from the window. And he knew he was probably in for a good caning, but he said nothing. As they crossed the field, he saw a uniformed man riding away, and for a moment Nathanael thought, *It's my father!* But he saw at once that it was not.

As they walked toward the house, Nathanael kept glancing at Hulda's face, which was filled with sadness. She was usually a cheerful woman, and he could not understand why she looked as though she could burst into tears.

When Nathanael entered the house, he went straightaway to the parlor, where his grandparents were waiting for him. As soon as he stepped inside, he could tell that something was terribly wrong.

"It was just a little scuffle, Grandfather," he said quickly. "I didn't really hurt Linus."

"It's not about that," Noah said slowly. "Come here, Nathanael."

Nathanael felt a shiver run up his spine, and as he went up to stand before his grandparents, he saw his mother sitting in a chair beside them.

Tears were running down her face. He had never seen his mother cry, and suddenly a great fear seized him. He ran to her at once, saying, "What is it, Mother? What's wrong?"

Awinita stood up. She reached out and hugged her son fiercely and whispered, "It's your father."

A chilling fear gripped Nathanael. "Is he dead?" he whispered, his face pressed against her bosom.

"Yes."

Nathanael clung to his mother as she whispered, "You must remember that your father loved us both dearly, you and me. And you remember also that he is with his Savior now. Never forget why he died—to make this land free for you, for me, and for others."

Nathanael clung to his mother for a moment, then finally drew back and said, "What will happen to us, Mother?"

"Havenwood will be our home. It's your legacy."

"It won't be a home without Father. . . ." Nathanael whispered.

PART I

A Home Lost

February 1784 – May 1784

"They wandered in the wilderness in a solitary way; they found no city to dwell in."

Psalm 107:4

Home at Havenwood

One

A light snow crusted the frozen earth, and the acrid smell of woodsmoke hung in the air as Fox stood stone-still behind a clump of elderberry bushes. He had remained in this position for half an hour, the only motion the involuntary blinking of his eyes and the slow, methodical rise and fall of his chest. He had grown taller and more sinewy than most boys of fourteen. In fact, he looked several years older than his actual age.

Overhead a red-tailed hawk lazily circled in the leaden gray sky, but Fox did not even lift his eyes. Twenty yards away a ten-point buck, as motionless as Fox himself, was standing in a grove of hickory trees. Fox knew he had not been seen. As he silently watched the large buck, he realized the deer would not have lived this long without being wary and cautious. The rifle in Fox's hands had grown heavy, but still he did not move. He had cocked the weapon earlier so as not to startle the deer by the clicking sound of the mechanism.

As Fox waited, his thoughts turned to the past two and a half years and how difficult they had been for him. Since the death of his father, his grandfather Noah's health had declined rapidly, and Fox had been thrown into the day-to-day work of the plantation. He had learned so quickly that Ezekiel, one of the hands, had admitted proudly to Noah, "That grandson of yours, he works like a grown man. And he's smart, too!" Ezekiel was not usually so free with his praises, so Fox had treasured his remarks when Noah had repeated them to him.

Suddenly the deer stepped out of the mottled shadows and slowly advanced to the small creek. He sniffed the air cautiously, then lowered his head to drink. Fox carefully raised the rifle until the bead was just behind the left leg, high on the buck's body. His finger tightened on the trigger, but then he hesitated. He had killed deer before, but now the strength of the large animal struck him, and he remembered the verse of Scripture he had read in his Bible the night before. *As the hart panteth after the water brooks, so panteth my soul after thee, O God.* The verse had made an impact on him, and without knowing why, he was unable to pull the trigger.

Suddenly Fox leaped forward and shouted at the top of his lungs. He delighted as the buck's head shot upward, and then the powerful body wheeled, bounding away with surefooted leaps until he cleared the creek. Something about the flight of the deer pleased Fox intensely. The deer seemed almost to fly on some of those long leaps. Fox watched as the buck disappeared into the thick woods, then sighed and shook his head. "I must be losing my mind. I could have gotten him easily."

Fox shrugged his shoulders and turned homeward, wondering to himself why he had not been able to pull the trigger. He had no trouble at all shooting squirrels or rabbits, but somehow the deer was symbolic of something too beautiful to kill. He was not so sentimental that he would refuse to eat venison, for he loved it, but the sight of that buck standing in the light of the February sun had touched him, and he knew that he and the deer shared a common bond.

As he made his way back toward the big house, he looked out across the large fields. He knew every foot of them intimately now, and already in his mind, he was laying out the spring planting. All of his life he had watched the overseer and the slaves work the land. He had learned quickly, and the cycle of the seasons was now second nature to him. His cousin Linus had no interest at all in learning how to run the plantation. He would simply say, "That's the overseer's problem."

Now as Fox approached the slave quarters, which were separated from the big house by a line of poplar trees, he felt a moment's disquiet as he thought of how he and Linus did not get along. Fox had tried his utmost to make friends with Linus, but he knew the boy's mind had been influenced by his parents. And Uncle Naaman and Aunt Julia despised Fox just as much as they had despised his father. They made little effort to conceal their hatred and their desire to see Fox and his mother leave Havenwood and return to their people so that Naaman and Julia could run the plantation as they saw fit.

As for Fox himself, he had no selfishness and could not understand why they could not all live together and share life at Havenwood. He and his mother were close to each other, as they were to his grandparents, but they had few friends among the white planters in the surrounding area. They much preferred the slaves who worked the land, which gave his uncle Naaman and his aunt Julia another reason to despise him.

As Fox descended the slight hill that led down to the slave quarters, his quick ears picked up the sound of an angry voice. He looked up, then hastened his pace. When he arrived at the line of whitewashed single-room slave cabins, the scene he saw made him bristle with anger. A large man was hulking menacingly over a prostrate slave. Fox shouted, "Stop that, Jasper!"

Jasper Tatum, a slovenly, unkempt man of forty-five, whirled to face Fox. He was short, no taller than Fox himself, strongly built, thick through the body with hamlike legs and a bulging stomach that strained against his belt. "You stay out of this, Nate!" he snarled. "It ain't none of your put-in!"

Fox looked down at the man on the ground, a fine-looking slave named Ezekiel. He had ugly red welts raised up on his ebony skin. Several of them had already started to ooze blood, and Fox's temper flared at the sight of the cruelty Tatum was known for all too well. He stepped between the two and said, "You know you're not supposed to whip any of the slaves!"

"Get out of my way, Nate!"

"You're not whipping him anymore." Fox stared at the man, whose little piggish eyes stared back at him as he added, "If you want me to report this to my grandfather, I will. We'll see how long you stay on as his overseer!"

Jasper Tatum longed to reach out and grab the boy and beat him to a pulp. It was not the first time the youth had interfered with his running of the plantation, and he hated Nathanael Carter with a passion. He often cursed the boy in the presence of others but never in front of Noah or his wife. He had quickly learned that Naaman and Julia Carter despised the boy and his Cherokee mother, but he also knew that Noah adamantly opposed the beating of slaves. Jasper had been warned by the old man at their last meeting—one more infraction and he would be dismissed.

For one moment Fox thought that the burly overseer would strike him, and he stood with his feet balanced ready to dodge a blow. He felt no fear as he slowly lifted the rifle across his body and drew the hammer back. He said nothing, but the clicking of the rifle made a sharp sound in the air. Ezekiel turned, his eyes large, and stared at the pair.

Tatum swallowed hard, then stepped back. "We'll see about this later," he muttered.

"We're seeing about it right now!" Fox said. "Get out of here and go on about your business!"

Tatum glared at the young boy and said between clenched teeth, "It's gonna be different when your grandpa dies."

"Go on! Get away from us!" Fox said. He watched as the overseer whirled and stalked away, cursing under his breath. Then Fox turned to face Ezekiel, who had gotten up.

"What was that all about, Ezekiel?"

Ezekiel was a tall, brawny man of thirty. He was one of the best workers on the plantation, smart, strong, and good-natured. But now he stood speechless. A line as tall and as strong as the walls of Jericho stood between white and black, but somehow Ezekiel felt a kinship with the young boy who now preferred to be called Fox. Perhaps it was because of his coppery skin. True enough he was half white, but the differences of race meant little to Fox. He had mingled with the slaves, eaten with them, slept in their cabins, and hunted with Ezekiel and others. As fearful and as apprehensive as the slaves were of white people, they had come to accept him.

Lowering his voice, Ezekiel said, "He was after Mercy."

Fox knew that Tatum abused the black women on the plantation, and his despicable behavior had brought him a strong rebuke from Noah. But the old man could not keep up with everything. Fox had seen Tatum's eyes following Mercy, Ezekiel's wife, and now he could only say, "I'm sorry, Ezekiel. I'll tell my grandfather. He'll speak to Tatum."

"Yes, Mr. Fox. That would be mighty thoughtful of you."

"You'd better have Mercy take a look at your back. And take the rest of the day off and rest up."

Ezekiel suddenly grinned. "Yes, sah, I'll do jist that!"

Fox turned and left the slave quarters and did not hear when Ezekiel said to Mercy, who had come up to touch his arm possessively, "That's one fine young man. Too bad he's got to put up with that Mr. Naaman. And his son, Linus, is gonna be jist like his father."

"They hates him, don't they? And his mama, too."

"Yes, they do, but he's gonna be the owner one day, and things will be different then. You jist wait and see."

Awinita sat in her room at the window looking out over the frozen ground and brushing her long, lustrous black hair. It fell down well below her waist and was a great deal of work, but she always remembered how much Titus had loved it, so she had vowed never to cut it. She still thought often of Titus and missed him so greatly that the pain in her heart felt like a twisting knife. Life had been good when they had married and then when Fox had been born. But now that Titus was gone, an empty sadness filled Awinita's heart, and nothing could assuage the grief she felt. Only the thought of Fox and his future gave her any joy at all. At the same time, she was aware that Fox's position at Havenwood was precarious. The planters were a closed society, and they had never accepted her into it, even though they were polite for Noah and Naomi's sakes. At times she wished that Fox resembled his fair-skinned father, but as providence would have it, he resembled her much more. As she continued to stroke her hair, a fierce pride for her Cherokee heritage burned in her heart and then a knock at the door turned her around. "Come in," she said.

Fox entered and Awinita immediately saw that he was troubled. "What is it, Fox?" She listened as Fox related the incident with Tatum, and finally she said, "You did the right thing, son."

"Mother, what do you think about owning slaves?"

Awinita did not hesitate. "Your grandfather was raised to think that it was not wrong for one human being to own another, but from all the suffering I have seen, my heart tells me it is wrong."

"Did the Cherokee have slaves?"

"Some of them did, but that didn't make it right, either. The Bible teaches that all men are equal in the sight of God, and the color of their skin doesn't matter."

"It may not matter to God," Fox said abruptly, dissatisfaction showing on his face, "but it matters to others. Uncle Naaman and

Aunt Julia, they hate us because of our Cherokee blood. So does Linus."

"They just don't understand," Awinita said without conviction. She had also felt the hatred from her brother-in-law and his wife and could see it in their son as well.

"I'm going to tell grandfather what Tatum did. And when I run this plantation, I'm going to free all the slaves, and they can work as free men."

Awinita rose, went over, and put her arms around Fox, marveling at how he had filled out, how strong he was. He was tall enough now that she had to look up when she spoke to him. "I'm proud of you, my son, and so would your father have been."

"Do you ever wish you could go back and be with your people across the mountains, Mother?"

Many lonely nights when she sat and silently mourned the loss of Titus, Awinita longed to return to her people, where she felt a sense of belonging. Here at Havenwood she felt cut off, surrounded by a sea of white faces. She was a perceptive woman and could sense the dislike and even hatred that lurked behind the polite demeanors of many of their acquaintances.

"Someday we may go back for a visit."

"I'd like that, Mother."

"And it's good, son, that you want to help the slaves. But stay away from Jasper Tatum as much as you can. We can't afford to antagonize him. Now," she said briskly, "go clean up for dinner."

"Do I have to eat with Linus and Lydia?"

Awinita smiled. "Yes," she said. "You be nice to them, and be nice to their parents, too."

"Linus is always calling me names and picking fights."

Awinita said, "Well, he hasn't been taught the ways of the Lord, as you have. So you turn the other cheek."

"What if he hits me on the other cheek? I've only got two," Fox said. "The third time I can hit him back, can't I?"

Awinita laughed and said, "Remember what your father taught you and try to set a good example." She pulled Fox forward, kissed him on the cheek, then smiled as he stomped out of the room grumbling. "You look like a man going to his own hanging," she called out.

He turned back and smiled, and for that brief moment he looked so much like his father that Awinita could have cried. After he left, she went over and sat down before the window and began to brush her hair again. She was troubled by the incident with Tatum, and an uneasiness chilled her heart as she thought of their future at Havenwood. Her people would see it as a portent of more trouble to come. The future seemed dark, and she wondered what would become of them once Noah and Naomi were gone. She knew of people among her tribe who claimed to read the future, but she did not believe in them. She knew Whom she had to trust, and as she continued to brush her hair, she prayed, "Oh, God, keep me and my son from harm. . . ."

Nathanael's Birthright

Two

The main dining room at Havenwood was a reflection of Noah Carter and his wife, Naomi. The room was efficient and attractive but not overstated, as at some of the other plantations. A large dining table made of oak with a molded top sat in the center of the room on a brown table rug, surrounded by oak chairs with solid backs and yellow woolen moreen upholstery. Lighting came from candles on the small pine chimneypiece, brass candle sconces on the walls, and brass candelabras on the table. There was a sideboard of mahogany behind the master's chair and to one side a single oak serving table.

Noah looked around the room with a sigh, reminiscing about the many happy meals he and his family had shared here in days gone by. His eyes touched on Naomi, and a deep love filled his heart as he thought of what a good wife she had been. He reached over and put his hand upon hers and said, "I've enjoyed every second of our married life, Naomi."

Naomi, caught off guard, suddenly flushed with embarrassment. "Why, Noah, what a thing to say!"

"Well, it's true enough."

"I can remember a few moments that you didn't seem to enjoy too well."

Noah was not feeling well at all. Weak and with no appetite, he had not once come down from his bedroom the previous day, and now as he sat there, he felt a feebleness that he despised. Still he managed to smile and say, "I've got a good forgettery. I love you more than I ever did."

At the end of the table, Awinita suddenly smiled. It did her heart good to see the love that her father-in-law had for his wife after all those years. At the same time it brought sadness as she realized that she would never again hear Titus say kind words like that to her.

Naaman glanced at his parents with a shock. He was not accustomed to hearing his father express his emotions so openly, and he suspected his mother was not, either. *He's getting senile. His mind's bad.*

Julia Carter viewed the scene differently. She studied the face of Naomi, now lined with hard years but still betraying her remarkable strength. *Will I be able to live as long as she has and keep Naaman's love?* she wondered. Deep down she grieved over their relationship, for she knew that Naaman was not capable of this kind of love. She had known so for a long time, even before she married him. Titus had been the one who was like his father. She did not know who Naaman was like. He certainly did not take after either of his parents. Her husband was a hard man. She had sensed this early in their courtship, and now, for one brief moment, regret filled her thoughts. But she spoke up and said, "That's a wonderful thing to say, Noah."

Noah was embarrassed by the attention and changed the subject. "Hulda, these are good biscuits. You always did make the best biscuits in the world."

"They ain't no better than Miz Naomi makes."

"That's right," Noah said, summoning up a grin. "The two of you, the world's champion biscuit makers."

The meal went on for some time, and finally Naomi said, "What was that argument you had with Jasper Tatum this morning? I could hear you shouting at him. You're in no condition to get so upset."

"Something Nate told me," Noah said. He was actually not hungry and toyed with the food on his plate. His chest was painful as he took another sip of his beloved sassafras tea and said, "Nate had to stop him from whipping Ezekiel."

"Why was he doing that? Ezekiel's the best hand we've got!" Naomi exclaimed.

When Noah did not answer, Awinita spoke up. "That Tatum's been after Ezekiel's wife, Mercy."

"You don't know that!" Naaman snapped.

"Yes, I do. All the slaves know it. Nathanael found it out some time ago." She always used Nathanael's proper name in front of his grandparents, although in private she called him Fox. Ever since his father's death, the boy had insisted on calling himself by his Cherokee name.

Naaman threw his napkin down and said angrily, "Ezekiel's just a troublemaker! If I had my way, I'd let Tatum beat him every day until he learned a little respect."

Noah suddenly stared at his younger son—his only son now. It had been exactly this attitude that brought about the division of the inheritance that Noah had planned to leave his sons. Titus was to have the plantation, and Naaman had already received the cash equivalent. It had strapped Noah financially and taken years to pull out of, and it was no secret that Naaman had lost most of the money in poor investments. Now Noah could only say, "I think Nathanael is to be trusted. He knows the slaves better than any of us, including Tatum."

Naaman wanted to argue, but he felt the pressure of his wife's knee against his, so he said nothing.

Lately, Noah was beginning to feel worse all the time. His hand shook as he ran it over his thinning hair, and he muttered, "Tatum's too hard on the slaves."

Naaman could not resist saying, "If you're not hard on them, they'll rebel and burn the place down."

"My conscience won't allow me to treat another human that way."

Naaman Carter felt a touch of bile in his throat. He was consumed by bitterness and couldn't care less about Havenwood were it not for the money it represented. Now he said shortly, "I don't think of slaves as humans!"

Naomi stared at her son in astonishment. "I can't believe I heard you say that, Naaman! You've been raised better!"

Naaman realized he had gone too far. "I'm sorry, Mother. I didn't mean it the way it sounded. I just meant," he explained glibly, "that they're not on the same level as we are."

Noah listened to this and said, "Well, it's probably a good thing that the inheritance was divided as it was. I've been talking with Nathanael—how he'll run the plantation when it's his. The boy plans," he said with a smile, "to free the slaves or let them work out the investment we have in them. Then they'll all be free."

"I think that would be a good thing," Naomi said quickly. "I've never liked this idea of owning another human being."

"It'll never work!" Naaman protested.

Noah suddenly rose in his seat and began to cough violently. Instantly Naomi stood and said, "You need to get to bed, Noah. You're not well."

Noah started to answer but could not for the spasms of coughing.

"Help him get upstairs, Naaman."

"Yes, Mother."

The two of them rose at once and came over to Noah. As they helped him up, Awinita sat very still, overwhelmed by the same sense of foreboding she had felt earlier. She could remember back in her days with the Cherokee when a certain woman would begin a death song—sometimes just hours before a person would die. She shut her eyes and prayed, *Lord, I've left all that behind. I ask you to be with your servant Noah. Thy will be done. . . .*

"Son, wake up!"

Fox awoke with a start. He had been dreaming, but he could not remember the dream. Now he sat up abruptly and stared at his mother. Her face was lit by the candle that she held. "What is it, Mother?" he whispered. "What's wrong?"

"It's your grandfather. He needs to see you."

"Is he sick?"

Awinita hesitated and then finally said, "You must know the truth, Fox. Your grandfather is going to meet his God."

His mother's words struck Fox like a blow in the chest. He loved his grandfather deeply, and the thought of losing him filled him with fear. "He's dying?" he whispered.

"Yes. And he wants to see you."

Fox swung his feet over the bed and pulled on his clothes without speaking. His mother waited in silence until he was dressed, then held the candle high with one hand and looked up at his face. She saw the strength of his father as well as his grandfather in the set features. "You will be a strong man like your father and your grandfather. Now go."

Fox turned and left the room. He was shaken by his mother's words and was thinking, *I'm losing everyone. First my father and now my grandfather.*

He made his way quickly down the hall and entered his grandfather's room. He saw that the rest of the family was there, and his mother came in quickly. The yellow light of the lamps cast an amber glow over the face of the sick man, and Fox was afraid. He saw how pale his grandfather looked.

"Come here. He wants to have a moment alone with you," his grandmother said.

As Fox advanced he did not notice that all the others had left the room. He paused beside his grandfather's bed, and for one moment he thought death had already come. Then the old man's eyelids fluttered and opened.

"Nathanael . . ." he murmured.

The boy leaned over, for the voice was very faint. "I'm here, Grandfather."

The dying man seemed to struggle for breath for a time but then grew somewhat stronger. Fox reached out his hand and Noah took it. The bones felt thin and brittle in Fox's own strong grip, and he held his grandfather's hand gently with both of his own.

"I have thought about you so much, Nathanael," Noah Carter whispered. "You have brought immense joy into my heart, and I thank the Lord daily for you." He paused, then continued faintly, "I must tell you something. . . ."

"What is it, Grandfather?"

"I had trouble accepting your father's choice of a Cherokee wife. You knew this, didn't you?"

"Yes, Grandfather."

"But your mother became like a daughter to me, and that love has also come to rest on you. I love your mother. And I love you."

Fox felt a sense of peace, for although he had been certain of his grandfather's love since his father's death, to hear him say it aloud was what he had longed for. Having lost his father, losing this man now was almost more than he could bear, but he said in a husky whisper, "I've always loved you, Grandfather."

"Love God, Nathanael. You'll have a home on this plantation. This is your heritage. It will belong to you as it would have belonged to your father." He squeezed Fox's hand with a surprising strength, and then his body arched. "Quick!" he gasped. "Go—get your grandmother!"

Fox sprang to the door and called his grandmother in. Naomi

came in at once and the others followed. Noah looked up at the faces surrounding him.

"My son, help your mother."

"I will, Father," Naaman said, moved more deeply than he had thought possible.

But then Noah said, "And help your nephew run the plantation."

Naaman took a deep breath but hid his anger and disgust and nodded. "Yes. Of course."

"Trust in God and love the family, my son." He then turned and raised his hand, and Awinita came to hold it. "You have been . . . a daughter in truth. I love you."

Awinita spoke only one sentence. "And I love you, Father," she whispered.

The time ran on, and at broken intervals Noah would speak. Always words of love and always full of confidence. Fox stood by watching, and the one thought that came to him was *I hope when I die I can do it as bravely as my grandfather!*

Finally Noah's eyes seemed to grow dim and he lifted his hand, and Naomi took it. "You have been a faithful wife. The joy of my life, Naomi, but now I must go to my Father."

Naomi held his hand, and he suddenly raised his head with one brief moment of strength and said, "I have loved you always, my dearest." He laid his head back, and then his lips moved several times as if in prayer, then he became still.

Fox knew that he was gone, and a single tear slid down his cheek. He felt his mother's arm around his shoulder and returned her embrace, oblivious to the angry stare from his uncle's ruthless green eyes.

Annabelle's Party

Three

Naaman Carter sat at the huge walnut desk carefully examining the man facing him. Philemon Dodd was highly intelligent, but that intelligence had nothing to do with morality. Dodd, Carter understood, was out for himself, and anyone who stood in his way was likely to get hurt.

Dodd met Carter's eyes with a hooded gaze. He was fifty-five years old, balding, and stocky, with pale green eyes that gave him an oddly sinister look. He kept his lips together like a tightly closed box most of the time, and now his mind worked quickly as he considered Carter's proposition. Finally he leaned forward and said, "You know the law as well as I do, Naaman."

"I'm no lawyer."

Dodd grinned suddenly, which gave him the appearance of a shark—he had small, sharp-looking teeth—and his laughter shook his bulky shoulders. "You may not be a lawyer, but I expect you have studied up on the law of inheritance."

Naaman shifted uneasily in his chair and tugged at the hem of his waistcoat. He was well dressed in a black pair of trousers, a white shirt with ruffles at the neck under a gray-and-black-striped waistcoat, and a coat of dark gray. There was something shifty in his gaze as he said, "This law of inheritance, it's unbreakable, I suppose?"

"Of course it is, Naaman. You know that." He thought for a moment and then said, "As I understand it, your father divided the property equally between you and your brother a few years ago. Titus got the deed to the land and the home, and you got all the liquid assets."

"Well, that's true enough."

"Noah was a pretty sharp fellow. I always admired him," Dodd said. He made a pyramid of his short, stubby fingers and examined them for a moment, and then his green eyes lit with ribald humor. "You made a big mistake doing that, Naaman."

"I know it was a mistake, but it's too late to do anything about it now."

"What did you do with all that money?"

"That's my business!" Naaman snapped.

"I heard you had made some poor investments. I suppose that's where it went. Anyway, for the time being you're a guardian of sorts for the boy and his mother, but when he's eighteen the property will all be taken over by him."

"Is there no way out of it? Are there no catches in the will at all?"

"Of course not. Your father wasn't a fool." Dodd leaned back and studied Naaman Carter carefully. What he saw was a man who had inherited his father's good looks but none of the character that had made Noah Carter a godly man of integrity. Dodd had also known Titus Carter well, and the two brothers had always been completely different. The man who sat before him was selfish, as was his wife, and from what he had observed, Philemon Dodd was certain that Naaman's children would grow up tainted by the same attitude. "What do you want from me, Naaman?" he asked finally.

"I want you to help me get my hands on that plantation."

"You're not going to get it—not unless Nathanael dies with no heirs of his own."

A silence hung over the room, and tiny motes of dust swirled in the golden bars of sunlight that slanted down from the window overhead. Naaman was silent for a long time, but Philemon Dodd was a perceptive man. When Naaman finally spoke, his words came as no surprise.

"Well, that may just happen. Life is a precarious thing and death often strikes the young as well as the old. . . ."

The heavyset lawyer did not reply. Over the course of his career, he'd become more than familiar with the baser instincts of human nature, but as he sat there examining the coldhearted man before him, he felt a shiver run up his spine. *I'll have to be more careful in my dealings with Naaman. I realize now he's capable of murder.*

As Naaman entered his house in Williamsburg, Julia met him and said in a harried fashion, "Naaman, why are you so late? We're going to have to hurry if we want to get to the party on time."

"I'm not interested in Annabelle Denton's party."

"Of course you are," Julia said with surprise. "We have to go."

Naaman pulled off his coat and headed for the bedroom. "I don't know why. I'll be bored to death and so will you."

Julia followed her husband into the bedroom and watched as he began to pull off his clothes. She saw that he was in an argumentative mood and knew that something had happened to disturb him. She knew better than to ask him, however, for he was a secretive man. In the years since they had been married, Julia had learned, to her disappointment, that her husband rarely shared his personal thoughts. At first she had pleaded with him to allow her to help carry any burdens or problems he faced. To her dismay, she learned quickly that it only caused more distance between them. It was better to change the subject than not have any conversation at all.

"We can't miss the party, Naaman."

"Why not? It's just another party."

"No, it's not," Julia said quickly. "Here. The clean shirts are in the armoire, and these pants would look nice, don't you think?"

"I'm old enough to dress myself, and I don't want to go to that party!"

Julia had also learned that the only way to handle Naaman was to simply refuse to argue. Instead, as she watched him pull his clothes from the walnut armoire, she began to speak of how important the party was and who all of importance from Williamsburg were going to be there. "Since her mother died last year, Annabelle has become one of the leaders of Williamsburg society. And you know Edward Denton is one of the most prominent citizens in the entire area."

Naaman actually had no intention of missing the party, but he growled and argued as he changed clothes. Finally, as he stood dressed, he said, "Well, I suppose you're right. We'll have to keep all the good connections we can. Besides, Edward may be able to help us untangle this situation we've found ourselves in."

Julia did not ask for more details. She understood well enough that the "situation" Naaman referred to was the shortage of funds that plagued them constantly. She had argued against risking his inheritance, but he had paid no attention. Now they both knew that their only hope was to find a way to obtain Havenwood. It was a valuable estate, and both of them were furious at the thought of an Indian woman and her son inheriting what was rightfully Naaman's. They had convinced themselves somehow that Awinita had robbed them of it, and now Julia said, "Edward Denton is one of the smartest men in Williamsburg. Why don't you ask him if there's anything that can be done?"

"I may do that," he said as he admired himself in the large mirror.

Julia nodded, for seeking Denton's advice was exactly what she had planned. "I'll go give the governess instructions about the children for this evening."

As Julia hurried off, Naaman Carter tied his cravat carefully. He was meticulous about his clothes. His mind was racing rapidly. He had become obsessed with the idea of getting his hands on Havenwood, and now that his father was dead, only the Cherokee boy stood in his way. His eyes narrowed as he studied his image, and he muttered, "There has to be a way—there just has to be!"

The room that Thomas Denton and his wife, Leah, shared was more ornate than either of them actually preferred. It was a medium-sized room, about fourteen by sixteen, with blue-and-gold carpet and two small windows covered in light blue velvet with gold tassels pulling the heavy material to one side. The walls were papered with large designs of peacocks and trees in blue, white, green, and gold, and the ceiling was painted a brilliant white and edged with gold paint on the raised moldings. A small, elaborately carved chimneypiece was decorated with polished brass fire irons and was flanked by two Chippendale chairs upholstered in blue silk damask. Above the fireplace hung a silhouette of one of the Denton ancestors, and on the mantel were silver candlesticks and vases of paper spills, which were used to light candles.

A large oak tester bed with a paneled canopy stood in the center of the room and was covered with a thick feather mattress with blue-and-white bed curtains and down pillows. A Queen Anne carved dressing table sat to one side of the bed and was covered with a snowy white Marseilles quilting. A large mahogany clothespress, a Hepplewhite tray-top commode, and a washstand, all of which were massive and elaborately carved, dominated the far wall. In the corner between the window and the fireplace stood a delicate oak cradle, holding the couple's two-month-old daughter, Sherah. She was fast asleep, breathing gently and soothingly.

"I never really liked this room, Leah," Thomas said suddenly.

Leah, who was putting the finishing touches on her hair, looked surprised. "Why not, Tom?"

"It's too fancy. I feel like I'm living in a museum."

Leah gave her hair one final pat, then went over to stand beside her husband. She was an attractive young woman, and the bloom of a happy marriage showed in her demure smile. She turned Thomas to face her and wrapped her arms around him. Looking up into his face, she said, "You just don't like fancy things, do you?"

"I like you and you're pretty fancy."

"Oh, really! You're telling me I'm a fancy woman?"

"Most certainly," Thomas grinned. "You're the best-looking woman around."

Sherah was now awake, and as if the child had understood and approved of her parents' flirtation, she began to make cooing noises. Leah pulled away from Thomas, went to the cradle, and leaned over, gently tickling her daughter. "Hello there, sweetheart. How did you sleep?"

Sherah Denton looked up with enormous blue eyes and suddenly gave a toothless grin.

"Look at her, Tom. Isn't she beautiful?"

"Not a tooth in her head and bald as an egg, and you think she's beautiful?"

"She's not bald. Look. She has this fine, silky hair. You know she's beautiful."

"Well, if you say so. She'll never be as pretty as her mother, though."

"I'd like to hear you say that when she's seventeen years old."

The two stood looking down at the cradle for a time, admiring their daughter. Thomas finally took a deep breath and said, "You know, Leah. God has been so good to me. Look at what I've got. A beautiful wife and a beautiful daughter."

"God has been good to us both," she said. "When I had to leave the frontier with my family, I was expecting a lonely life and figured I'd be an old maid for quite some time." Leah put her arm around her husband and smiled at him. "I didn't know I'd meet the best friend of Jacob Spencer and fall in love."

Indeed, after Thomas Denton had fought with the British during the war, he had given up the idea of ever finding a wife. But the first time he had laid eyes on Leah Foster, he had lost his heart to her. Their courtship and marriage had been a whirlwind affair, much to his family's dismay, but he was blissfully happy.

Leah's parents had recently moved to New York. Leah had received a letter from them stating that they were doing well but that they were missing her and her brother, Joseph, considerably.

"You ever hear from Joseph?"

"No. Not a word."

"That was a pretty strange affair."

"You mean Annabelle and Joseph?"

"Yes. It must have been pretty hard on Annabelle getting stranded at the altar like that. She thought she had finally found someone."

"I think it was very hard on her, but she pretends that it didn't hurt. It had to, though," Leah murmured. "Any woman would be deeply hurt by that kind of humiliation in front of family and friends."

Joseph Foster, Leah's brother, had met Annabelle Denton, Thomas's sister, after Leah had married. He had won Annabelle's heart, and in a few months, she had agreed to marry him. The wedding, which was to be at Christmas, promised to be one of Williamsburg's gala social events. One week before the wedding, however, Joseph had simply disappeared and had not been heard from since.

"I miss Joseph terribly. I just can't imagine what's happened to him."

Thomas said gently, "Well, you know you have to consider the fact that he . . . well, that he might not be alive."

"I've thought about that, Tom. It just isn't like Joseph to run off."

"Well, we'll have to keep praying for him and trusting God. In any case, it has been very hard on Annabelle—our mother dying, and then getting left at the altar. . . ."

The two said no more about Joseph, for it saddened Leah to

think of what may have happened to him. As he finished dressing, Thomas said, "Leah, have you thought any more about moving west?"

"Yes, I have. It doesn't seem quite right to leave your father all alone."

"Well, my father does have Annabelle," Thomas said. "Although why they choose to stay here I don't understand. You know, those who sided with the British, as we did, are never going to be accepted here in Williamsburg. The colonists are not going to soon forget the British atrocities during the Revolution."

"I know," Leah said. "I, too, have been surprised that Edward and Annabelle want to stay." She hesitated for a moment, then turned to Thomas and said, "Do you really want to go over the mountains, Tom? To the frontier?"

"There's plenty of land and endless opportunities over there."

Leah could see the excitement in his face whenever he spoke of starting over on the frontier. And in her heart, she knew she wanted to return to the place she had loved as a young girl. She waited until he finished and then said, "If you want to go, Tom, I'd love to move over the mountains."

Thomas Denton grew excited. "Do you mean it, Leah?"

"Yes. I can see your heart is already there, and even though you've had some success here, you would always feel as though you had missed something."

"That's exactly right, Leah. I just never quite knew how to express it. It's such a great land. You know that better than I do. I feel all cooped up here in the city."

The two talked excitedly about it for a while, and finally Leah sighed and said, "Your father won't like it."

"No, but he has his life to live and we have ours."

"But how would we get there?"

"We'd find a group that was making the trip. Later in the summer when Sherah will be stronger."

At that moment, the Dentons' governess knocked on the door to come take care of the baby for the evening. Thomas and Leah gave Sherah good-night kisses and then went downstairs, where they found Thomas's father, Edward, speaking with Annabelle. Annabelle was looking especially glamorous. She was wearing a lightweight azure velvet gown with a square neckline edged with white lace and with elbow-length funnel sleeves ending in love-lace ruffles. The tight-fitting bodice had embroidery down the front and down the edges of the overskirt, and the petticoat, made of layered white lace, was full.

"You're still the prettiest sister I ever had, Annabelle," Thomas said.

Annabelle glared at him. "I'm your *only* sister!"

"Well, it's still true enough."

Thomas hesitated, then said, "I hate to spring this on you, but tonight Leah and I have made a decision. We're moving over the mountains to the frontier."

Instantly both Annabelle and her father stiffened. "You can't do that!" Edward Denton said. "Why, it's foolhardy! It isn't wise, Thomas."

Annabelle joined in with her father, and the two argued for them to change their mind. But after explaining why they wanted to follow their dreams, Thomas and Leah realized that Edward and Annabelle would never be happy with their decision.

Secretly Leah was happy to leave for other reasons. Ever since meeting Edward Denton, she had felt uncomfortable with him and equally so with Annabelle. She did not know whether Thomas could see it or not, but they were very shallow, selfish people. Both of them were attractive and accustomed to success, but they lacked a generous spirit, which often showed in their demeanor with others. Thomas, on the other hand, had not taken after either of them in that aspect. Perhaps he had inherited his goodness and generous spirit from his mother or, perhaps, from a grandparent. In any case, Leah would not miss the tension she sensed, although she would never dare mention her feelings to Thomas.

The argument was put aside when Naaman and Julia Carter arrived. Annabelle met them smiling, and her father came to shake hands with the pair.

They talked for a moment about the party, and then Julia Carter had a moment alone with Annabelle. "I am so grieved over the way Joseph Foster treated you, Annabelle."

Annabelle laughed and said, "Probably for the best. I'm too good for him." She tried to make a joke out of it, but Julia took her seriously.

"You certainly are. He is just a nobody, and although I've never said a word, I've always thought that Thomas could have done much better than to marry Leah."

Annabelle was taken aback at Julia's comment and said nothing, but she secretly concurred.

Soon the guests began to arrive, and the party was in full swing. The small string ensemble began playing and filled the ballroom with lively music. Many couples moved out onto the floor in one smooth motion for a waltz. The room swirled with colorful gowns that sparkled in the candlelight, and laughter and lively conversation filled the room as the women enjoyed the social gossip and the men discussed the political problems that stirred in the land.

Thomas danced with his sister. As they glided around the room, he grinned down at her, saying, "We make a handsome pair, don't we?"

"Yes. But, Thomas, I can't believe you're leaving Williamsburg for the savage frontier."

"It's what I want to do, Annabelle. You and I are different. You like it in Williamsburg, but I don't fit here. I'm miserable."

"But why? You have everything here."

"No, I don't. I want to be my own man, make my own decisions, and I could never do that here."

"Are you saying that Father is domineering?"

"Well, he is a little bit, you know."

"I think that's unfair, Tom. He only wants what's best for you."

"Maybe so. But in any case, we've decided to go."

"I suppose Leah put you up to all this."

"Of course not. It was my idea."

They were moving around the floor in time to the music, and finally she said sprightly, "That's what you think! A woman can use her wiles to influence a man to do anything. Why, Leah's little better than a savage herself, having grown up on the frontier."

"Wait a minute! I won't hear that kind of talk about Leah," Thomas said sternly. "I know you were hurt by what her brother did, but you have no right to take it out on her."

Annabelle was accustomed to having her own way, and her face grew red as her brother continued to explain why he couldn't stay in Williamsburg any longer. "I found out, Annabelle, that material things are worthless. God has blessed me with a loving wife and a new daughter, and I want what's best for them. On the frontier we can face life's challenges and trust God to lead us. Every decision seems already made for me here."

Annabelle would have argued more, but at that moment the dance ended, and Thomas walked across the room to claim Leah for the next dance.

Inside the library of the Denton home, Naaman Carter and Edward Denton had met. Naaman had murmured, "Could I see you alone, Edward?" and Denton, surprised, had led him to the large room. When they were seated, the two talked for a while about politics. "Well," Naaman said, "North Carolina finally ceded her western lands to the Confederation Congress. I think the government only wanted the land to use it to pay off the debt incurred by the war."

Edward took a drink from the heavy cut-glass tumbler and smacked his lips. "It'll never work. This new government will fold, and the Colonies will be begging England to take them back."

"Oh, I agree with you, Edward! Can't go any other way."

Finally Edward said, "What's on your mind, Naaman? I can see something's gnawing at you."

"Well . . . you know about how my father's estate was divided."

"Yes. I heard about it." Privately he thought Naaman had made a foolish mistake, and now he studied the man carefully, wondering what he was up to.

"You know there are attacks still being made all over the country," Naaman said. "Why, the plantation next to Havenwood was attacked just last week."

"That's right. I've heard about the attacks on Tory homes. It's one reason I'm inside the city. They won't attack here, but the plantations are wide open." Edward took another drink and nodded. "Havenwood would probably have already been raided if it hadn't been for your father's loyalty to the Continental Congress."

Naaman dropped his head for a while and then looked up with a cunning light in his eyes. "It would be a shame if my nephew was killed in a raid on Havenwood."

Instantly Edward Denton understood the purpose of this meeting. "Yes. Although, it would be rather . . . convenient . . . for you and Julia. The property then would rightfully be yours, wouldn't it?"

"That boy doesn't deserve Havenwood anyhow. He and his mother are strangers. If anything happened to him, of course, I would take care of his mother. Give her enough money to get back to her people."

Edward said suddenly, "So you think there's going to be a raid. What makes you think so?"

Both men knew exactly what was in Naaman Carter's mind. It would not be difficult to hire some of the riffraff who had developed a taste for pillage and rampage during the Revolution. Naaman did not speak further of this but simply said, "It would be a shame if we were raided, but who can tell how these things will happen?"

Edward Denton had never been sympathetic toward Noah's Cherokee daughter-in-law, nor to her son. He strongly felt that Indians needed to be kept in their place, and now his eyes glittered as he said, "Such raids happen. Sometimes, though, they have to be, shall we say, 'arranged.' "

Instantly Naaman understood that the idea of procuring "his" property was a real possibility. As he left the library he thought, *It won't be any trouble to arrange a raid.* With a smile on his face he shook Edward's hand and thanked him. Then he left the library and returned to the party.

For the rest of the evening, Naaman seemed so happy that Julia noticed it. As they were enjoying some of the food that had been prepared, she smiled and said, "You seem to be very pleased."

Naaman Carter looked across the room at Edward Denton, and they exchanged knowing smiles. "It's going to be fine, dear. Just fine," he said with barely hidden excitement.

Secret Plans

Four

"Mother, I really think you ought to come and stay with Julia and me for a few days."

Naomi Carter looked up with surprise in her faded blue eyes. She had said little since the death of Noah. She had kept to herself for so long that even Awinita was troubled about her. Now she sat in her chair with her hands clasped together, the sewing in her lap forgotten for the moment. Finally she said, "I don't think I'd care to do that, Naaman."

"But, Mother, I really think you should. It's been hard on you since Father's death, and you need to get away to get your mind off of him."

"I'll never do that," she said as she picked up her sewing again.

"Well, I didn't mean it like that exactly." Naaman stumbled over the words and tried again. "But we'd love to have you come for a visit. We've made some improvements to the house that I'd like you to see. You'd be able to get out a little bit. You never see anything different here at Havenwood."

"And what would I see in Williamsburg?"

"Why, people and . . . and all the new buildings that are going up! There's a new inn with great food service where Julia could take you to. Lots of activity going on."

A faint smile turned the corners of Naomi's mouth, and she murmured, "I think I'm past all that, son."

"Mother, you're still grieving over Titus, too, aren't you?"

"Yes, I am. I suppose I always will."

"You've got to learn to turn loose of him and of Father, too."

Naomi said nothing. She had been greatly disappointed at Naaman's seemingly indifferent response to his father's death. It had seemed to mean little to him, although he had put on an air of mourning for a time. She knew that Naaman was not a man capable of showing much feeling. He had always been self-centered, even as a boy. It had been hard for Naomi knowing that Titus had been her favorite and that she had not always been able to keep that fact hidden from Naaman. *Perhaps*, she thought, *if I had not spoiled Naaman, he might have been different.* Rationally she knew this was not true, but she could not stop the pangs of guilt, the sense that she was partly to blame for Naaman's poor character.

Naaman pulled a chair up and sat down in front of his mother. After his talk with Philemon Dodd and later with Edward Denton, he had made up his mind that he was going to own Havenwood at any cost. The thought of an Indian having part of his heritage infuriated him. Even as he talked with his mother, pleading with her to come and visit him, he thought of the plans he had already put into motion. He had arranged for a raid to strike at Havenwood, but it was carefully planned. He had given strict orders to the outlaw in charge of the ruthless band he had hired. "No destruction of property. You understand that? You won't harm any of the slaves. They're worth money. You've got one job, that's it. There's an Indian boy there and I don't want him left alive."

The cold-blooded order had troubled Naaman for a time, but his greed and hatred eventually blinded him from all reason. He had convinced himself that he had been cheated all of his life by his parents. He had known well that Titus was the favorite son and that a special love had passed on to Nathanael, his half-breed nephew. Now his heart was hardened, and he had rationalized his deed, thinking, *If Nathanael had been living with the Cherokee, probably he would have been killed in a raid already by this time.*

"Please, Mother, do this for me."

Naomi was surprised by her son's persistence. She and Noah had visited Naaman and Julia for brief periods, but their stays had never been relaxed and pleasant. Noah had said after the last visit, "Let them come and see us. There's a bad feeling about that house." Nonetheless, the grief of losing a son and a husband had taken its toll on her. Though Awinita had comforted her like a daughter, perhaps a short spell away from everything that reminded her of her losses might help lift her spirits. Setting the sewing aside, she looked at Naaman and said, "All right then, son, if that's what you really want."

A gust of relief washed through Naaman. The final piece of his evil scheme was now in place. He was determined that nothing should happen to his mother or any of the slaves. He had deliberately left out any instructions for dealing with Awinita, but he secretly hoped she would suffer a tragic fate the night the raid took place.

"Good. You'll have a good time with us in Williamsburg."

Jasper Tatum's eyes narrowed as he listened to what Naaman Carter had to say. He was not entirely surprised at the proposal, for he had long known that Naaman hated Awinita Carter and her son. Finally, when Naaman finished, he grunted with satisfaction. "Let me get this straight," he said. "There's going to be a raid on this place?"

"Not so loud," Naaman whispered nervously. He and Tatum were standing outside the barn, and looking around nervously, he was relieved to see no one else in sight. "You want the whole world to know about it?"

"Ain't nobody here," Tatum said. "Now, tell me more about this raid."

"All right. Here's the way it will be. Tomorrow night I'm taking my mother to spend some time with my wife and me in Williamsburg. After we leave there's going to be some men who'll come. They'll do lots of shooting and screaming and carrying on, but they've got strict orders not to hurt anybody."

"What's that all about?"

Naaman hesitated, then shook his head. "Just stay out of the way and you won't get hurt."

Suddenly Tatum's eyes narrowed. "Wait a minute," he said. He grinned broadly then, and a hoarse chuckle issued from his thick lips. "Ain't nobody going to be hurt, you say? What about that Indian kid that thinks he's such a big man?"

Naaman did not answer. He did not want to take Jasper Tatum into his confidence, but he couldn't have him interfering, either. "The boy will just have to take care of himself," he said quickly. "Never mind about him."

Tatum was a shrewd man, and he laughed aloud, saying, "So the Indian gets shot, his mama gets taken out, and you and your wife own Havenwood."

"Keep your voice down, you fool!" Naaman whispered angrily. He could not resist another look around but again saw no one. "Keep this all to yourself! After the raid's over, you go into town and spread the word around of what's happened. Nobody will be too surprised. There's been enough raids in this part of the land. Then you send word to me in Williamsburg."

"And who's going to run this plantation?"

"Why, you are, Jasper. I'll own it, and you'll be my overseer. You'll have a pretty soft life here."

Jasper Tatum thought of the power and control he'd finally have over the slaves with Nathanael gone. He smiled and said, "All right. But tell those fellows to be careful with their guns."

"Don't worry. They know exactly what to do."

Naaman turned and walked away, and Jasper Tatum moved over to the horse he had tied to a hitching post. He mounted it and rode off with a fixed smile upon his face as he passed the slave quarters.

For some time after the two men disappeared, all was quiet. Only the rooster crowing over to one side disturbed the silence of the barnyard. But then the door to the barn creaked and slowly opened.

Mercy, Ezekiel's wife, emerged into the sunlight and looked fearfully in every direction. She saw no sign of them. She had been inside the barn looking for guinea eggs, which the hens laid anywhere they chose. The voices of the two men had caught her attention and she had crept up to a crack in the planks where she could watch them. She had held her breath, listening to the conversation, and now she ran toward the big house as fast as she could. "I got to tell Ezekiel. He'll know what to do," she panted.

"What's the matter with you, Ezekiel?" Hulda stared at the huge black man who had appeared at the back door and banged on it incessantly. "You gonna knock the door down."

"Hulda, I got to talk to you."

"Come on in."

"No. You come out here."

Puzzled, Hulda stepped outside the door and followed until Ezekiel stood some thirty feet from the house, behind the smokehouse.

"What's all the big secret about?"

"I got to tell you what Mercy done heard."

Hulda listened as Ezekiel repeated the tale Mercy had told him, and then Ezekiel said, "You got to do somethin', Hulda."

"What I'm gonna do?"

"Go tell Miss Awinita."

Instantly Hulda knew that was the answer. "All right. Don't you say nothin' about this to nobody, Zeke."

"I don't aim to."

Hulda went back into the house at once and hastened upstairs. She burst into Awinita's room without knocking.

Awinita looked up from her writing table and saw the frightened look on the woman's face. "What's wrong? Somebody hurt, Hulda?"

"No, ma'am. Zeke done come and told me somethin' you gotta hear about."

"Zeke? What is it?"

"You gotta do somethin', Miss Awinita," Hulda said. She then repeated the story and ended by saying, "Dat man hates you real bad! I ain't never had no love for Mr. Naaman. He wasn't nothin' at all like Mr. Titus. He wasn't like Mr. Noah neither nor his mama, but you gotta tell Miss Naomi."

"I can't do that, Hulda."

"Why not?"

"Because it would be overwhelming for her to find out just how cruel her son is."

"But you gotta do something."

"I can't tell her," Awinita said firmly. She stood up and her face was set. Her mind raced quickly, and she said, "We don't have any proof. If I went to anyone with this, Naaman would just deny it. They'd call off the raid, and they would try it again some other time."

"You really think Mr. Naaman would kill you and that boy?"

Awinita did not answer for a moment, and then she said, "Yes. I think he would. He wants this plantation, and he'll do anything to get it."

"What you gonna do, then?"

"I've got to talk to Fox. We'll have to get away, so you'll have to help me, Hulda."

"I do what I can and so will Zeke and Mercy."

"Have you seen Fox?"

"He was out in the south pasture early this morning."

"Send someone to get him."

"Yes, 'um. I'll have Zeke go. He's still waitin'."

"I . . . I don't believe it, Mother," Fox said. He was already showing signs of having a deep chest and wide shoulders, and he had an instinctive quickness in his movements. His dark brown eyes were very deep set, and now as he stood before his mother, he was puzzled. Yet at the same time, his heart told him that his uncle was capable of turning on them. He listened as his mother explained what Mercy had heard and then said, "Uncle Naaman always hated me—and you, too."

"I know. But we can't stay here, Fox."

"Where will we go?"

"We'll have to go back to my people, to the Cherokee."

Instantly Fox's eyes lit up, and they seemed to burn with pleasure. "I've always wanted to go over the mountains."

"Well, you're going to have your chance now. We've got to leave quickly. Go get everything you want to take over the mountains. We'll need a wagon, too. I'll pack my things while you're fetching it."

"What about Grandmother?"

"I'll write a letter and leave it with Hulda. She won't get it until we're far away."

"Are you going to tell her about Naaman?"

"No. Her heart has carried enough grief already. She couldn't stand it. I'll tell her that staying here is too hard without your father. And I'll also tell her that I want to show you your Cherokee heritage."

"All right, Mother. The wagon will be ready when you are."

Awinita moved quickly. She wrote the letter, explaining why she felt they must leave, adding that she would come back in the future. In her heart she knew they could never come back as long as Naaman was alive.

She folded the note carefully and then began to pack her clothes. She would not need many, for once back with her people she would once again adopt traditional dress.

Sitting on the edge of her bed, she looked wistfully about the room, then picked up her Bible, holding it in her hands for a time before opening it. She read for a while, seeking comfort, and finally came to the phrase concerning Abraham in the book of Hebrews: "And he went out, not knowing whither he went."

She put her finger on the verse and prayed softly. "Lord, I do not know the way, but you do. Guide me and my son and keep us safe, for I ask it in Jesus' name."

Flight From Havenwood

Five

Awinita moved forward and put her arms around Naomi, holding her so tightly that the elderly woman gasped.

"My goodness, Awinita!" Naomi cried as she was released. "You don't have to squeeze a body to death."

"I'm going to miss you so much, Mother!"

"Well, after all, Awinita, I'll only be gone a month. That's not too terribly long."

Fox was standing beside Awinita, and he knew what was going on in his mother's heart as she said good-bye to her mother-in-law. He himself felt a lump in his throat, for he loved his grandmother dearly, and he knew that this might be the last time he would ever see her. She was frail and elderly and not in good health, and he knew that the long journey over the Appalachians might take the two of them away from her forever. He stepped forward and put his arms around her, something he rarely did.

Once again Naomi was surprised. Her grandson had been very demonstrative as a young boy, but with the nature of an adolescent, he was shy about showing his feelings now. She reached over and patted his cheek, saying, "Well, this is one way for a grandmother to get a hug, but it's not so easy."

"I'll miss you, Grandmother," Fox said, his voice unsteady. He was trying to fix his grandmother in his mind's eye so that he would always remember her kind and gentle face.

The three were standing beside the buggy that Naaman had brought to drive his mother back to Williamsburg. Naaman stood waiting to help his mother in, and finally he said impatiently, "We'd better get going, Mother. It's a long drive and it will be dark soon."

Naomi leaned forward and suddenly took Awinita's hands, and tears filled her eyes. "Take care of Nathanael," she whispered.

"I will," Awinita said. Then she added with a tight voice, trying to control her emotions, "You've always been like a mother to me, Naomi."

"Let's go. There's no more time," Naaman said roughly and almost pulled his mother away from Awinita's grasp. He helped her into the buggy, as well as Huldah, who came out of the house with a lunch packed in a basket. Huldah was to travel to Williamsburg with Naomi to see to her needs. She was misty-eyed as she said goodbye to Awinita and Fox, knowing she might never see them again, then stopped for one moment and looked at Fox.

Naaman smiled strangely and said, "You take care of things while I'm gone, Nate."

"Yes, sir, I will."

The two stood watching the wagon as it moved off down the road, raising a plume of dust behind it. Fox turned to his mother and asked, "Have you thought that we might not see Grandmother again?"

"Yes, but that's in God's hands, Fox. Come. We've got to get ready."

Fox followed his mother up to her room, and while she was selecting a few last personal items that she would take, he seemed restless. Finally he said, "I'm worried about Ezekiel and Mercy."

Awinita turned to face the boy. "I've been thinking about them, too, and I've decided that we're going to have to take them with us."

"Oh, Mother, could we? I know Tatum. He'll beat Ezekiel terribly if we leave him here, and he's after Mercy, too. You know what kind of man he is."

"Yes, I know. I thought about whether it would be legal or not, so I'm going to send a letter to the lawyer who handles our affairs saying that we're taking them with us as servants."

"Do you think they'll go with us?" Fox said.

"Why don't you go talk to them while I finish packing. Tell them how bad it will be if they stay."

Fox had already gathered his few belongings together, including his rifle. He immediately left the room and ran to the slave quarters. Finding Ezekiel and Mercy at their small cabin, he stepped inside and began without preamble. "Get your things together. We've got to get out of here."

Ezekiel stood straight, his eyes wide with shock. "What do you mean, Mr. Fox?"

"We've got to get away. My uncle's trying to kill me, and you know what Tatum will do to you if we're not here."

"He's right, Ezekiel," Mercy said quickly. "I've been worried sick about it."

"My mother and I want you to go with us over the mountains."

"But we belongs to Miss Naomi."

"That's all taken care of," Fox said, and he went on to explain that the lawyer was being contacted and that they would be going as servants. "But once we get over the mountains we'll all be safe. Now get everything ready. We're going to take a wagon for all of our belongings."

"Which horses you want to take, Mr. Fox?"

"Take Bess and Nellie. They're the strongest."

"That's right. They is. I go get 'em hitched up."

Fox hurried back to the house and found his mother ready. He helped her move her luggage downstairs and said, "This is too much to haul over where the wagon is. We'll come around the back way, and Ezekiel and I will load it up."

"All right. I'll go with you."

The two made their way through the falling darkness and found that Ezekiel had hitched the wagon up and Mercy was busy loading their few personal possessions inside.

"Are you sure you want to do this, Ezekiel?" Awinita asked. "It's dangerous over the mountains. There are hostile tribes, and any of us could fall into their hands. We'll be risking our lives."

"Yes, ma'am, I wants to go and so does Mercy. As long as Mr. Naaman's alive and that man Tatum is here, it wouldn't be safe for us."

"All right we'll—"

"You stand right where you are!"

The four turned quickly, and Fox was shocked to see Jasper Tatum suddenly appear out of the darkness. He had the pistol in his hand he always carried when he went anywhere close to the slave quarters, and he held it high on cock. "Where do you think you're going with that wagon?"

"That's none of your business, Mr. Tatum," Awinita said quickly. "You go on about your business. We're taking a short trip."

"You're not going anywhere," Tatum said. "Boy, you get that wagon unhitched."

Ezekiel did not move, and Tatum snarled, "Runaway slaves get shot, and that's what you're going to get right now!"

Fox saw the pistol rise and knew that Tatum meant to kill Ezekiel. He lunged forward and managed to shove Tatum's hand up. The gun exploded with a deafening sound, and he suddenly was struck in the temple with a fist that knocked him to the ground.

Instantly Jasper was standing over the boy, shaking him like a rat and lifting his fist again. "You've had your own way around here, but that's over now!"

Awinita ran forward, but she was shoved aside and fell to the ground. Quickly she called out, "Ezekiel, he's killing Fox! Help!"

The huge slave moved quicker than Awinita would have thought possible. His hand shot out and he grabbed Jasper's uplifted fist and hauled it down. Jasper Tatum let out a yell, then regained his balance. He threw a mighty blow that caught Ezekiel on the chest and drove him backward. The overseer was short and powerful, and he moved forward, pummeling Ezekiel. Ezekiel had never struck a white man in his life, for he knew that it would cost him his life. He merely tried to protect himself as he was driven to the ground by one of Tatum's powerful blows. He felt Tatum fall upon him, and then he heard Awinita call out, "Ezekiel, you have to protect yourself!"

Ezekiel gave a mighty lunge that threw Jasper off of him. The burly overseer came to his feet roaring, but he was met with the full force of Ezekiel's fist. It caught him directly between the eyes and knocked him to the ground. His head hit a rock and he lay absolutely still.

By this time Fox had arisen and came running over to stare down at the overseer. "Is he dead, Ezekiel?"

"I . . . I don't know!" Ezekiel was trembling, for the thought of killing a white man terrified him. He knew it would mean certain death. They would hunt him down with dogs and string him up from the nearest tree.

Awinita went over at once and knelt down beside the overseer. She could not tell if he was breathing, and when she touched his head, she found blood on the back of it. "He hit his head on a rock. I think he's dead."

"What'll we do, Mother?" Fox asked in a frightened tone.

Awinita thought quickly. "We've got to get out of here."

"But what'll we do about him?" Fox asked.

"We'll leave him where he is. Come on. Get the wagon loaded."

Quickly they drove to the house and loaded the things Awinita and Fox had decided to take. Without a moment's loss of time, they leaped into the wagon, and Awinita herself took the lines. Fox settled beside her, and Ezekiel and Mercy scrambled into the back. Awinita spoke to the horses sharply, "Up, Nellie! Up, Bess!" And the horses shot out of the yard.

As they cleared the driveway and turned down the road, young Fox Carter turned for one last look before the house was hidden by a grove of poplar trees. A sadness came over him, for he realized he was leaving the only home he had ever known, although it hadn't really felt like home since his father had died. Still, this was the first time he had been truly homeless.

Turning to his mother, he said, "Mother, will your people have us?"

"We will see, son," Awinita said. She sat up firmly on the seat and did not look back. She knew that her fate and that of her son lay not in this place but somewhere over the Misty Mountains.

Escape to the Frontier

Six

Naaman's face was stern, and his mouth was drawn into a straight line as he faced Edward Denton. "I don't know what happened, Edward," he said. "All I know is that one of the hands found Jasper unconscious. He was beat half to death. It looks as though someone tried to kill him. I have my suspicions it was a slave."

"But you say that Cherokee squaw and her son are gone?"

"Yes. Along with two slaves, a male named Ezekiel and his wife, Mercy."

"Well, where could they be going?"

"I don't know. Who knows what's going on in that crazy Indian woman's mind?"

Denton paced the floor and puffed on his pipe. His mind worked rapidly, and finally he said, "Well, I'd guess they're going over the mountains back to the Cherokee, back to the woman's tribe."

"Do you think so?"

"Where else would they go?"

Naaman Carter seemed to relax. "That's dangerous country over there. There's always war between the Indians and the settlers. I doubt if any of them will survive the trip."

"Well, even if they don't, I think there's now a perfectly legal way for you to take over the plantation once your mother is gone," Denton said slowly. "I mean, they're both gone, and you could have them declared dead by a court. Then Havenwood would belong to you."

"That's right, isn't it?" Naaman laughed aloud. "Now I can run the plantation as I see fit." Then his eyes clouded. "But I'll never be truly at ease there until I know for certain that the boy is dead and unable to ever return and claim Havenwood as his."

The fire red sun was dipping below a far-off mountain range as the wagon cleared a crest, and Awinita smiled at the beautiful sunset. The small company had kept off the main roads to avoid being seen. They had camped at night beside small streams and cooked their meals over an open fire. In a way it was one of the best times Fox had ever had in his life. The dense forests were filled with game, and he managed to find fresh meat—deer, squirrel, and rabbit—whenever they needed it. Now as the days rolled by, he grew more and more anxious to meet his mother's people.

"How long will it take to get there, Mother?"

The sun was almost down now, and the last rays of light began to fade. Before she answered, she said, "There's a stream up there. We'll make camp for the night."

But Fox repeated his question. "How long will it be? Another week or two?"

"It's going to take quite a while. It's farther than you think, and the trail gets harder. We may have to trade the wagon for pack animals and horses."

"I don't care," Fox said. His youthful face was filled with a look of adventurous excitement as he gazed off into the distance. For a long time he remained silent.

"What are you thinking about, son?"

"Well, where will we live? We won't have a house or anything."

"We'll go to my brother. Sequatchie's a good man. A godly man. He'll take us in and care for us."

His mother's calm assurance that they would have a place to stay assuaged his concerns. After the death of his father and then his grandfather, Havenwood lost much of the meaning it had held for young Fox Carter. Secretly he had been longing to turn west, and his mother had told him so many stories of Sequatchie, his uncle, and of others among the Cherokee that he had dreamed many dreams about them.

Now as they pulled up beside the small stream, Fox sat there for one moment. The darkness was coming quickly now, but his mind was far ahead. *It won't be long,* he thought, *until we'll be over the mountains, and then I can really find out what it's like.*

To Dwell in Franklin

August 1784 – July 1785

"And ye shall dwell with us: and the land shall be before you; dwell and trade ye therein, and get your possessions therein."

Genesis 34:10

The New State of Franklin

Seven

As always, Elizabeth Spencer woke slowly. In contrast to her husband, who seemed to leap from a sound sleep into full watchfulness, Elizabeth had to weave her way through several layers of sleep before full consciousness came. Now as she lay curled up in the crevice she had created in the soft feather bed, the first sign of the real world that came to her was the sound of a mockingbird outside the window. It was a sound she loved to hear, and as she emerged from the world of dreams, she smiled at the bird's cheerful song.

Another sound came to her—a rasping that she had to think about for a moment to identify. Then coming completely into the world of consciousness, she opened her eyes just enough to see her husband standing before the washstand and peering into a tiny mirror. He hated shaving, and Elizabeth smiled more broadly as she heard him muttering under his breath.

"Dull razor! Wouldn't cut its way through hot lard!"

The song of the mockingbird grew more pronounced, and Elizabeth pulled the quilt back and sighed.

It was a very slight sound, but it caught the quick ears of Hawk Spencer. He turned to her, one side of his face clean, the other covered with a foamy white lather, and suddenly grinned. As he did so, Elizabeth thought, *What a handsome man he still is.* At the age of forty-nine, Hawk Spencer was an impressive specimen. Exactly six feet tall, his thick coal black hair, slightly wavy and worn short, had a few speckles of gray, but his face was smooth and unlined. Dark blue eyes looked at her, so dark that they appeared black at times, especially when he was angry. He had a square face with a strong cleft in his chin and a straight English nose. Wearing only a pair of drawers, the muscles of his upper body swelled upward from a deep waist. His face and hands were dark from years of exposure to the sun.

"I know what you're thinking," he said.

Elizabeth was startled by Hawk's statement. "What?" she demanded.

"You're thinking what a fine-looking husband you managed to trap."

"Oh, you're getting to be absolutely swollen up with pride!"

Hawk put the razor down and went over to her. He drew the cover completely back, crawled into the feather bed, and pulled her toward him.

"Hawk, you're going to get shaving soap all over me!"

"A small price to pay for attention from such a handsome husband."

Elizabeth could not resist Hawk when he was in a playful mood—which was often, it seemed. She had been married once before, and happily, but had lost her husband in an Indian attack. She had not sought a second husband, but her relationship with Hawk had been a true godsend, and this marriage was especially sweet to her. For all his toughness, which a man needed to make it out here on the frontier, Hawk Spencer was a gentle man with her and with their children. Now he pulled her even closer and kissed her firmly, smearing shaving soap on her face.

"Hawk!" she protested.

"What?"

"I've got to get up and fix breakfast. You're going to get a late start as it is."

"Who cares?" Hawk kissed her again and then lifted his head and propped it on one elbow. "You're the most beautiful woman in Watauga. You know that, Elizabeth Spencer?"

Indeed, Elizabeth was a beautiful woman. Her thick blond hair fanned over the pillow. It had brown highlights, and she kept it cut just below her shoulders. Her eyes were large and green, and she had a heart-shaped face with a pert nose and a smooth complexion. She smiled up at him now and reached up and touched the cheek that was not covered with lather. "Not many husbands are as sweet as you are."

"*Many?*" Hawk grinned at her. "Name one."

"I don't have time for your foolishness."

"It's not foolishness. Men are supposed to pay attention to their wives and tell them how pretty they are."

"But you've got to go to Jonesborough."

"Jonesborough can wait. I'm romancing my wife."

Elizabeth lay against Hawk, pleased with his tender affection. She was truly fortunate. Not many wives out here on the frontier had a husband as loving and considerate as this one!

"How many geese do you suppose?"

Elizabeth stared at Hawk. "What are you talking about? What geese?"

"I was thinking about how many geese you had to pluck to make this feather bed. It must have been hundreds."

"I don't have time to count geese with you."

"Well, I've been thinking how nice it was of you, Mrs. Spencer, to make such a generous feather bed for us." His eyes glowed mischievously.

"Hawk Spencer!" Elizabeth began. "I never met such an incorrigible—"

"Shh . . ." Hawk interrupted her with a finger to his lips, then pulled her close and kissed her as if he were a young bridegroom.

"Get up, Josh. I hear Mama."

Joshua Spencer groaned and muttered, "Leave me alone! It's too early to get up."

But Hannah would not leave her brother alone. Being two years older than Joshua, she felt she had a mandate to give him orders—something that Joshua firmly resented. He rolled over in the bed, and his movement was accompanied by the rustling of the shuck mattress. For a minute she thought about the feathers she was saving to make herself a bed like her parents'. But that was many geese away. Joshua, she knew, did not care whether he slept on the ground or in a feather bed. He could sleep anywhere under all conditions. Now she reached over and shook him, but he simply pulled the cover over his head and curled up in a ball. Beating on his back, she said, "Josh, get up. Papa's going to Jonesborough and we've got to tell him good-bye."

This stirred the boy somewhat, and he pulled his head up. His eyes were half shut, and he muttered, "What time is it?"

"Time for you to get up."

At the age of twelve, Hannah was still thin and had her mother's heart-shaped face. She gave her honey brown hair a few strokes with a brush she had carried from her room and watched as Joshua slowly emerged from his bed like a bear coming out from a winter's sleep. He pulled on his deerskin pants, then his buckskin shirt, and finally slipped moccasins onto his bare feet.

"Those buckskins are bound to be miserably uncomfortable! Why don't you just wear linsey-woolsey like the rest of us?"

In all truth the buckskins were not as comfortable as the garments his mother spun together from linen and wool, but Joshua loved to dress as much like a long hunter as he could. He scratched his tousled brown hair that was somewhat darker than his sister's and stared at her. "I'm going to be a hunter. This is what hunters wear." His build was rather stocky, and he had freckles and dimples, which he hated.

"Hannah—Joshua! Come on. Breakfast is almost ready."

"Come on," Joshua said and ran from his room, tripping over a rug and almost falling. He looked over at his mother, who was standing by the fireplace and smiling at him. "You're going to fall and break your neck someday. Why don't you walk more carefully like Hannah does?"

"Ah, girls can walk all prim and proper. Men do it different."

Elizabeth could not restrain a smile. "You think the sign of a man is falling down, I take it?"

Joshua did not answer, for his father had come in from the outside. His face was bright, and he was wearing buckskins almost identical to Joshua's. "Hello. What's this about falling down?"

"Why, Ma's always tellin' me to be careful, but I almost never get hurt."

Hannah giggled and said, "You're always banging your fingers or dropping something on your foot or burning yourself at the forge."

"I am not!"

"You are, too!"

"Stop that fussing! Your father's going to be gone. I want you both to be sweet."

"Yes. Like me," Hawk said. He came over and picked Hannah up and squeezed her until she squealed.

"Papa, you're crushing me!"

"That's because you're such a sweet girl, just like your ma." He kissed her soundly, put her down, then went over and grabbed Joshua, lifting him up off the floor.

"Ah, Dad, don't be whirling me around!"

"I will until you get too big for me to do it. When you can put me flat on my back, I'll stop." He kissed Joshua firmly on the cheek and laughed at the boy's protest.

As Elizabeth watched them while she finished making breakfast, she suddenly thought of her first husband, Patrick. He had also been as openly affectionate with Andrew and Sarah, the two children she had borne him. She was happy that the older Hawk got, the more willing he seemed to show his feelings in ways that pleased her—and the children.

"You sit down now. Breakfast is almost ready."

As Elizabeth set plates heaped with food on the table, Hawk looked at it all and said, "Well, I won't starve to death on this trip if I eat all of this."

Elizabeth had prepared a larger breakfast than usual. There were platters of fried ham with gravy, dressed eggs, buttermilk biscuits, fresh apple butter, johnnycakes, and hot coffee.

"Pa, I want to go with you to Jonesborough."

"Not this time, son."

"But why not? I never get to go anywhere."

"It's going to be a tough journey. I've got to make a quick trip. And besides"—Hawk winked at Elizabeth—"there's got to be a man on the place."

Joshua was pleased by Hawk's words, and his mind was averted. "And do I get to load the rifle?"

"Sure. Just be careful you don't shoot anybody with it that doesn't need shooting."

"I will, Pa. I'll be real careful."

"He's too young to be loading that musket, Hawk," Elizabeth protested.

"Oh, he'll be careful. The boy's got to learn how to take care of himself."

After breakfast was over, Hawk reached up above the door and plucked his best musket from the rack made of deer antlers. He slung his powder horn around his neck, slipped his bullet pouch inside his shirt, then said, "I've saddled my horse. Why don't you two fetch him for me."

The two children raced out, and Elizabeth went over at once. She put her arms around Hawk's neck and pulled him down and kissed him. "I'm always afraid when you go," she murmured, placing her head against his chest.

"Why, there's no problem."

"I know. The Indians are quiet right now and all, but I can't help it."

"Where's your faith, woman? I'm going to tell your pastor on you."

Elizabeth forced herself to smile. "Don't do that," she said.

He suddenly wrapped his arms around her and held her close. He put the top of his head on her soft hair, and the two stood there for a long moment. Finally he whispered, "You're the best thing I have on this earth, Elizabeth Spencer."

Elizabeth's eyes blurred. She blinked the tears away, then looked up and said saucily, "Well, I just might let you back into my feather bed when you return—if you've been well behaved!"

Hawk winked at her and said, "I'll be the best husband you ever saw."

He kissed her again, then moved outside the cabin, where he found Sequatchie already mounted on his gray stallion and smiling at him.

Sequatchie, in his middle fifties, could have passed for a much younger man. His face was smooth and he was lean and fit. His quick brown eyes studied Hawk, and he said, "You white men sleep late. I could have been halfway to Jonesborough by now."

"Iris wouldn't like that. I'll bet she made you a fine breakfast."

"Good to have a squaw. They do all the work."

Elizabeth laughed. "I'm going to tell her you said that."

"No. Don't tell her," Sequatchie smiled. He had remarried late in life to a woman named Iris Taylor, and now there was a contentment in him that had not been there when Hawk had first met him. Hawk had been fleeing from himself after the death of his first wife and would have died if Sequatchie had not found him in the wilderness. The Cherokee had taught Hawk all he knew about hunting, and now the two were fast friends.

As the children returned with his horse, Hawk swung into the saddle. Hawk pushed his coonskin cap back and, holding the reins, said, "Josh, you take care of your mother and your sister, now."

"I will, Pa. I sure will."

As the two men rode out away from the homestead, Hannah came over and stood beside her mother. She took her hand and said, "I don't like it when Pa goes away."

"Don't worry. God will take care of him."

Hannah smiled then. "He will, won't He. Come on, Josh. Let's go down to the creek and catch some fish for supper."

Something about the journey from Virginia to the distant lands beyond the Appalachians brought fear to Thomas Denton. He had lived in a city for most of his life and had little concept of the tremendous distances that had to be covered before reaching the lands that lay beyond the Misty Mountains.

As they passed through the canebrakes, unbelievably tall and dense at times, there was not room for another wagon, so that when two met it was necessary to cut a space wide enough for both to pass. He had been shocked by the thickness and immensity of the canes, which reached up to twelve feet tall and more.

Thomas had also been amazed by all the wildlife that lived off of the cane. He had passed through an immense forest, with teeming flocks of turkeys that seemed to have no fear, and deer as numerous as birds had been back in Virginia.

Now as Thomas awoke, the thought of the hundreds of miles that the three of them had covered pleased him, and yet he was anxious to reach his destination, as the immense spaces left him with a sense of loneliness—in spite of the abundant game he had seen.

He lifted his head and was startled to find that Leah was not beside him in the wagon. He sat up abruptly and saw that Sherah was sleeping peacefully. Outside he heard the ring of metal on metal, and he slipped into his pants and pulled his shirt on, then his boots. Getting out of the wagon carefully, he found Leah had started a small fire.

"Good morning," she said, turning to smile at him. "You're a sleepyhead."

"Well, it was a long trip yesterday," Thomas said as he stretched. He had discovered that Leah was tougher than he, but then she had grown up in this world and he had not. "I meant to get up with you," he said and went over to stand beside her.

"Why don't you shave. I've got some water heated."

"What for? Nobody here to see me except you."

"Well, don't I count?" Leah pretended to frown.

"Yes, you count." He put his arm around her, kissed her thoroughly, and then proceeded to shave. He had not intended to shave every day of their journey, but once, early in the trip, when he had threatened to grow a beard, Leah said, "You'll look like a bear. I won't have it." That had been the end of that.

Leah had fried ham and the last of the eggs they had bought at a settlement back down the trail. As Leah finished her breakfast, she said, "I want to have lots of chickens when we get settled. All kinds. I love eggs."

"Well, you'll have plenty of them," Thomas promised. "We'll have milk cows, beef critters, chickens, and pigs, and we'll eat until we're fat as pigs ourselves."

"How far will we have to go?"

"Well, according to what that hunter we met yesterday said, we ought to get to Jonesborough by noon."

"I'll be glad when we get to Watauga." Leah started to say something else, but a cry reached her from the wagon and she laughed. "There's Sherah wanting her breakfast."

"Well, I can't take care of that, but I'll clean up and we'll be ready to go pretty soon."

Thomas quickly cleaned the dishes and hitched the team, and by the time he had everything packed, Leah was up on the seat holding Sherah on her lap. Picking up the lines, Thomas said, "Here we go. Won't be too long now and you'll be back home."

Leah nodded thoughtfully. "It'll be good to see everyone again."

Thomas jerked at the sound of a twig snapping. He was surprised to see an Indian woman staring at him. "Hello," he finally said.

"Hello. I am Awinita. I am traveling with my son and servants to meet my brother, Sequatchie."

"I know a Cherokee named Sequatchie," Thomas replied. "He travels with a man named Hawk."

"That is my brother."

"You can join my wife and me if you would like. We are headed that way."

Jonesborough was the seat of Washington County, a sparsely settled section of the western lands claimed by North Carolina. The small village was packed with wagons and horses, and buggies of all sorts gathered around the courthouse. The settlers had come for a meeting to discuss whether they wanted to join with two other counties in North Carolina's western territories—which had recently been ceded to the Confederation Congress—to form a new, independent state.

Sequatchie leaned against the rough logs that composed the courthouse and studied the people milling around. Beside him, Hawk whittled idly on a piece of cedar, using his long knife, sharp as the razor he shaved with.

"I don't know what's going to happen here, but something's got to be settled!" Hawk declared. "We should be able to govern ourselves and have control over our own land."

Sequatchie nodded but was silent for a long time before he said, "My people have lived on this land for generations, and yet we are not consulted about these decisions that are bound to make things harder for us."

Abruptly Hawk stopped whittling and turned to ask, "Why do you say that?"

"Now that the war with England is over, there will come many white people over the mountains, especially if a new state is formed in these western territories. My people will be pushed out, but I have always known this. It is not just, but it will surely happen."

The two men waited for another hour, and finally one of the representatives came out and shouted, "It's all over! We're going to petition Congress to recognize us as a new state, and we're going to call our new state Frankin or Frankland—after Ben Franklin."

The crowd of settlers were all shouting, and several men fired guns off in celebration. Others went to the tavern to celebrate, but Hawk said, "I'm ready to go. I have a few things to get at the store. You want to get the horses saddled while I do that?"

"Yes. I'll be ready."

Hawk shouldered his way through the yelling crowd and entered the small store, which was also filled with people buying supplies. It took him some time to get his purchases, but finally he emerged and stepped out into the bright August sunlight. Perspiration dampened his face, and as he stepped down, he heard someone call his name.

"Spencer—Hawk Spencer!"

Quickly Hawk turned and his eyes flew open with astonishment. "Well, what in the world are you doing here, Tom Denton?"

Thomas had pulled the horses up and leaped to the ground. He ran over to Hawk, his face alight with pleasure. "Mr. Spencer, I'm glad to see you."

"Just Hawk. What are you doing here, Tom? Does Jacob know you're coming?"

Jacob, Hawk's son by a previous marriage, and Thomas Denton were the closest of friends. They had grown up together, and even now that Jacob was married and settled in the Watauga area, he still spoke often of his old friend.

"No. He doesn't know. You know how hard it is for mail to get through, but he'll know soon enough. We've come out to settle here. To buy land and make our home."

"Your family is with you?"

"Yes. Come along. I want you to see my daughter. Oh, and I've got something special for your friend Sequatchie."

"What's that?"

"Come along and I'll show you."

Hawk stepped across to the wagon and spoke to Leah, whom he already knew. He properly admired the new baby, and then Thomas said, "Come here. Sequatchie's in for a shock." He led Hawk back to a second wagon behind the Dentons' and stopped abruptly before an Indian woman. "This is Awinita, Sequatchie's sister!"

Awinita smiled and put her arm around her son. "Yes, it is I. It is good to meet you. And I want you to meet my son, Nathanael, but he prefers to be called Fox."

"Well, your brother's going to be surprised. He's gone to get our horses."

"He's here with you?" Awinita said eagerly.

"Yes. I'll go get him."

Hawk made his way through the crowd and found Sequatchie back in front of the courthouse holding the two horses. "Come along, Sequatchie. Tie the horses up."

"But are we going?"

"Not yet. I've got a surprise for you."

"Surprises are usually bad," Sequatchie muttered.

"Not this one. You're going to like it. I think it's kind of a Christmas present for you."

"Christmas! It's August. Christmas is a long way off. Anyway, who would be giving me a Christmas present?"

"Come along and see." Grabbing Sequatchie's arm, he tugged the reluctant Cherokee through the crowd. They came up from the side, and Sequatchie did not see who was on the wagon. He turned to say, "Well, what's the surprise?"

At that moment, Awinita heard his voice and turned. She came out of the wagon quickly and approached her brother, saying quietly, "Sequatchie!"

Sequatchie froze, then whirled. When he saw his sister standing there, he could not believe his eyes. "You are here, Awinita!" he whispered.

"Yes. I have come home."

Hawk grinned as he saw his friend shocked beyond words for the first time. "I didn't think it was possible for you to be surprised, Sequatchie," he murmured.

Sequatchie, however, said nothing. He reached out and took Awinita's hands and held them for a long time. Looking into her eyes, he said in a low, pleased voice, "I was so sorry to hear of your husband's death, but now you are here. We are together again."

"Yes, and this is your nephew. His name is Nathanael, but he prefers to be called Fox. I have written you of him."

Fox had come down out of the wagon, also. He had heard many stories about his famous uncle Sequatchie, and now he stood there embarrassed and not knowing what to do.

Sequatchie released Awinita's hands and came to stand before his nephew. He put his hands on the boy's shoulders, which brought Fox's head up, and held his eyes. The man studied his nephew for a long moment while the others watched, and finally he said, "It is good to see you, nephew. We must get to know each other."

"Yes, Uncle Sequatchie," Fox said quickly. "I want to learn everything about the Cherokee."

"I do not know if any man knows that," Sequatchie said, smiling faintly. "But I will be able to teach you a few things."

"This is Ezekiel and Mercy," Awinita said. "They must find a place to stay, too."

Sequatchie studied the two, who were watching him curiously, and then he nodded. "You will stay with me and my wife."

"All of us?" Awinita said with surprise. "Your wife might not like that."

"You will see. She is a fine woman."

"And you and your family will stay with us, Tom," Hawk said quickly.

"When can we leave?" Leah asked. "I'm so anxious to see everyone."

"Well, we'll feed and water your horses, and then we'll be ready to go," Hawk said.

An hour later the small procession moved out, the two wagons being led by the Cherokee and the long hunter. As they left the noise and excitement of Jonesborough, Thomas Denton turned to his wife and put his arm around her. His eyes were bright, and he said, "I feel like I'm coming home, too, Leah."

Fox's New Home

Eight

As the wagon rattled along the trail, Fox sat beside his mother, his eyes fixed on the two men riding ahead. He had not known what to expect when he saw his uncle, but something in the bronze features and the piercing eyes of Sequatchie had caught Fox's imagination. In truth he was lonesome for his father, and he saw in the Cherokee a man he could trust.

They had traveled steadily ever since leaving Jonesborough, and finally Fox saw Sequatchie say a word to Hawk, then turn and ride back toward them. He pulled his horse up beside the wagon and smiled. "Nephew, get behind me. You and I can get acquainted as we travel."

Instantly Fox jumped from the wagon with an agile leap and landed astride the powerful withers of the gray stallion. "It is all right, sister," Sequatchie said. "My nephew and I need some time alone."

Fox held on to the waist of his uncle as the gray stallion suddenly broke into a gallop and then into a dead run. They passed Hawk, who laughed and called out, "Don't get lost, Sequatchie." The two continued at a dead run for at least half a mile down the trail.

Finally Sequatchie pulled the stallion to a halt, and Fox released his grip. He did not speak for a time, for he had the feeling that Sequatchie did few things without a reason. He waited until finally his uncle began naming off trees. He pointed out oak, maple, hickory, chestnut, poplar, ash, black gum, and black locust.

"How many of these trees do you know?"

"Most of them," Fox said. "Lots of these grow back in Virginia."

"Show me some more and name them off."

"Well, there's a red oak, that's a basswood, and that one over there is a cherry tree. . . ."

When the boy paused, Sequatchie said, "That's good. You have learned much in your world."

"I've wanted to come here for a long time, Uncle."

"I am glad you are here. It is good to have family."

The boy sat on the broad back of the horse, and soon they passed through a river bottomland, where Fox identified sycamore, river birch, sweet gum, and willow for his uncle. Later on when they passed onto higher ground, he named several nut-bearing trees—hickory, walnut, and pecan.

"There's no country like this!" Fox exclaimed.

"I'm glad you think so. I trust it will be your home for a long time."

"I want to be a Cherokee, Uncle."

Sequatchie did not answer for a time. His eyes, as always, moved from point to point as they rode along. He had developed the habit of being wary of enemies, and now, although there appeared to be little danger, he remained alert. Finally he said, "It is getting harder all the time to be a Cherokee."

"Why is that?"

"Because our ways are dying out. In the days of my father, the Cherokee lived simply. We had wars from time to time with our neighbors, but with the white man it is different. All of the tribes in this country shared the land, but white men do not see that. They believe in owning a parcel of land for their own, and no one else can come upon it."

Fox thought about his uncle's words and then said, "We could move west."

Sequatchie smiled. "You are not the first to think of that. But no matter how far west we move, the white man still advances. I have heard of a big water far to the west. What will we do when we reach that and can go no farther? The white man will still keep coming."

The thought of the Cherokee being pushed out of their land made Fox unhappy. He had built a dream in his mind about how he would become a true Cherokee, and now that dream seemed to be falling apart. He did not speak for a long time, and Sequatchie knew that what he had spoken of to his nephew had caused the young boy's heart to carry a burden now.

"This is still God's world, Fox," he said quietly. "It is a big world, and in your time there will be plenty of woods with much deer and bear to hunt. One day all of the land, I think, will be filled and crowded, but that may be as God wills."

Fox pondered all these thoughts as his uncle Sequatchie took him back and deposited him in the wagon with his mother.

"Did you have a good talk with your uncle?" she asked him.

"He's a very wise man, but some of the things he said made me sad," Fox said.

Awinita put her hand on Fox's sturdy shoulders. "There's a sadness in being a Cherokee," she said. When he did not answer, she squeezed his shoulder and said, "But then, there is a sadness in being human. One day God will have us in His house, and there will be no sadness. So be happy, my son. Learn from your uncle. You can become a Cherokee, though a part of your father will always be in you. That may bring grief to you now, but I think one day it will bring much joy."

"Ma! Ma, they're here! Pa's back, and he's got somebody with him!"

Hannah Spencer had been boiling clothes in the black pot out beside the cabin, poking the garments with a stick. She had thrown the stick down and run to the front of the house, calling out as her father and Sequatchie emerged from around the bend, followed by two wagons.

As her mother came outside and Joshua came sailing around the house with dirt on his hands from digging fishworms, Hannah said, "Who are they, Ma?"

"I have no idea," Elizabeth said.

When the travelers reached the cabin, Sequatchie proudly introduced his sister to Elizabeth.

"It is so good to finally meet you, Awinita."

"Thank you," Awinita replied. "It is good to be back home."

"It's going to be a hot day," Jacob said. As he stretched, Amanda looked over and thought, *What a striking resemblance this older son of Hawk Spencer has to his father.* He was almost an exact copy with the same coal black wavy hair and dark blue eyes. He was the same height, though leaner and less muscular than his father.

Amanda herself was slight, very slender with an olive complexion. The daughter of Iris Taylor, who was now married to Sequatchie, Amanda had become a very attractive woman. She had been abused by her father during her early years but had blossomed after his death, and nothing in the world could have pleased her more than to have been sought as a wife by Jacob Spencer, whom she adored.

The two sat on the porch of their cabin, which Jacob had fixed up with his own hands along with considerable help from his father and Sequatchie, and waited for the sun to come up. They usually got up before dawn to sit on the porch together and watch the sun rise, after which Amanda would go in and fix breakfast. After eating they would both begin work on their homestead.

"I wonder what news Pa brought from Jonesborough," Jacob said. He leaned back on the bench he had made out of walnut, and balanced his back precariously against the smooth logs of the cabin. "He thinks we'll become a state."

"Will that make any difference to us?"

"Not as long as the title's clear."

The two sat there talking, and finally the sun, red and glowing, pushed its way up over the fog-covered mountains. "You know, that sun reminds me of an old man climbing up out of a hole," he sighed. "Old Man Sun. Sure gonna be a hot day."

At that moment Jared, their two-year-old son, suddenly appeared, running around and making a great deal of noise. His parents ignored him, for Jared always made a great deal of noise. He had such similar looks to those of his father and his grandfather, it was almost comical—the black hair, the dark blue eyes, and the sturdy frame. The three generations of Spencers made quite a picture when they lined up—Hawk, Jacob, and Jared.

Like most two-year-olds, Jared was quite a handful. Suddenly Amanda screamed, "Jacob, he's got a snake!"

Jacob came down off the porch with one movement and hit the ground running. Quick as a flash he reached out and pulled the snake out of Jared's hands. "It's all right," he said. "It's just a garter snake."

"But it's a snake! It could have been a ground rattler."

"That's right. Son, you mustn't pick up snakes."

"Why?"

This had become Jared's favorite word. He was intensely curious and would listen with all of his might as people explained, but he always wanted to know why. Now he stood looking up at his father, who had stooped down beside him and still held the snake.

"Because some snakes are very bad. They can hurt you when they bite you. So until you get old enough to know good snakes from bad snakes, promise me you won't pick up another one. Your ma and I wouldn't want you to get hurt."

Jared looked over at his mother, who was standing on the porch, her hands clenched together, still not over the fright. The little boy said calmly, "All right." Then he turned and darted off around the corner of the building.

Jacob tossed the snake down and shook his head. "Nothing troubles him."

"Well, it troubles me!" Amanda said.

"Snakes are just a part of life around here, along with bears and mountain lions and deer. He'll just have to learn how to take care of himself, and we'll have to pray for him every day."

"Well, I'm going in to fix breakfast."

"All right. I need to chop some wood for the fire. The woodpile is getting a little low."

Jacob went over to the pile of logs and began splitting one. He had become an expert log splitter, the best in Watauga, it was said. Picking up a heavy ax, he drove it lengthwise into the log, creating a tiny crevice. Bending over, he picked up a locust wedge, the wood of which was almost as hard as iron. He grabbed a short-handled sledge and pounded the wedge in until the crack ran farther down the log. Moving along, he drove the locust wedge in deeper and deeper until he heard a satisfying cracking sound and the log fell into two pieces.

As he worked he thought about how he had ended up on the frontier. Jacob had grown up with his father's parents in Virginia. He had had a difficult life, for upon the death of his mother, his father, Hawk, had practically lost his mind. He left him with his grandparents until the boy was almost grown. It had left some deep scars in Jacob, but finally his father had returned and claimed him and taken him to Watauga, where he had become an expert woodsman. He had also found a good wife and now had a fine son. Life was good to Jacob, and he began to sing aloud as he picked up the wedge and prepared to split the log in quarters.

He had split only one of them when he looked up to see a wagon, and he heard a voice crying out, "Jacob! Jacob Spencer!"

For a moment Jacob could not believe what he was seeing, then he cried out, "Why, Tom Denton!" Dropping his ax, he ran forward and the two men leaped toward each other and wrestled each other around. They had been the best of friends in Williamsburg, and Jacob was delighted to see him. "What in the world are you doing out here in the back woods?"

"I'm doing what you did, Jacob," Thomas grinned. "I'm going to be a backwoodsman. Come along and see my new daughter. She's my pride and joy." Jacob knew Tom's wife, Leah, of course. He and Amanda had been surprised, but very pleased when Leah had written of their marriage. It had seemed strange to Jacob that Leah had met his best friend after leaving Watauga with her family and had fallen in love with him. He could see now that both were very happy. He greeted Leah warmly before admiring their daughter, Sherah.

Soon the two families were seated inside and eating a big breakfast. The two men talked rapidly, reminiscing over old times as Leah and Amanda did the same. Finally Jacob said, "What's it like back in Virginia, Tom?"

Thomas was eating a biscuit. He swallowed the morsel and then said with a worried frown, "It's changed a lot now that the Revolution is over. Everybody that was on the British side is in trouble. The patriots have seized their property in many cases."

Thomas spoke on for a time and then shrugged his shoulders. "After my mother died, I began to think that I needed a change. Leah always loved this place, and to tell the truth, I guess I've just got an adventurous streak in me."

"Jacob, do you think that we can make it out here?" Leah asked quickly.

"Why, of course you can."

"What I mean is . . . Tom's family were Tories," Leah said anxiously.

"Nobody knows that. In any case, other Tories have come over the mountains to make a new life. Most of the time folks out here just struggle to live from day to day and don't get too fussed about politics after the fact."

Amanda had been listening closely to all this and asked quickly, "How is Annabelle?"

Thomas smiled wistfully. "Well, she's still throwing parties and trying to be the prettiest girl in Virginia. I guess maybe she might be, too . . . now that I've stolen Leah away, that is!"

"Did you get to see my grandmother before you left?" Jacob asked.

"Miss Esther? I sure did. I made a special trip, and I've got letters for you in the wagon."

"She's the finest lady I've ever known. I'm sure she misses my grandfather, James," Jacob said with some sadness in his voice. His grandfather had practically raised him, and even though Jacob had not been able to see James Spencer very often after moving to the frontier, he still grieved over his death.

"She seems to be doing very well. She's happy to have Anne Martin living with her, especially now. She misses you, of course."

The talk went around to Awinita and Fox, and Thomas said, "We met them on the trail here. It was surprising we were coming to the same country, but then maybe not so much so. A lot of people are headed over the mountains toward Watauga and even farther west."

"Well, Sequatchie will be glad to have Fox around," Jacob said.

"Fox has already made an idol out of his uncle. He talked about nothing else all the way here."

The visit lasted all day, and finally when their company had left, Jacob said, "You know, it's so good to see Tom again."

"Yes. And good to see Leah, too. They've got a good marriage. Who would've believed they would find each other after Leah left? You can tell they love each other, and Sherah is a sweet baby girl."

"I think we ought to have one that sweet, too."

"Oh, you do?"

"Yes, I do. I've been thinking a lot about that lately." Jacob pulled her to him and said, "What do you say?"

"I think it would be a good idea, too. But what if it's another boy?"

"Well, we can only keep on trying. I'll tell you what. We'll try ten times, and if we end up with ten boys I'll just give up!"

As soon as Thomas got back to the Spencer cabin, he began to write a letter to his sister, Annabelle. After telling her of their safe arrival, he ended the letter, saying, "A woman named Awinita and her son, Fox Carter, are here. I remember Father mentioning some friends, I think, who had that name. They may be related to Fox. I just thought I'd mention it. You might ask around."

Awinita had found time to speak to Sequatchie, and she had told him why they had to leave. Sequatchie had listened as she told the story of how Fox's uncle Naaman would have killed them if they had stayed.

Sequatchie made no comment, except to say, "You will stay with me as long as you need to."

"I've worried about Ezekiel and Mercy," Awinita said. "They were so good to us on the way. I got sick, and I think I would have died if it hadn't been for Mercy's care."

"They'll be safe on this side of the mountains."

"It wouldn't have been safe for them to stay at Havenwood," Awinita said quickly.

Sequatchie, later on, spoke to Fox, saying, "You're going to have a good time here, Fox. I will teach you what you need to know to be a good woodsman, and Hawk Spencer will teach you much, too."

"People back home didn't like it because I was half Indian and half white. Will that make a difference here, Uncle?"

"It may with some people." He put his hand on his nephew's shoulder. "But God doesn't know black or white or red. He only knows those who are His people and those who are not. Let that content you, nephew."

A Home With Christ

Nine

Fox was awakened abruptly out of a deep sleep by the rustling of a hunting bird's wings as it took flight from its perch outside the attic. The moon shone into the small room with the roof coming to a peak over his head. One small window admitted light and air, and Fox came off his bed and went to the window and stared outside. The moonlight poured its silver light over his uncle's homestead, and the boy's eyes sought the night sky for signs of the owl, or whatever bird it had been. He saw nothing, however, but he was wide awake. He had no way of telling time, but he knew that dawn was not far away. A faint line of light had already begun to show in the east.

Growing restless, Fox slipped into his clothes and moved as quietly as he could down the ladder that led to the lower part of the house. The house consisted of one large room used for a kitchen, a dining room, and a living area, with two good-sized bedrooms. Fox slipped outside, closing the door carefully behind him, and moved along the path that led toward the deep woods. He had made this trip several times, and now he followed the well-worn trail that led down to a small stream full of plump, juicy sunfish and bass. Reaching the stream, he waited as the sun slowly came up. He had no gun, but he longed to be out-of-doors. As he stood there he was dreaming of the hunting trip that his uncle had promised to take him on shortly.

The water gurgled over the round stones in the small stream, and the line of light grew thicker and broader and finally began to filter down between the leaves, throwing a pattern of light and shade on the earth all around. The leaves stirred with a rising morning breeze, and Fox began to walk as quietly as he could beside the creek. He followed a path for a time, but then it disappeared, so he made his way carefully along the bank, placing his feet as quietly as he could. All the while he wished he had a gun so that he might bring something back from a hunt.

He had not gone more than two hundred yards down the creek when suddenly he heard an odd noise. Stopping in his tracks, he held his head high and sniffed the air almost as an alert animal would. Perhaps much like his namesake, the fox. The sound seemed to come from directly ahead, and he slowly moved forward on the sunlit forest floor.

It sounded almost like a man grunting from trying to move a heavy weight.

The woods along the creek were filled with briars and wild berries that impeded him. They scratched his hands, and he blinked once when a twig slashed across his open mouth, but he uttered no sound.

He was slowly closing in on whatever was making the noise. Finally he reached a huge cedar tree that rose majestically into the sky. Quietly he pressed himself against it, for he could hear the noise very plainly now—just on the other side of this tree. Slowly Fox eased himself around and took one slight step—and then he froze.

An enormous black bear was feeding on the remains of a calf. Instantly Fox knew that this calf belonged either to Sequatchie or the Spencers. Black bears did not usually attack something as large as a calf. Fox figuered this one must have been very hungry. The bear suddenly lifted his head, and his small eyes seemed to bore right into those of Fox.

Fox remained absolutely still and even held his breath. The bear continued to stare at him and then sniffed the air. Fox was thankful that he was downwind from the bear, but he had also heard that bears would charge for no real reason. They could be fierce, deadly creatures. Sequatchie had told him so.

For a moment Fox thought that the bear started to advance, but then he seemed to change his mind and with a grunt began tearing at the carcass.

Fox pulled himself behind the tree and found that his legs were unsteady. Making as little noise as possible, he kept the tree between him and the large animal and retreated until finally the sound was faint. Then he turned and fled at full speed along the trail beside the creek. He ran toward the cabin, and as soon as he reached it, he began to call, "Uncle! Uncle!"

Sequatchie had risen and now he stepped out on the porch, anxiety on his face. "What is it, nephew?"

"A black bear. It's eating on a calf."

"Where did you see this?"

"There. Down by the creek." Fox pointed.

Sequatchie turned without a word and went inside. Awinita and Iris came out wearing robes, and Iris said, "What is it?"

"A bear. Fox saw him eating that calf."

"Oh no, not our calf!"

"Well, I hope he enjoyed it. At least we'll get some good bear steaks. But I know you loved that calf."

Fox watched breathlessly and finally whispered, "Uncle, could I go, too?"

Sequatchie suddenly turned. He had loaded his musket and held it in his left hand. He studied the boy and then nodded. "Yes. It is time." He looked over at Awinita, who nodded at him, and said, "Here, take this rifle. I will load my other." He quickly loaded the other musket and said, "We will be back soon."

Awinita wanted to call out to Fox to be careful, but she knew that would embarrass him. When the two had left, she said, "It's such a hard life out here. It's so dangerous."

"Yes, but he will learn. Sequatchie will teach him," Iris said.

Fox and Sequatchie hurried along the path through the woods until they reached the creek, and then Sequatchie asked, "This way?"

"Yes. About two hundred yards."

"If you shoot, shoot for the head. A black bear as large as this one can take a dozen bullets in his body unless you hit a vital spot. Try for the head."

"All right, Uncle, I will."

As the two moved quietly along the creek, Fox admired the way Sequatchie seemed to move effortlessly and without a sound. His own footsteps were clumsy by comparison, no matter how hard he tried.

Sequatchie moved slower as the bear's grunts got louder, and he put his finger to his lips. The two moved closer and finally they reached the huge cedar tree. Fox nodded and pointed just on the other side. Sequatchie agreed. The two stepped out and almost at once the bear saw them.

Fox expected Sequatchie to shoot. Instead, he was stunned when his uncle said, "Take the shot, Fox."

Hardly daring to breathe, Fox blinked with astonishment. He watched the bear rise up on its hind legs, over six feet tall. And then it lowered itself and moved forward slowly but snarling.

Fox put the bead right on the bear's head, held his breath, then pulled the trigger. The retort of the rifle disturbed the silence of the forest, and the recoil of the weapon kicked Fox's shoulder back, making him wince. He waited for Sequatchie to fire, but when he looked he saw that the bear was down.

Sequatchie put his hand on the boy's shoulder. "A fine shot," he said quietly. "Come."

The two approached the bear, Fox with awe at the sheer size of the bear. He watched as Sequatchie knelt beside the massive head in silence.

Sequatchie reached over and touched the wound in the bear's head. Blood was on his finger and he arose. Fox watched him, not knowing what he was going to do, and then he felt his uncle's finger on his forehead and then on his cheeks. He felt the hot blood of the bear as it ran down his face.

"It is the mark of the first blood for you, Fox," his uncle whispered. "You will be a great hunter. Greater than your father, greater than I."

Fox knew that something had changed for him. He looked deep into the eyes of his uncle. Sequatchie's eyes seemed to bore into him with an unsettling steadiness. He knew that his uncle wanted to impress upon him the significance of this moment, and he did not know what to say. Suddenly he felt tears well up. He blinked them away and turned so that his uncle could not see them.

But Sequatchie had seen. Now he came and put his arm around the boy. "I wept when I killed my first bear," he whispered. "Now you are the true son of a Cherokee."

Three days after the slaying of the bear, Fox got into the wagon early on Sunday morning and found himself sitting beside Hannah Spencer. The men were riding horses, so Fox drove the wagon with the women. He wished he could have ridden with the men, but Sequatchie had asked it of him, and that was enough for Fox.

"Tell me again about the bear," Hannah said.

Fox felt uncomfortable around Hannah Spencer. He did not know what to make of her. She was over two years younger than he and had attached herself to him from the moment he had stepped foot on the Spencer homestead. He liked her well enough, but for some reason felt awkward around her. She had no apprehensions at all about asking the most intimate questions, and he felt somewhat pressured by this.

"It was just a bear."

"But it was such a big one, and it filled the smokehouse up, too. Tell me again how you killed it."

Fox spoke to the horses, for the men had pulled out, and as they moved along he began to tell the story of the hunt.

Awinita, seated behind him with Iris, Elizabeth, and Joshua, listened with amusement and yet with pride. Sequatchie had told her that not many men could face a charging bear and calmly put a bullet through its head. "He will be a great hunter, sister," he had said.

Now as they rolled along, Elizabeth and Iris talked about their children. Awinita listened passively. She caught a glimpse of her son's profile from time to time, and a sadness pricked her heart as she remembered Titus and longed to have him back. Losing him had been like having her heart torn out, and she had never revealed the depth of her sorrow and grief to anyone, least of all to Fox. She knew that he, too, was struggling with the loss of his father, and it was a great joy to her to realize that Sequatchie could, in some ways, be a father to her son.

"Weren't you afraid?" Hannah asked breathlessly.

"I didn't have time to be afraid."

"Didn't have time! It doesn't take long to be afraid. Why, I stepped on a snake the other day. I was so afraid I screamed. I didn't have to think about it."

Fox could not help laughing. "You sure have a funny way of putting things, Hannah."

"But were you afraid?"

"No, I wasn't afraid."

"But what if you had missed? The bear would have eaten you."

"No. Sequatchie was right beside me. I doubt if he's ever missed a shot in his life."

"That's right. I'd forgotten about Sequatchie. What are you going to do with the hide?"

"Sequatchie's going to show me how to cure it out, and then I'll make a rug of it and put it beside my bed."

"Why don't you give me half of it. My feet get cold in the morning. It would be nice to get out on a nice warm bearskin rug."

"I want the other half," Joshua demanded.

"That makes three halves," Fox grinned. "Pretty soon I'll cut the thing up in so many pieces it won't even look like a bear." He found himself enjoying talking with Hannah and Joshua, but he knew he would never cut the bear up—he would keep it forever. Perhaps give it to his son if he ever had one.

"What's the preacher's name?" Awinita asked as the wagon jolted along.

"It's Reverend Seth Donovan. He comes from Scotland."

"Is he a good preacher?"

"Oh yes, he is," Elizabeth said quickly. "One of the finest we've ever had. Of course, I'm a little prejudiced. He's my son-in-law."

"Well, he's still the best except for Reverend Anderson, I think."

The women went on talking about Seth Donovan, and Awinita listened carefully. "So he came over to fight for the king but decided not to."

"Yes, he did, and when he met my daughter, Sarah, the two fell in love and that was it," Elizabeth said.

By the time the group had gotten to the church, which was made of logs, as was everything else in Watauga, Fox had learned a great deal about the community. Iris knew everyone, as did Elizabeth Spencer, and both Fox and his mother listened avidly, trying to remember all the names. Of course Hannah was right there chattering at his side, and as he got out of the wagon and tied the horses, she came and said, "Come on, Fox. You can sit with me."

"No. He's going to sit with me," Joshua said firmly.

"He can sit between the two of you," Awinita said. "Go along, Fox. Make sure you behave yourself."

Fox gave her an injured glance. "Behave myself! Don't I always?"

"Yes, you do."

"Well, Joshua doesn't," Hannah said. "You can make him behave."

The argument about who was going to make who behave continued until finally they were inside. Fox looked around at the church, which was about thirty feet wide and no more than forty feet long. The benches were made of half-split logs with pegs for legs, and a simple table stood at the front with a pitcher and a glass of water on it. Fox was accustomed to an ornate church back in Williamsburg, but somehow he found this roughhewn church on the frontier pleasing.

A young boy came up and said, "Hello, Hannah."

"Oh, hello, Ethan. This is Fox." The two boys studied each other warily. Ethan Cagle had dark hair and sea green eyes and appeared to be slightly younger than Fox.

"We're the same age," Hannah said, as if reading Fox's mind.

Ethan was staring at Fox, and finally he turned his head to one side and asked, "Are you an Indian?"

Fox felt his face grow warm. Several people around had heard the question, and he nodded. "Yes. I'm a Cherokee."

"He's only half Cherokee, Ethan," Hannah said quickly.

Ethan did not comment. He stood staring at Fox for a time, then walked away without another word.

"He's usually nicer than that. Some of his kinfolk were killed by Indians in a raid, so he's a little wary around Indians. But don't let him bother you. He'll like you fine when he knows you better."

Fox was accustomed to this sort of treatment in Williamsburg, but he had hoped it would be different on the frontier. Now he saw that it would not be. He tried to shove it out of his mind and listen as Hannah described other people and as Joshua interrupted with his own comments.

Finally a large man stood up and entered the room and went to stand behind the table. "That's Reverend Donovan. Isn't he fine looking?"

Seth Donovan was indeed a fine-looking man. His golden blond hair would have reached to his shoulders, but he had it clubbed. It was thick as a lion's mane. He had blue-green eyes and was very broad shouldered and deep chested.

"He's married to my half sister," Hannah said. "I think he's the handsomest man in all of Watauga, but he doesn't seem to know it."

At this point Elizabeth reached over and thumped Hannah on the head and whispered, "You be quiet! The service is starting."

The singing pleased Fox exceedingly. He had a fine, clear voice that had only recently changed, and now he joined in the hymn. They sang "Great God of Wonders," by Samuel Davies, one of Fox's favorites, and his voice rose clear and pure above the others:

Great God of wonders! all thy ways
Are matchless, Godlike, and divine;
But the fair glories of thy grace
More Godlike and unrivaled shine.
More Godlike and unrivaled shine.

Many people were turning around to see whose fine voice it was, and Awinita felt a gush of pride.

In wonder lost, with trembling joy,
We take the pardon of our God;
Pardon for crimes of deepest dye,
A pardon bought with Jesus' blood;
A pardon bought with Jesus' blood.

And then the chorus came:

Who is a pardoning God like thee?
Or who has grace so rich and free?
Or who has grace so rich and free?

"The boy has a fine voice," Sequatchie whispered to Awinita. He was sitting next to her and reached over and touched her hand. She turned to face him and saw the smile that reached even his eyes. "He doesn't get that from me."

"Nor from me. But his father could sing like that."

The song service went on for a while, concluding with "O God Our Help in Ages Past," a hymn based on the Scripture lesson for the morning. Then Seth Donovan rose and greeted his congregation. After a short prayer, he said, "We have visitors with us today, and we are happy to welcome them." A smile touched his broad lips, and he went on, "In large churches in big cities, people can go for years and not be noticed. But here where we are small, we all know each other. After the service I would like to meet all of you who are new to this part of the world, to this community, and we trust that God will bring you here often."

Fox felt a warmth for the preacher. He had a strange way of speaking with his Scottish accent, but Fox easily understood him. Donovan had a powerful voice, but he did not shout, exuding warmth and confidence as if he were speaking to Fox personally.

"My text this morning is found in the book of Psalms. We know that Moses, the great man of God, wrote one psalm—the Ninetieth Psalm—and it begins with a verse that I have always loved. 'Lord, thou hast been our dwelling place in all generations.' The last hymn we sang was based on this psalm."

Reverend Donovan spoke for some time about the background of the psalm, and at one point in his sermon, he said, "When Moses wrote this, the Israelites lived in tents and were wandering in the wilderness. Every morning they got up and followed the pillar of cloud God provided to lead them. No man or woman knew which way they would go. Day after day, week after week, month after month, and year after year they followed the cloud, and all of that time not a single house was built. Not a cabin, not a lean-to. They lived in tents made from the hides of their herds of cattle and sheep."

Fox listened carefully as the preacher went on to talk about the wanderers in the wilderness, and he felt a sadness. *That's what I am. I don't really have a home.* The thought troubled him, and he glanced at his mother, who was listening intently to the minister, then turned his attention back to the sermon.

"But Moses is telling us that, even though we may not have a house of wood or stone, yet we always have a home, for God himself is our dwelling place. Isn't that a wonderful thought!" Reverend Donovan exclaimed. "They had no homes built of wood, but they dwelled in God. And that is what I want to stress this morning. None of us knows whether we will have a house to live in tomorrow. Houses burn down, floods sweep them away, but nothing can ever change God. He is the unchangeable One, and that's why I want my habitation to be in Him. A house that I cannot ever lose. While I'm here on earth He is my home. Christ is my home, and when I die I will go to my home who is Christ."

The sermon was the best Fox had ever heard and it moved him. Seth Donovan made it clear that houses did not matter. Things did not matter. Only being in Christ mattered, and Fox found himself entranced by the words of the preacher.

Finally the sermon came to an end, and Reverend Donovan said quietly, "I would ask you one question this morning. Is your home in Christ? If it is not, then you are a wanderer. You may own the biggest home in the world, which may be worth a lot of money, but it will not last. Only Christ lasts, and the only house we can have is in Him. So I encourage you this morning to turn your hearts to Jesus Christ. He is the answer. Make *Him* your home."

After the sermon was over, Fox filed out with the congregation, and immediately Hannah grabbed his arm and turned him around so that he had to face her. "Isn't he a great preacher?"

Fox did not have time to answer, for suddenly Ethan Cagle was there. He said, "Hannah, come here. I want to talk to you."

"But I'm talking to Fox."

Cagle simply reached out and took her arm and led her away protesting.

For one moment Fox was tempted to challenge Cagle. He did not understand the boy's motivation, but he did know that Cagle disliked him because he was a Cherokee.

Fox's mother came to stand beside him. She had seen the whole thing, and she said, "That was a wonderful sermon, wasn't it?"

"Yes it was, Mother."

Awinita hesitated, wanting to say something about the Cagle boy's behavior, but she knew that Fox would face worse, so she said only, "Come. Let's join the others."

Of Children and Grandchildren

Ten

The Spencer cabin had been enlarged twice. The last addition, a huge room, was designed especially so all the family could enjoy being together. As Hawk had put it, "Now we've got children and grandchildren and sooner or later great-grandchildren. I hope one day, wife, to see this room packed to the walls with Spencers and Donovans and MacNeals."

Now as Elizabeth moved around the huge fireplace, she took an opportunity to gaze about the large room with satisfaction. *Well,* she thought with wry amusement, *there's plenty of room here to satisfy even Hawk.*

The room itself was twenty feet wide and twenty-five feet long. At one end of it, the fireplace, built of stone from the river, dominated the room. It was fully equipped with tongs and shovels and cooking implements that hung from iron hooks. The fireplace was big enough to take almost full-sized logs. Although the weather was hot, the cooking fires had been lit, and Elizabeth went over to check the huge pot that was bubbling with beans, which had been soaked overnight in preparation for the family's Sunday lunch.

One of her implements, a bread toaster, had been designed by Hawk. She picked it up and admired the delicate work. It was made of iron with twisted links to hold slices of toast. It had three legs, two under the toast itself and one farther back on the long arm. All of the other women in the Watauga settlement were envious of the contraption, and Hawk had laughed, saying, "If I ever want to stop being a farmer, I can go into the toaster business."

The cooking pots that hung from rods near the back of the fireplace were also made out of iron and had been forged by Hawk. She had decided to make some dressed eggs and had put her salamander, or long-handled shovel, in the fire until it was red-hot. Quickly she cracked the eggs, threw them into the frying pan, and cooked them over the fire. When the eggs were set but not hard, she held the salamander over the eggs to cook the tops. She had found it to be the best way of broiling food.

After the eggs were done, she set them aside under a cloth and then began making johnnycakes. Johnnycakes were the main item of the Spencer household's diet, and Elizabeth made them expertly. She heated water and butter in a saucepan, then added cornmeal, salt, and sugar. She poured it all into a large bowl, added milk, and stirred it until the batter was well mixed. Then after greasing the skillet, she dropped six spoonfuls of batter onto it. She busied herself until the cakes had cooked about five minutes and were golden brown, then turned them over. She made enough of these to fill a large platter, and just as she was finishing, the room was invaded by the screams of youngsters. Elizabeth's grandson Abel dashed in, followed by his little cousin Jared, and rushing in after them was Abel's mother, Abigail MacNeal. The two boys ran around the room screaming like wild animals.

"Elizabeth, I know these boys are driving you crazy," Abigail said.

"Not at all. Let them holler. We need a little excitement around here."

Abigail had just managed to harness Abel and was lecturing him on being quiet, but Elizabeth just laughed. "Trying to get a two-year-old boy to be quiet is like trying to tell the sun to come up in the west, Abigail."

Elizabeth went over to her two grandsons. She saw in Abel's face traces of her first husband, Patrick MacNeal, and although she said nothing, she had a fondness in her heart for him still. She had loved him dearly, and she saw in Andrew and Sarah, his children, traces of him every time she looked at them.

After a time the men trooped in, and once everyone was seated, Hawk asked a rather lengthy blessing. When he had finished, he looked around and grinned. "That blessing was a little longer than usual."

Sarah had come to visit with her husband, Seth Donovan, and

now she teased her father. "You're just showing off because the minister's here."

Reverend Donovan laughed and winked at Sarah. His face was flushed from his play outside with the youngsters, and he put his arm around Sarah and gave her an affectionate squeeze. "That'll be the day when Hawk Spencer tries to impress me."

"You're wrong about that, Parson," Hawk said. "I always like to impress the preacher. We have such bad people in our family." Here he leaned over and looked directly at Elizabeth. "One of us has to be good to balance out the rest."

Elizabeth laughed and shoved him away. "I think everyone knows," she said, "exactly who's the good one in this house."

Sarah loved to watch her mother and stepfather tease each other. Her husband, Seth, had been impressed by this relationship also, and now he squeezed Sarah and whispered so low that no one could hear, "I love your parents. I hope our marriage will be as happy as theirs."

Sarah took Seth's hand and squeezed it, and as she did, Andrew nudged Abigail and said, "Look, Abby, the preacher's making up to his wife. Isn't that just graceful?"

Everyone laughed. They all admired Seth Donovan and knew that he was destined to become a great preacher. Hawk and Elizabeth were both as proud of him as they could be, and now Hawk said, "Which of the men in the Spencer family do you think is the best looking, Reverend?"

"I am," Andrew said, winking at his mother. "Everyone knows that. I'm surprised you would need to ask, Pa."

Hawk leaned over and pretended to examine his stepson's features. Although Andrew was not his blood kin, he felt as strongly about him as he did about his own sons, Jacob and Joshua. He had never treated the three of them any differently, and now he pretended to be puzzled. "I don't know. Jacob has the looks of his old man—mighty handsome indeed. Of course, it's hard to beat the original!"

The foolishness went on for some time, but after the meal was over, Elizabeth noticed that Sarah seemed sad. When the others had gone outside to watch the children play games, she said, "Come now, daughter, let's have a cup of tea."

"All right, Mother."

They sat down and drank the strong tea, which was a treat. Real black tea had to come all the way from the coast, so usually they just drank sassafras tea. Elizabeth tried to make conversation, saying, "Imagine, somewhere over across the world in China, the tea leaves were grown that made this. I wonder what the names of the farmers were?"

Sarah smiled. "You think of the oddest things, Mother."

"I suppose I do, but we're out here so far away from everything. We never know what's going on in the rest of the world."

"No. I suppose it's all most of us can do just to survive. It's hard living on the frontier."

"Have you ever been sorry that we came out here and left Boston, Sarah?"

"Not a bit. God was in it, Mother."

"Yes, He was." She was silent for a while, and then she said quietly, "I still think of your father so often. He was such a good man."

"So do I. I think of him almost every day."

"He would have been proud of you and Andrew. As a matter of fact, I think he still is."

"Mother," Sarah said, "do you really think people in heaven know what we're doing down here on earth? That Father knows about me and Andy?"

"Only God knows those things, but I like to think that they do. After all, they loved you on earth. Why wouldn't they love you in heaven?"

"That's a good thought," Sarah smiled. She took her tea and poured a little honey in it. Stirring it with a pewter spoon, she said, "God's been good to us. All of our family is healthy, and your grandchildren are strong."

Elizabeth studied her daughter, and finally she asked bluntly, "Is anything wrong, Sarah?"

"No. Not really, Mother."

"Oh, come now. I know you better than that. What is it?"

A slight flush tinged Sarah's cheek, and she said with some embarrassment, "I had thought that Seth and I might have a baby by this time, but we haven't."

Well, that's it, then, Elizabeth thought. *She's worried about not having any children. Perhaps she even thinks she's barren.* Quickly she said, "You mustn't worry about that. You and Seth have been married only a short time."

"I know, but when I see Abel and Jared and how happy Amanda and Abigail are with their babies, and both of them already expecting again, I feel left out somehow."

The sounds of the children shouting outside floated in through the room, and Elizabeth sat there praying quietly that she would have the words to say that would give comfort to this daughter of hers. She loved Sarah dearly and wanted her to be happy in every way. Finally she said, "It's hard for us to remember, Sarah, that God doesn't always move in the way we think He should. We know we like things to be orderly and to go as we like them to, but sometimes they don't. Just think about Abraham and Sarah longing for a son all those years."

"I've thought about her so much lately, Mother," Sarah said. "We have the same name, so I suppose she's always been one of my favorite characters in the Bible. And I thought about how she was a lovely woman, how men found her attractive, even the Pharaoh of Egypt, and yet she didn't have a child for years and years."

"But when she did, it was right in line with God's will," Elizabeth said.

"I know that, and I'm trying to be patient." Suddenly she laughed and said, "I was always an impatient little monster, wasn't I?"

"You never were a monster," Elizabeth smiled. "But you always were a little quick."

"That's a nice way to put it—quick."

"Well, you were impulsive—much more so than Andy. I can remember you always got him into all sorts of pickles. You were always the instigator."

"That's what I was, an instigator but not a monster," Sarah smiled. Then she grew sober and said, "I love children so much, and Seth wants a family, too. We're both praying for a child, and I want you and Pa to pray with us."

"We'll do that, of course, and I'll also pray for patience for you."

"Well, that's a dangerous thing, for the Bible says tribulation worketh patience."

"Oh, so you want the patience but not the tribulation. Is that it?" Elizabeth laughed. "Well, I guess we're all that way. Come now.

Let's go outside and watch the children play. I think I can hear your father over all of them. He loves games better than the youngsters do."

They moved outside and found the yard crowded with their own family as well as with neighbors and their children. Hawk, out of breath and dripping with sweat, had joined Sequatchie, Paul Anderson, and Will Martin, Elizabeth's brother, all of whom were watching from the shade of a tree as the young people raced after a ball.

For a time the two women watched too, and then Sequatchie came over and sat down on the porch beside them. "That was a fine meal, Elizabeth," he said.

"You think any meal's fine, Sequatchie."

"Well, when you've gone for as long as I have at times without food, you appreciate most meals. But this one was particularly fine." Sequatchie had abandoned, for the most part, his Cherokee dress, which in the summer consisted mostly of a breechcloth with leggings. Now he wore a simple gray linen shirt that Iris had woven for him and a pair of blue linen trousers. The loose shirt was fastened around his waist with a broad belt, making his waist look even narrower than it was. He watched the game for a while, and finally he said, "I wish Fox would join in more."

Elizabeth had noticed that Fox was standing on the outside, and she said, "You'll have to give him time. You know how young people are. They have to find their place in the circle."

Sequatchie said slowly, "I'm not sure, Elizabeth. I'm worried about him. He doesn't seem to be able to fit in."

"He will. Don't worry about it, Sequatchie," Sarah said quickly.

They watched for a time, and Rhoda Anderson, Paul's wife, noticed that her daughter, Rachel, who was only ten, seemed to be more active than some of the boys.

"Look at that Rachel," Elizabeth said. "She's climbing a tree."

"Yep, she's more like a boy than she is a girl," Sequatchie said. But then as they watched, Rachel got into some sort of argument with Joshua, and the two went wrestling around on the dirt, both of them yelling.

"She does think she's a boy," Rhoda sighed. "She's gonna break Josh's arm." Rhoda went to tend to her daughter.

Sequatchie laughed and said to Elizabeth, "Well, she's going to be a beautiful woman when she grows up. One of these days she'll be breaking boys' hearts instead of their arms."

The early afternoon sun was hot, and Elizabeth and Sarah had brought out refreshments for all of the youngsters. There was plenty of blackberry punch and cookies baked in the Dutch oven.

Hannah went to where Fox was standing alone and said, "Come on over, Fox. These are good cookies."

Fox, indeed, had felt left out. He had not seemed to find his place with the young people. Joshua had introduced him to his cousins, Eve and David Martin, and to Rachel Anderson, but Fox had remained somewhat distant, partly because Ethan Cagle was also among the group.

As Fox took a cookie and ate it, then reached for another one, David suddenly said, "You know, we're all going to be attending that new school called the Martin Academy." He turned and asked, "Where did you go to school, Fox?"

Fox was embarrassed, for he had never gone to a formal school. He had told Hannah about this, however, and now she said quickly, "Fox had a private tutor back on the plantation in Virginia."

Fox nodded. "Yes. That's the way it was."

"Well, school will be different," Eve said.

"It'll be fun," Hannah agreed. "We'll get together every day. Pa's going to let us ride a horse to school."

"Sequatchie said I could use one of his horses, too."

It was discovered that most of the youngsters had obtained similar permission from their parents, so they would all be riding, some with younger brothers and sisters behind them.

As the group began to break up and families started to head toward home, Hannah moved closer to Fox. "It'll be fun going to school, Fox."

"I don't know. Teachers can be pretty hard, I heard."

"Oh, this is Mr. Samuel Doak. He's a fine teacher."

"Do you know him?"

"Yes. He's also a minister. He's been teaching around here, just individuals, for a long time. I really like him, and you will, too."

"Maybe it will be all right," he said.

"You're always worrying about things, Fox. I wish you wouldn't."

"Well, if you were half Indian, you'd be worried, too, Hannah."

Hannah's feelings were hurt. "I never said anything about you being half Indian. I love Sequatchie and his Cherokee friends."

Suddenly a wave of remorse swept over Fox, and he said quickly, "I'm sorry, Hannah. I didn't mean to snap at you."

Hannah brightened up at once. "That's all right. It's going to be lots of fun."

Trouble at Martin Academy

Eleven

Fox found Martin Academy more difficult than he had thought. Perhaps this was because he had not applied himself back in Virginia. For whatever reason, he found himself having to work harder than others. And although Samuel Doak, a tall man with level dark eyes who could pinpoint laziness without effort, was not a cruel teacher, still he was demanding. Fox wanted desperately to prove himself in his studies. He did not want to embarrass his mother or his uncle by falling behind the rest of his classmates.

September had come, and the cool air was now sweeping over the countryside. Fox sat at his place in the small log schoolhouse listening as Mr. Doak spoke of geography, pointing out pictures of North America on a large map fastened on the wall. Fox was interested in the country and had dreams about what lay beyond the vast distances to the west.

Finally Mr. Doak laid his pointer down and said, "Now we're going to talk about your assignments. I trust you've all spent some time on your work."

Fox shifted uneasily, for the assignment had been for each student to write a brief essay on his background. Fox had struggled with this and found it difficult. He hoped that Mr. Doak would pass him by without comment.

Hannah, as usual, had her work done. She, Eve, David, and Joshua had worked on the project together as they were cousins. She stood up and read in a clear voice the history of her family as they came from Virginia and Massachusetts and ultimately from England.

"That's very good, Hannah. I'll check your spelling." Mr. Doak smiled, took Hannah's paper, and began to call on other students. Most of them, Fox noted uneasily, had no trouble with the assignment. Finally, when Fox was asked to read his paper, he got up reluctantly and mumbled so badly that Mr. Doak had to say sharply, "That's no way to read a paper, Nathanael. Stand up straight and read it loudly."

The two boys who sat directly behind Fox, Eli Harrison and Isaiah Tompkins, snickered, and one of them said, "Maybe he doesn't want to read about his family, Mr. Doak."

Surprised at Eli's remark, Mr. Doak said, "Whatever do you mean by that?"

"Well, I mean what's he going to say? His family was a bunch of savages. Don't know how anybody could write anything about that."

"That's enough from you, Eli!"

"I was just commenting, Mr. Doak," Eli said, trying to look innocent.

But Isaiah Tompkins snickered, and Fox felt a flicker of anger growing in him. He turned and said, "Don't you say anything about my family, Eli!"

"You're mighty proud of them redskin savages you come from," Eli snapped, his face growing red.

"Eli, that's enough! You go stand in that corner."

"Why, I didn't—"

"You heard what I said. Go stand in the corner!" Mr. Doak watched as the boy flung his books to one side and stomped to the corner. He did not face the wall, however, but turned a baleful glare on Fox.

Mr. Doak hesitated. He did not want to make an issue of this, and he was well aware that some of the citizens of Watauga did not take kindly to Indians. They felt they had to put up with Sequatchie, for he was a prominent member of the Cherokee nation, and everyone wanted to remain on as good terms as possible with that tribe. *But this boy is another problem*, Doak thought. *If I press this too hard, Harrison and Tompkins will take it out on him after school.* Finally he said, "You stand there until the class is over, and I'll hear no more smart comments about anyone's background."

Though they went on with their lessons and Mr. Doak seemed satisfied with Fox's paper, Fox was embarrassed. It was late in the afternoon when all this took place, and an hour later Mr. Doak dismissed the class. He stopped beside Fox long enough to say, "Don't let those two bother you, my boy."

Fox looked at the schoolmaster, his face rigid. "I can't ignore them, sir."

"I know it's hard, but do the best you can. Everyone who matters respects your family. You'll have to remember that Eli lost an older brother during an Indian attack. That's no excuse, of course, but hard to explain to a boy his age. Try to keep a good spirit."

"Yes, sir. I'll try."

When Fox walked outside the schoolhouse, Hannah was standing there waiting for him. Fox saw quickly that Eli and Isaiah were waiting, also, and his lips drew into a white line as they approached him.

Hannah saw the two boys coming and yelled, "You leave Fox alone!"

"Get out of the way, Hannah," Eli said, grinning broadly. "I'm gonna bust up this Indian."

Hannah immediately began to call some of the students to come around. She yelled for Joshua and David. "Josh, you and David have to look out for Fox."

"I don't need any help," Fox argued, quickly facing his two adversaries.

The two older boys laughed and Joshua said, "Calm down, Fox. Eli, you and Isaiah scoot out of here. Your own families are certainly nothing to brag about."

In truth, the families of the two boys consisted primarily of shiftless never-do-wells who spent most of their time carousing, and both fathers had been placed in jail for minor infractions.

David said, "That's right. Be on your way or you'll be the one that gets busted up."

Fox wanted to get away, so he went to his horse and mounted. Hannah, Joshua, Eve, and David were almost as quick. Hannah said, "Don't run off and leave us, Fox."

"I won't," Fox said.

As they all left the school yard, Joshua, who admired Fox, was still angry and said, "Don't mind what those two say. What do they know?"

"Are you all right, Fox?" Hannah asked.

"Yes, I'm all right," Fox mumbled.

As they rode along, Ethan came riding up. He had a fine buckskin that his father let him ride to and from school, and as he pulled up beside them, he gave Fox an odd look. He finally said, "I know you're mad, Fox, but remember Eli lost a brother last year. Killed in an Indian raid."

"Well, that doesn't have anything to do with Fox," Hannah said. "He didn't kill Eli's brother."

"Well, he shouldn't be that way, but you know how he is. It's hard to lose a family member."

Fox stared at Ethan for a moment, remembering that he had lost a cousin to a Cherokee attack as well, and said nothing. His heart seemed to have grown cold. He had left Virginia hoping for a true home and true friends, but thus far, he had not found a place where he could be himself and belong. He leaned over, patted the horse on the shoulder, and spoke quietly. "Come on, girl. Let's go home."

Christmas in Franklin

Twelve

Hawk Spencer had always enjoyed Christmas, and on Christmas morning of 1784 he had risen early and gone outside to begin his preparations for the day. He was somewhat surprised to see Fox standing on the porch and wondered what had gotten the boy up so early. Giving him a friendly smile, he said, "Well, you are up early for Christmas, Fox."

"Couldn't sleep." It was a crisp morning, and Fox's breath lingered in the air.

The boy's brevity troubled Hawk. He had spoken with Awinita and discovered that she was concerned about his inability to fit himself into his new setting. Now, thinking it would be good to spend time with the boy, he said, "How about helping me do the cooking?"

"You're going to cook the Christmas dinner?"

"There's not enough room in the fireplace to cook everything that Elizabeth and your aunt want to cook. So we'll just take care of this outside and I could use some help."

Fox gave Hawk an odd look. "I thought women were supposed to do the cooking," he said finally.

"Well, a long hunter learns to cook for himself. You'll have to learn, too, Fox. You and Josh and Sequatchie and I are going to be going on some hunting expeditions. Your mother or aunt won't be there, and my wife won't be there. It'll just be us men."

Fox swelled with pride at the phrase "just us men," and he nodded. "I hadn't thought about that," he said. "But I don't know anything about cooking."

"Well, you're not too old to learn."

"What are we going to cook?"

"What do you think we've been saving these wild turkeys for? You got one of them yourself."

"Oh, that's right!" Fox said, remembering the hunt they had been on two days earlier. He had not dreamed how hard it would be to bring down wild turkeys. They were shy creatures, and he and Sequatchie had sat still as stones for what seemed like hours before they finally had success. He had brought one down and Sequatchie another, and after hunting all day, Sequatchie had finally shot a third as it rose into the air. "Hard to hit a bird in the air with one of these smooth-bore muskets," Sequatchie had said. "Maybe you can get a rifle someday, a Kentucky rifle. I think they're the best ones."

"I'll tell you what, Fox. Let's get the worst part over first," Hawk said.

"What's that?"

"Dressing them. I hate to pluck feathers, but it's got to be done. Can't eat feathers, can you, Fox?"

The two went out far from the cabin, where, for some time, the feathers flew. As they plucked the birds, Hawk entertained Fox by telling him stories about some of the adventures he had had on the frontier.

"I grew up just like you did, Fox. In town. When I came over the mountains I didn't know a thing. It was your uncle who taught me all I know about the woods. You've got about the best teacher in the whole settlement of Watauga."

Fox pulled out the soft underfeathers and watched as the rising breeze took them away. The sun was up now, but it was still cold outside, and his fingers were growing numb. But he did not care. "I'm glad to be here," he said. "I like it better than the plantation."

"You think you'll ever go back there? I mean, your mother told me that when you get to be of age, the place will be yours."

Fox did not answer for a while but plucked the bird he held firmly with his left hand. "I don't know," he said finally. "I think I like it better here."

"Well, maybe you can sell it to your uncle in Williamsburg and use the money to buy some land out here. It's plenty cheap. Might even go all the way to the other side of Kentucky. Daniel Boone's found some likely spots there."

Fox felt as comfortable with Hawk Spencer as he did with his uncle. As they finished plucking the birds, he wished he could be as accepted by the young people as he was with these two men.

Hawk took out his knife, gutted one of the birds, and allowed Fox to do the others. When they were all clean, Hawk said, "Well, let's go get started." The two carried the birds back by their feet, letting them hang downward, and when they reached the cabin, they placed them high in the crook of a tree to keep the dogs away.

"What'll we do now?" Fox asked.

"We dig holes," Hawk said.

The two began digging holes using shovels, and when they were done, they lined the bottoms of them with red-hot coals from a fire Hawk had started the night before with huge logs. "Now we smear these little darlings with mud. Go get some from the creek in these buckets."

"We're going to put mud on those birds?"

"You wait and see. There's a thing or two you haven't learned about cooking out in the woods. Go on, now."

Fox made a quick trip to the creek and came back with the buckets filled with mud. He watched as Hawk carefully encased one bird with mud, and then he did the same with the other two.

"All right. Now we put them on top of these coals," Hawk said as he put one bird on and allowed Fox to do the others.

"What do we do now, Hawk?"

"We cover them with red-hot coals, the hottest you can find. Be careful, now. Don't burn yourself."

The two worked diligently, piling the hot coals on until the birds were completely buried, almost up to the rim.

"Now put a few shovelfuls of dirt on top and we're all done."

They could hear laughter coming from the cabin, and Hawk said, "Let's go in there and see if we can argue some breakfast out of the women this Christmas morning."

Fox was hesitant, but just as he was about to say no, Sequatchie appeared out of the woods and joined them. He leaned his musket against the cabin and smiled. "Come over to get your Christmas gift early, Fox?"

"I been helping Hawk with the cooking."

"Well, I wish I'd been here. I can cook better than he can."

"You can't, either!" Hawk said.

"Of course I can!" Sequatchie grinned. "I was cooking before you were born, white man."

The two men joshed each other, and Fox envied their easy companionship. Finally Iris appeared at the door and said, "Come on. We're going to have a very small breakfast."

The three went inside and found that the breakfast was small indeed. Just a small piece of cooked ham and two biscuits for each of them.

"Why, this is no meal for a man!" Hawk said, grabbing Elizabeth as she walked by. "I married you because you could cook."

"You're not going to spoil your appetite," Elizabeth scolded, "by eating a lot now! By the time you get through, the others will be here and we'll have our Christmas."

Before the three of them had scarcely finished their breakfast, the room seemed to be swarming with people. Fox had trouble keeping up with everyone. Jacob, Amanda, and Jared were there. Seth and Sarah Donovan came in, along with Andrew and Abigail with their son, Abel. Will and Rebekah Martin, Elizabeth's brother and sister-in-law, were there with their children, Eve and David, and neighbors George and Deborah Stevens, who were Abigail's parents, came to join the celebration.

Awinita looked around at the cabin she had helped the other women decorate. Smiling, she saw that Fox was happy and was grateful for the friends he had here. Leaning close to Elizabeth, she said, "I'm glad to see Fox joining in. He's not able to make many friends at school, it seems."

Elizabeth shook her head. "It's just a matter of time," she said. "It's all new to him."

The presents were not expensive ones. The stores where city people bought their gifts were many miles away, and most of the gifts were homemade.

Fox had been shown by Sequatchie how to tan hides, and he had spent hours tanning the hide of a rabbit and making mittens out of it for his mother. When he gave them to her, her eyes lit up and she hugged him. "Why, how clever you are, Fox!"

"Well, Sequatchie showed me how to do it. And he trapped the rabbit, too."

"They're so soft. My hands will never be cold again. Thank you, son."

Fox received several gifts from his mother, from Sequatchie and Iris, from Hawk and Elizabeth, and from Mercy and Ezekiel. Most of them were small, but when all the gifts were given, his mother gave him one more package.

"What is this, Mother?" he asked. "It's heavy."

"You're really too young for this yet, but I want you to have it for your first Christmas in Watauga."

Fox unwrapped the package and stood there speechless. In his hands he held a beautifully balanced pistol. He looked up and whispered, "It was Father's, wasn't it?"

"Yes. It belonged to your father. He always said he was going to give it to you when you were seventeen, but I want you to have it now."

Everyone gathered around to look at the pistol, and it was handed around until finally Hawk took it and examined it. "I've never seen a finer weapon, Fox," he said. He aimed it, pulled the hammer back, and pulled the trigger. The click sounded through the room and he shook his head. "Fine piece of workmanship. I know you'll treasure it."

Fox moved back to the wall and sat there holding the pistol in his hands. He ran his fingers over the smoothness of the barrel, worked the mechanism, and thought of his father. It brought a sadness to him as it always did, for he missed him greatly.

When all the gifts were given, Elizabeth said, "Now all of you men take these children and go outside. We've got pies and cakes to make, and we don't want you underfoot."

"Are you sure you don't want me to stay here and help?" Hawk grinned. "I do most of the cooking around here anyway."

Everyone hooted at that, and Elizabeth said, "That'll be the day when I eat a pie of yours. Now, get out of here, Hawk Spencer, and take these youngsters with you."

The men and children moved outside as the women began preparing the cakes and pies. Elizabeth had asked Awinita, Iris, and Deborah to make the cornbread dressing and some of the other vegetables while she, Abigail, Amanda, and Sarah worked on the desserts. "I've always wanted to make a baked pumpkin pudding. I've always liked that and the men love it," Elizabeth said.

"Yes. Seth loves that, too."

"All right. Let's work on that first."

The two women gathered the ingredients, then Sarah cracked some eggs and dropped them into a large mixing bowl. She beat them with a fork and then added the pumpkin.

Elizabeth added cinnamon, ginger, and allspice, and finally they poured in molasses and milk.

"An hour ought to be enough to bake this," she said. "What else shall we make?"

"I brought over a sack full of pecans and walnuts," Sarah offered. "I've been cracking them and shelling them for a long time. Let's make spiced nuts. The children love them. Seth would be fat as a pig if I let him eat all he wanted to."

"You're better at that than I am, Sarah. You go ahead and make them."

Sarah measured out cinnamon, sugar, and nutmeg into one of the small bowls. Then she separated the egg whites and beat them with a fork. She stirred a few of the nuts into the egg whites, then took the nuts out and rolled them in the sugar-and-spice mixture. Finally she put them on pans and baked them over the fire for about twenty minutes.

As they were working together, Elizabeth noticed that Sarah was strangely quiet and kept looking at the two-year-olds, who were playing together on the floor. She paid special attention to her nephew, Abel.

Finally she said wistfully, "Abel's such a fine boy."

"He certainly is. A woman couldn't ask for a finer boy than that." Elizabeth hesitated, then said, "You're not still worried about the fact that you haven't had a baby yet, are you, Sarah?"

"I try to be patient, like we talked about." Sarah gave a wistful look at Abel and said, "Other women just seem to be more fortunate than I am."

"Well, having babies and raising them isn't all fun, you know."

"I know. Amanda and Abigail are always telling me about how hard they are to keep clean and how they keep you up at night. I wouldn't fuss about that, Mama, if I had a baby of my own."

"Your time will come, daughter," Elizabeth said. "Don't fret yourself about it."

"I'll try, Mama. I know God decides who has children and who doesn't. 'Children are an heritage of the Lord; and the fruit of the womb is his reward.' I memorized that Scripture."

"Seth will love you, baby or no baby. Don't you worry about that."

Suddenly Sarah straightened up. "I know it, Mama. I don't intend to fuss."

"We'll just keep on praying for you to have a child."

"I know. My heart hurts sometimes, but God knows best."

While the women were inside talking, the men had gathered outside and were watching the young people play. Hawk was talking about politics, and the others listened carefully. "Well," Hawk said deliberately, "have you heard that they finally settled on a name for our state? It will be Franklin, and not Frankland, as some wanted."

"It's a good name," said Andrew. "I always liked Ben Franklin. Any word yet on whether Congress is going to recognize our statehood?"

"From what I hear, it's not looking hopeful," Hawk replied. "Still, we're apparently going to go ahead and draw up a state constitution—Governor John Sevier's idea."

"What will happen next?" Seth asked. He was not at all certain about politics in the New World. "It seems strange not having a king, but I'm glad of it. I had enough of kings back in Scotland to do me a lifetime."

A murmur of agreement went around among the men, and Hawk said, "I think there'll be a convention next year to adopt a constitution."

"I don't know that North Carolina will go along with this. We'll have to give up some of the land to settle it, won't we?"

Hawk shrugged. "I don't know. It looks that way, but I hope it all goes smoothly."

The only two black faces in the crowd, Ezekiel and Mercy, were not left out. Mercy went inside to help the women cook, and it was soon discovered that Ezekiel could play a fiddle. He had been a favorite back on the plantation, and now when he drew out his fiddle and began to play lively tunes, all the youngsters were entranced by it.

"I wish I could play a fiddle like that," Fox said.

"Why, I reckon you can," Ezekiel said. "I'll be right proud to give you lessons."

"Would you, Ezekiel?"

"Why sho. Why not?"

"Would you give me lessons, too?" Hannah said. She had come up to stand beside Fox, and her face was beaming.

"Why, missy, I'll do it. Here. Do you want to try it?"

Hannah took the fiddle and let Ezekiel place it under her chin. "Now you hold the bow like this and your two fingers right here. Now pull it across it."

A screeching sound made everyone flinch, and Joshua said, "That sounds awful! Here, let me try it."

Soon all the children had to have their turn with the fiddle, and all of them produced the same result.

"I guess it's going to take a lot of lessons to learn to play the fiddle," Fox said. He had had no more success than the rest, and finally he said, "Let's play another game."

"Let's have a hoop race," Joshua said.

The hoop race proved to be quite exciting. The hoops were used to bind the wagon wheels together, and they had only three of them, so only three people could race at a time.

Fox was the swiftest of all, and he had to slow down to let some of the other children win.

It was midafternoon before all of the turkeys were ready and the pies and cakes were baked. They had all been placed inside on two large tables, and the room was crowded. A fire burned merrily in the fireplace, and the smell of fresh bread and pies and cooked meat stirred everyone's appetites. Thomas, Leah, and their baby, Sherah, had arrived. Paul and Rhoda Anderson, along with Rachel, had also joined the celebration.

"Everyone quiet down now," Hawk said. "We've got to have the blessing." He turned and said, "Paul, would you please ask the blessing?"

The room grew quiet and Paul Anderson began to pray. It was a brief prayer, but obviously his heart was in it. He ended by saying, "O Lord God, we are your children, and you have provided for us this food. We thank you for it. And we would not forget that Christmas means the coming to earth of God himself. So we honor the Lord Jesus Christ, and we thank you for everything you have given, especially for your gift of salvation. Amen."

"All right. Sequatchie, you carve that turkey. I'll do this one. Seth, you can try that one, and, Jacob, try to keep from messing up that last one."

The men carved the turkeys, and soon everyone had a plate full of turkey, green beans, dressing, and sweet potatoes. The smell of spiced tea filled the cabin.

Fox was sitting beside Hannah, and she talked rapidly all the time. Finally she said, "How do you feel about this new state?"

"I don't know anything much about it," Fox said.

"I think it's exciting," Hannah enthused. "One day there's gonna be states all the way to the Mississippi River."

"Oh, I doubt that. It'll stop somewhere."

"No, it won't," Hannah said quickly. "You wait and see. This is going to be a big country."

Fox did not speak but ate his food, chewing it slowly.

Hannah spoke again. "How do you like your new home, Fox?"

"I'm not sure where home is," Fox muttered.

Hannah stopped eating and looked over and said suddenly, "You know, that's what Joseph and Mary must have felt on the first Christmas. They didn't have a real home, either, but were outside in a stable. But that doesn't matter because Jesus was born there."

Fox didn't answer, and Hannah went on, "I always think about the baby Jesus this time of the year, don't you?"

Actually Fox could not answer that question honestly. Christmas had always meant to him a time to eat and a time to have fun and to get presents. He said now, "I guess so."

Hannah talked for a time about the baby Jesus and then said, "Look. Father's going to read the Christmas story out of the Bible. Come along. I've always loved that story. I think I know it by heart."

Fox had heard the Christmas story, too, but later, after the meal when Hawk Spencer read it, something seemed to tug at his heart. The idea of God becoming a man and being born as a tiny baby was more than anything he could grasp. He listened carefully and finally, when it was over, he listened as Hawk prayed for everyone in the cabin individually. He heard his own name being called and heard Hawk say, "And give young Fox Carter a special calling from you, O Lord, and let him know that you love him more than anyone on earth could ever love him."

The words sent a thrill down Fox's back, and he felt tears rise in his eyes. He quickly blinked them away, for he knew that Hannah was watching him closely.

"Wasn't that nice of Papa to pray for you like that?"

"Yes, it was," Fox said. He could say no more, and looking up, he met his mother's smiling eyes.

Sarah and Drusilla

Thirteen

Seth Donovan inhaled deeply, enjoying the biting air of winter as he drove their wagon over the frozen ground. January of 1785 had brought freezing weather and difficult times. While others may have groaned over the hardship, Seth Donovan thrived on it.

As the wheels rattled over the stony trail, he looked up and said, "I think there's snow in the air."

Sarah lifted her head and gazed at the gray sky. It was marked by a few white clouds that scudded along the edge of the horizon, almost touching, it seemed, the tops of the mountains that rose over in the west. She was wearing a fur coat made from skins that Sequatchie had trapped, and she herself had helped to sew them into the coat. She snuggled down and looked up at her husband, struck once again by his rugged good looks. His Scottish blood showed in the golden hair that reached to his shoulders. It was as thick as a lion's mane, and although he himself had no vanity about it, Sarah did. She kept it carefully trimmed, which thoroughly amused him.

Seth suddenly turned and looked down at Sarah and for a moment wondered what was in her mind. He had not yet reached the depths of Sarah MacNeal Donovan's feisty spirit, and he suspected he never would. She had fiery red hair that her father had passed along to her and a temperament that matched it sometimes. Usually she wore her hair in long ringlets that cascaded down her back, but now it was all tucked up underneath a cap made from the same fur as the coat. Her eyes were pale green, and the few freckles that would appear in summer were now very faint, so that he could barely see them sprinkled across her nose. "What are you thinking about, wife?" Seth asked cheerfully.

"I don't know. About what a handsome husband I have, I suppose."

Seth grinned down at her and put his powerful arm around her. Drawing her close, he gave her a squeeze and said, "I never thought I'd have to come all the way from Scotland to America to find a bride."

"Did you have lots of girls in Scotland?"

"Hundreds of them. They were all crazy about me. You wouldn't believe it."

"Oh, you always say that!"

"You always ask me that, and no matter what I say, you don't like the answer. Are you worried about me, Sarah?"

"Of course I am. A handsome preacher is irresistible to many women. You think I haven't seen some of the younger women and the widows looking at you while you're preaching?"

"That's love for the Lord, you see."

"No, it's not. They're not thinking about the Lord, I can tell you that," Sarah said firmly.

"How do you know? Have you become a mind reader?"

"I think I know a little bit about women. I used to notice handsome men myself. There was a preacher who came in once to preach a meeting for us. Oh, he was the handsomest thing! He had hair as black as a raven's wing and dark eyes—soft sometimes, so soft you wouldn't believe it. My, he was handsome!"

"Was he a good preacher?"

"I don't know. I was too busy admiring him."

"Well, that's a fine thing to admit! I'm ashamed of you, Sarah."

"I'm just honest, that's all. You know those young women look at you. Don't you try to fool me, Seth Donovan!"

Seth suddenly laughed. "You know me pretty well, don't you? Well, if you know me that well, you know that no matter how they look at me, I'll not be looking back at them."

This was what Sarah wanted to hear. She moved closer under his arm and enjoyed the stout muscular form and the strength that seemed to flow from him.

There were no roads to speak of in Watauga, only trails that wound around between the huge trees. Seth's eyes were constantly on the alert as they ambled along in the buggy, and his musket was on the seat to his left. There was little enough danger of attacks here, but still caution became a way of life out on the frontier. If for nothing else, the bears and cougars that roamed the area were warrant enough for carrying a loaded musket.

As they rode along, the two talked of the spiritual well-being of the community. Sarah had learned that being the wife of a preacher was not easy. She was not accustomed to all the burdens that came her way, but the Lord had given her such happiness in her marriage that she was willing to endure the hardships of the job.

As they were drawing nigh to the Mullinses' place, Sarah asked, "Why couldn't Paul Anderson make this visit?"

"He had commitments over at the Piney Wood settlement," Seth answered.

Seth understood at once that Sarah did not want to talk to Drusilla Mullins, because she was afraid of what to say to her.

As Seth pulled the buggy up in front of the small cabin, Sarah said, "Maybe it would be better if I just waited out here."

Giving his wife a look of surprise, Donovan shook his head. "That wouldn't be right. They'd be hurt." He leaped off the wagon, tied the team, and then went around to help Sarah down. "Don't you like the Mullinses?"

"Oh, they're very nice. I just feel uncomfortable around Drusilla."

"So do I. It's hard to know what to say at such times as these. There's nothing you really can say, but visiting makes a difference. At least we can show our love by that."

Drusilla Mullins had lost her third child two nights earlier. She and her husband, Clement, had already suffered through the painful loss of two stillborn children. They had looked forward to the hope of a new baby with such joy that now both Seth and Sarah hated to face them. But Seth led her to the doorway, saying, "We'll do what we can, Sarah." He knocked on the door and it opened at once. Clement was a large man with dark hair, and sadness marked his face.

"Come in, Reverend," he said. "And you, too, Mrs. Donovan."

"How are you, Clement?"

"Not so well, as you can imagine."

Sarah slipped out of her coat and hung it on a peg on the wall. "Let's go in and visit Drusilla."

Clement led the way to the single room, opened the door, and the two went in. Drusilla was a small woman of twenty-five with brown hair and light brown eyes. She was in bed and looked up at the two as they entered. "Why, how nice of you to come," she said and managed a smile.

Seth went over and took her hand. He said, "We know we can't do anything to ease your pain, but we wanted you to know that we are grieving with you."

"Thank you, Reverend."

Sarah took a stool beside the bed and said, "How are you feeling?"

"Clement is taking good care of me."

"We would have come earlier but—"

"Oh, that's all right. The neighbors have been coming and bringing food."

"I brought some Brunswick stew. It's out in the wagon. I forgot it."

"I'll get it," Seth said quickly.

Clement moved to follow Seth. "I'll go with you, Reverend. I'll show you that new foal that came last week."

As soon as the two men were gone, Sarah did not know exactly what to say. Finally she asked, "Is there anything I can do for you, Drusilla?"

"No. I have everything. I'll be up and about pretty soon."

"You must not be too quick to do that."

"I won't be, but I'll get my strength back soon." She was quiet for a time and then said, "Clement named the little one Mary Hannah after his two favorite Bible women."

Suddenly the tragedy of their loss brought tears to Sarah's eyes. She tried to hold them back but to no avail. For the life of her, she could not tell if her sadness and sorrow were for the small woman who lay before her or for her own lack of providing a baby for Seth.

Drusilla suddenly reached over and took Sarah's hand. "Don't cry. Little Mary's with Jesus, and we will see her one day."

Sarah finally controlled herself and produced a handkerchief out of the pocket of her dress. She wiped her face and then shook her head. "I don't know why God keeps people who want them from having babies," she murmured as she dabbed her eyes again.

"God always knows best. The Scripture says that. You know it better than I, Sarah."

"I know, but I want a child so desperately."

"Your life is in God's hands, as are both mine and Mary's."

"But why would He deny you and me the desires of our hearts?"

"You remember the story of Hannah in the Bible?"

"Yes."

"Well, she prayed and God gave her a son. He became Samuel, the great prophet of Israel. You just have to be like Hannah and wait on God."

Sarah suddenly shook her head, and her lips grew tight. "I was never good at waiting, Drusilla."

"I know. I'm not good at it, either. 'But they that wait upon the Lord shall renew their strength.' You remember that verse from Isaiah?"

"Yes. I remember it."

The two women talked for a long time, and finally Drusilla said, "Sarah, in good time God is going to give you and Seth what you need. It may be that you'll never have a baby, but God will always be there. He'll always provide for you."

Drusilla suddenly began to pray softly, but there was an intensity in her voice. Mostly her prayer was for Sarah and for Seth that whether they had a child or not, they would find their peace and their rest in the Lord Jesus.

As Sarah listened a strange thing began to happen: A peace began to settle on her heart. She had been distraught for so long that she could not understand it at first. She had spent sleepless nights, she had walked the floor, she had prayed and cried unto God, and yet nothing had happened.

Now as the soft voice of Drusilla Mullins filled the small bedroom, Sarah knew that she had found a new peace with God. Something within her own heart had changed. The situation was no different. She still was not pregnant, so far as she knew, but somehow the prayer of this simple woman who lay on the bed with her own loss so keen and fresh had touched Sarah's heart.

Finally Drusilla said, "God did something, I think. I felt it."

"Yes, He did, Drusilla." Sarah leaned over and hugged Drusilla. "I came over to comfort you, but you've been doing the comforting." Drusilla felt almost like a child in Sarah's strong arms.

Finally when Sarah drew back, Drusilla said, "I'm glad you came. We never know how God is going to work, do we? I'll bet you didn't think when you were leaving your house that God was going to minister to you through a grieving mother."

"No, I didn't. I've been doubtful about God, Drusilla, and I know that is wrong."

"I think you're right," Drusilla nodded. "Ingratitude and unbelief grieve the Lord. So I'm just going to be grateful to God for what I have and believe Him that He will do what is best."

Sarah sat for a long time, and the two women did not speak. Something new had come to Sarah Donovan, and she was certain she would not doubt God again no matter what happened.

A Visit From the Governor

Fourteen

You know, there's something about a new baby that always makes me want to cry."

Elizabeth lifted up her new grandchild and smiled into the round face. Taking advantage of the first warm days of spring, Jacob and Amanda had brought their new daughter, Emily, to visit her grandparents and her young aunt and uncle, Hannah and Joshua, for the first time. While Joshua kept little Jared out of harm's way, Elizabeth held the month-old morsel of humanity, and indeed tears glistened in her eyes. She was so grateful to God for all He had blessed her with on this lovely day in April 1785.

Hawk glanced at his wife's face, then said roughly, "Here. Give me that young'un." Reaching out, he snatched Emily from Elizabeth and held the baby high in the air. He laughed aloud and said, "Why, she looks just like you, Amanda. That's a relief."

Amanda was used to her father-in-law's teasing. "Why's that?" she asked, knowing that she would get a jocular answer.

"Why, I've been having nightmares," Hawk said, looking at Jacob. "Thinking she'd look like this ugly fellow here—or me. Most of my prayers have been for her to look like you or her grandmother Iris. I declare, I think she looks like both of you."

As the grandparents were making much of Emily, little Jared tugged on Elizabeth's skirt to be picked up as well. He didn't stay long, however. After a kiss and some assurance that he wasn't being ignored, he wriggled out of her arms and began running around once again. Laughing at his grandson's antics, Hawk insisted that it was time to get an artist in to draw pictures of all four of their grandchildren. Abigail and Andrew had presented them with a new grandson, Caleb, two months earlier, a brother for Abel.

Elizabeth sighed in thankfulness at thoughts of her four beautiful grandchildren and finally took the newest member of the family back from Hawk. She sat down and held Emily closely. "She's the sweetest thing!" Elizabeth crooned, rocking back and forth.

"She probably gets her sweet nature from Pa," Jacob grinned.

"Oh, don't be foolish!" Elizabeth said. "You know what an old grouch he is."

"A grouch! Me? Why, I never have a cross word for anyone," Hawk protested.

The two families visited for a time and shared a meal together in the Spencer cabin. Then finally Jacob and Amanda had to make their way back home with their little ones.

"I'll be over to visit you tomorrow," Elizabeth said.

"You come and bring Pa with you," Jacob said. "He can help take care of his new granddaughter. He always was good with women-folk."

Elizabeth shut the door after they had left and then said, "Let's go out by the creek, Hawk."

"By the creek? What for?"

"Oh, I don't know. It's so pretty this time of the year. I think April is my favorite month."

"All right. If you say so." Hawk took his musket off of the wall and said, "Maybe we'll see something good to eat on the way. A wild pig or something."

"You're always thinking of your stomach."

Hawk reached over and grinned at her. "No. Sometimes I'm thinking about how pretty you are."

Elizabeth shoved him away and said, "Don't be foolish. I'm an old grandmother now."

"Prettiest grandmother I've ever seen. What big eyes you have," Hawk grinned.

The two walked to the stream and sat down where it made an elbow, almost as if it encircled the couple in its arm. Silently, they listened to the water gurgle over the rounded rocks.

Hawk set his rifle carefully up against a tall walnut tree, leaned back against the trunk, and pulled Elizabeth closer. "Tell me what you're thinking," he said.

Elizabeth was quiet for a moment, then said, "I'm just thinking how wonderful it is to have a family. I'm as excited now over grandchildren as I ever was over my own."

"You know, I feel the same way about it. It's just like beginning life all over again."

"Why, that's exactly what it is!" Elizabeth exclaimed. "Every time a new life comes into the world, especially one of our own, I think of what God is going to do in that new life."

The two sat there speaking quietly. From time to time a bass would rise slowly to the surface, sometimes snatching a dragonfly in its large mouth as it came out of the water with a lusty splash.

"You keep on splashin'," Hawk murmured. "I'll get you, old boy, as soon as I get time to do a little fishing."

"What's happening about our new state?"

"Well, John Sevier is still serving as governor, and all the other officials and their salaries have been set."

"I think that's wonderful."

"I did get some other good news. The state has officially recognized Martin Academy."

"Joshua won't like that," Elizabeth laughed. "He's been hoping the school would have to close."

"You know, that boy's a good scholar. He fusses a lot, but he's as smart as you are."

"Oh, I hope he's a lot smarter than I am. I want him to be a real scholar, Hawk. Maybe go off to college back east."

"Wouldn't it be something if he turned out to be a lawyer or a judge?"

"He's a handful right now, but he's like you. When he gets his mind set, nothing dissuades him."

At that moment they heard a faint cry, and Hawk suddenly grew alert. "That came from the cabin. We'd better get back. I think we've got more visitors."

Hawk reached down and pulled Elizabeth to her feet, then picked up his musket, and the two hurried back down the worn path toward the cabin.

"It's Sarah and Seth," Hawk said, catching sight of them.

"Well, we haven't seen much of them lately. I hope they can stay for a visit."

"I doubt it. That Seth is a whirlwind. He's going all over Watauga preaching everywhere he can get two or three people together."

As they approached the cabin, Hawk murmured, "Look how happy Sarah is. Something's different."

"And Seth, too. Look how he's smiling."

"Hello," Hawk called out. "Good to see you two. Where are you bound?"

Sarah did not answer, but she ran forward and without warning threw herself into her mother's arms.

Elizabeth was nearly overbalanced. She caught herself and cried, "Well, what in the world is it, Sarah?"

Sarah lifted her face, and there were tears like diamonds in her eyes. "It's . . . it's . . ."

Instantly Elizabeth knew what the news was, but she would not spoil Sarah's pleasure in telling it. "What is it?" she said.

"Seth and I . . . we're going to have a baby."

"You don't mean it! Well, praise God!" Hawk cried out.

"We wanted to tell you as soon as we were sure. We wanted you to be the first to know," Sarah said. "You've been so good to pray for us to have a child."

"Well, I'm so happy I could cry. I never know whether to laugh or cry when such good news comes," Elizabeth said. "But I'm just going to decide to laugh. Now you've got your heart's desire."

Hawk slapped Seth on the shoulder and said, "What do you think about becoming a father, Seth?"

"I haven't had time to get used to it yet," Seth Donovan said. He looked stunned, but then he laughed out loud. "I've had to learn so many things, I guess I can learn one more. But I just praise God for sending this child into our lives."

The two couples stood there for a time, and then Elizabeth said, "When do you think the baby will be born, Sarah?"

"Some time in the fall, I think. As you know I've had a bad attitude about this. But that all changed when I went over to talk to Drusilla a couple of months ago."

"I knew something was different after your visit with her, but I didn't know what it was," Elizabeth said.

"I'd begun to think that women without children are cursed by God, but that's not so. Drusilla helped me to realize that."

The four talked excitedly for a while, and then finally Sarah said, "God has answered our prayers. Especially Drusilla Mullins' prayer."

One week after Hawk had gotten the news that he was to have yet another new grandchild, he and Sequatchie were working on the roof of Sequatchie's house. The two men were arguing, as they frequently did, about which one was the best roofer.

"I was roofing before you were born," Sequatchie said, driving a nail in. He had to be very careful with the nails, for they were a precious commodity. Since all of them were handmade, often an old house was burned down just to get the nails out of it.

Hawk fastened one of the cedar shakes and made a grimace of disgust. "You always say that. That you were doing something before I was born. That doesn't mean you do it better. Just longer."

The two men actually enjoyed their arguments, but finally Sequatchie said, "Listen, somebody's coming."

Hawk lifted his head and listened. "I don't hear anything."

"That's because you're not an Indian. You white people are half deaf. Can't see as well as we can, either."

At that instant Hawk's ears, which were unusually good, caught the sound of approaching horsemen. "I knew they were coming all the time. I just wanted to make you feel better."

The horsemen drew up, and Sequatchie said, "Why, that's Governor Sevier."

"It sure is. Let's get down and find out what the governor wants and who all that mob is with him."

The two men quickly climbed down off the roof by means of a ladder and went forward to meet the group, who had dismounted. Sevier, a tall man with handsome, aristocratic features, put his hand out and shook hands first with Sequatchie and then with Hawk. "I'm glad to see you both," he said.

"How are you, Governor?" Hawk asked.

"Well, I could do without some of the hassles of trying to establish a new state."

"You mean being governor's not all pleasure?" Sequatchie grinned. "I thought you'd get to tell everybody what to do."

"It seems like everybody wants to tell me what to do."

"Well, you sit down with all your friends at that table, and I'll have my wife bring out some refreshments."

Thirty minutes later the group was finishing off the last of a peach cobbler and the hot sassafras tea that Iris had produced. They had been talking about politics steadily, and finally Sequatchie said, "What are all of you doing out this way? We're pretty far off the beaten track."

"I've come to see you two."

Sequatchie and Hawk grew alert. "What about, Governor?" Hawk demanded.

"I want to have a meeting with the Cherokee next month, and I want you two to lead the delegation."

"Where will it be?" Hawk asked.

"Over by Major Hugh Henry's station. You know where that is?"

"Yes," Sequatchie said. "That's by the mouth of Dumplin Creek."

"That's right," Sevier said. "We can make our own treaties now without interference from North Carolina."

Sequatchie and Hawk both agreed with this, and Sequatchie said, "Are you sure you want me to go?"

"Especially you. You know your people better than anyone else, and I want it to be a fair treaty."

They talked for some time about the meeting the following month, and after the governor and his attendants had ridden out, Sequatchie said, "I hope this treaty means good things for my people. They're getting restless. There's going to be more bloodshed if some of the wrongs are not righted."

Hawk was quiet for a time, and then he said, "You know, I'm thinking it might be good for Fox to go with us."

"Fox?"

"Yes. What do you think?"

"I'm not sure," Sequatchie said, taken by surprise.

"Well, it'll be a good chance for him to meet your people—his people."

Sequatchie nodded abruptly. "You're right, of course. We will take Fox."

The two men went back and began roofing, and Sequatchie worked silently. The thought was going through his mind, *I hope everything goes well, or Fox may become even more disillusioned about his life and about his Cherokee heritage.*

Meeting at Dumplin Creek

Fifteen

The settlement of the vast lands across the Appalachian Mountain Range proved to be more difficult than those who lived on the eastern seaboard ever dreamed of. Indeed, the whole effort and attention of the Colonies were so taken up by the long, bloody, and difficult Revolution that little thought had been given to the particulars of how the land would be settled.

The French and Indian War had been waged over this very territory. The crux of the struggle was whether or not the western lands would be controlled by France or by England.

The cost of the French and Indian War had been high for England, and she had insisted that the colonists pay for part of it. This, to a great extent, was one of the causes that had brought on the Revolution itself. England felt her claim was just. They had fought the war, and now those Englishmen who happened to live in the Colonies should help shoulder the cost. Americans had not seen it this way, and finally the Revolution, after smoldering for some time, had burst into flames.

But now a new country existed, the United States of America, and a vast region larger than Europe itself stretched out across the continent. It is doubtful whether any foresaw the one nation reaching from the Atlantic all the way to the Pacific, but certainly the lands just over the mountains were on the minds of many Americans.

All during the Revolution, settlers had gone through the Cumberland Gap, led by men such as Daniel Boone. They had settled on the land without permission, and now these settlers and their children were fearful about their claims. Several treaties had been drawn up with the Indians, but none seemed satisfactory or authoritative, and questions of land ownership and title remained cloudy and uncertain.

The victims of westward expansion were, of course, the Native Americans, who had lived on the land for generations and whose customs had evolved over long periods of history. Now they were being pushed inexorably out of their heritage. The Cherokee had, along with other nations, already engaged in several bitter wars. During the Revolution itself, some of the Native Americans had joined with the British in fighting against the colonists, leaving a bitter taste in the mouths of many of the new Americans.

And now all of the concern for land ownership in western North Carolina was further complicated by the emerging territory of Franklin, which had claimed statehood, formed a government, and begun negotiating treaties independent of North Carolina. A bitter struggle had ensued in Congress, with the advocates and opponents of Franklin almost coming to blows. The representatives from North Carolina particularly were adamant in their denial of the right of Franklin to become a state.

All of the land disputes hung heavy on the minds of Hawk and Sequatchie as they arrived at Dumplin Creek. Along with Governor Sevier, seven other men made up the commission. Hawk and Sequatchie had been included not because they were surveyors or politicians but because they understood the problems of the Cherokee better than most. Sequatchie, of course, was highly favored among the entire Cherokee Nation. Hawk, too, had won the grudging admiration and acceptance of Sequatchie's people.

As the meeting got under way, Sequatchie was approached by Governor Sevier. "What do you think, Sequatchie?"

"I think it would be best if we dismissed and went home."

Sevier was taken aback. "Why do you say that?"

"Because there are only a few chiefs here."

"We tried to get the word out to as many as possible," Sevier defended himself.

"My people move slowly, and it is difficult to get them together. But whatever is done here, it is unlikely that those chiefs not represented will feel themselves bound by the treaty."

Sevier chewed on his lip and then shook his head. "We'll just have to do the best we can."

Sequatchie did not argue, for he saw the governor's mind was made up.

As the meeting went on, Fox Carter was enjoying himself tremendously. Although the Cherokee representatives were not large in number, he was fascinated by them and talked to as many as he could. Sequatchie introduced him to many who knew his mother well, even his whole family.

"What do you think of your Cherokee brothers, Fox?" Sequatchie asked.

"I like them," Fox said sturdily. "I wish I could spend more time with them."

"We will do that. I will go with you, and we will spend some time with your mother's and my people."

"When?"

"As soon as possible. Right now I'm worried about this treaty."

"But it's a good thing, isn't it, Sequatchie?"

"I think it could be, but it's happening too fast. Governor Sevier means well, but he does not understand the Cherokee mind. Our people need more time to think, and besides, they have been mistreated by the white men so many times that they will need much assurance."

Fox thought about his uncle's words as the meeting continued. He listened carefully and was now glad that his mother had taught him the Cherokee tongue. He was not fluent in it yet, but he was determined to study hard until he could speak as well as Sequatchie. Once he asked about a Cherokee he had met named Adahy, and Sequatchie gave him a curt answer: "He is a friend of the warrior Akando, who answers to Chief Dragging Canoe. Stay away from these men, Fox." Obviously Sequatchie had misgivings about Adahy and Akando, and Fox was curious as to why.

The meeting finally ended, and the Indians received clothing and other articles in exchange for the lands included in the treaty. Most of the chiefs agreed with what Sequatchie had already said and told Sevier that those chiefs not represented would be unhappy and would repudiate their action.

The treaty itself was put in a document and signed on June 10, 1785.

As soon as the Dumplin Treaty was signed, new settlers began flocking into the area. This new incursion was exactly what the Cherokee had feared, for settlers now entered part of the territory that the chiefs who had not been present to sign the treaty claimed as their own.

As Fox, Sequatchie, and Hawk made their way back to the Watauga homestead in the days that followed, Fox asked his uncle, "When will we go back to be with the Cherokee?"

Sequatchie had been evasive. "We will go soon, but right now there may be trouble."

"Trouble between the colonists and the Cherokee?"

"I'm afraid so."

So it was that Fox began to feel himself more and more pulled away from his father's heritage toward the plight of his Cherokee brothers and sisters.

Unbeknown to Hawk, Sequatchie, and Fox, Adahy watched the delegation leave with much interest. As they passed out of sight, Adahy mumbled to himself, "I must send word to Akando that Awinita is back and living with her brother." He smiled cruelly as he added, "I'm sure he will be interested to know she has a son as well."

Plots and Schemes

Sixteen

"Mother, who is Adahy? And who is Akando?"

Awinita had been making soft soap outside of the cabin, but she lifted herself up now and stared at her son, who had approached and blurted out these questions.

"Why do you ask that, son?"

"I met Adahy at the council meeting. Is he an old friend of yours?"

"No."

"I didn't think so," Fox said. "I could tell he and my uncle don't like each other."

"And did your uncle tell you why?"

"No. I didn't want to ask. Did you know him back before you married my father?"

"Yes, I did. He is a good friend of a man called Akando."

"Who is he?"

For a long moment Awinita seemed to be uncertain as to what to say. Finally she took a deep breath and said, "Akando is a fierce warrior of the Cherokee. Many years ago, when I was a girl, he asked my father to let me be his wife."

Fox was startled. "I never knew that! You never told me anything about it."

"It was not a happy time," Awinita said slowly. "Akando is a cruel man, and I wanted nothing to do with him."

High overhead a hawk circled. A flock of doves flew by below, alerting the predator, which suddenly plummeted into their midst. The hawk struck one of them, scattering feathers and killing the dove instantly, then followed the body down and was lost to sight.

Fox had watched the hawk and was fascinated, but not so much as by what his mother was telling him. "What happened?"

"Akando became almost a madman. He was used to having his own way, and then I met your father."

"My father?"

"Yes, and I loved him from the first. And he loved me."

Fox's mind was working quickly. "Oh, I see! Then that's why he hates Sequatchie, too, I suppose."

"Yes. My brother never wanted me to marry Akando. He, too, was against him and told my father it would be a bad marriage. He always liked your father, but Akando hated him. They fought once, and both of them nearly died."

This bit of history intrigued Fox, and the next day, he asked Sequatchie, "Do you think Akando will come for my mother now that she doesn't have a husband?"

"He's a cruel man, and she would have nothing to do with him. He will go to Dragging Canoe and try to stir up trouble, I think."

"I've heard of him. That's an odd name."

"Dragging Canoe is the fiercest of the Cherokee warriors, and he hates white men the worst."

Somehow Fox had had the idea that he would come to a peaceful village and learn the ways of the Cherokee, but now he saw that it would not be that simple. "What will happen? Will you meet Akando again?"

"Yes. We have encountered each other several times. We do not speak, but now that your mother has no man, I would not be surprised if he approached her."

Fox shivered. "She wouldn't have anything to do with a man like that."

"No. She would not, but Akando would take her forcibly if he saw the chance."

Summer had come to Williamsburg bringing hot weather, and Annabelle Denton felt perspiration gather on her face as she walked up to the house of Julia Carter. Removing a handkerchief, she wiped her face and remembered that Julia had not really wanted to meet with her. But Annabelle had insisted and now she had arrived. She was met at the door by a maid, who took her to the parlor, and soon

Annabelle and Julia were sitting drinking tea from fine china cups.

Julia said more quickly than necessary, "What is this you have to tell me, Annabelle?"

"I've just gotten a letter from my brother, Thomas."

"Yes. How's Thomas doing?"

"Very well. He likes it out on the frontier, but he tells me he's met an Indian woman with the last name of Carter. They live close to them near Jonesborough."

Annabelle knew without doubt that this would cause trouble for Awinita because her father had told her of the trouble between Naaman Carter and his nephew, Nathanael, after he and his mother had fled.

Annabelle Denton rarely had any compunction over hurting others. Even though she was a beautiful young woman, she could, at times, be very cruel.

The two talked for a while, and finally when Annabelle left, Julia went at once to Naaman, who was in his study. He looked up when she walked in and said with some irritation, "What is it, Julia? I'm busy."

"Annabelle Denton was just here."

"What did she want?"

"She wanted to tell us about something her brother, Thomas, had discovered."

"I'm not particularly interested in the Dentons, Julia. I'm busy!"

"You'll be interested in this, Naaman." Julia smiled suddenly, but it was not a pleasant smile. "You'll never guess who's living very close to Thomas and his wife."

"Nobody we know."

"Yes. Awinita and Nathanael."

Instantly Naaman sat up straight and scowled. "I don't believe it!"

"It's true enough. I saw the letter. Of course, Thomas didn't have any idea of the trouble we've had with those two. But Annabelle does."

Naaman stood up and began to pace the floor. He stroked his chin and then turned to his wife. "This is bad news. I had hoped we'd never hear of the pair again. If they stay gone long enough, they can be declared dead."

"Well," Julia said, "they're not dead."

Naaman did not answer, but the intent was plainly written on his face. Finally his wife said, "I know what you're thinking."

"You don't."

"Yes, I do. You're thinking that the frontier is a dangerous place and a lot of people get killed by Indians and wild animals."

"Well, that's exactly what I hope, Julia. I don't want my nephew coming back to claim Havenwood. If he tries, I'll just have to do something about it!"

No Place to Call Home

May – December 1787

"And Jesus saith unto him, 'The foxes have holes, and the birds of the air have nests; but the Son of man hath not where to lay his head.'"

Matthew 8:20

The Foxes Have Holes

Seventeen

Hawk and Sequatchie had returned from a hunt that had been only partially successful. They had managed to bring down only two deer, rather small does, and neither hunter was in a particularly good humor.

When they arrived back at the homestead, they sat about dressing the animals. As they worked, the conversation turned to the frustration that both of them felt over the political misfortunes of the state of Franklin.

"Things could not have gone worse for my people," Sequatchie said as his knife flashed in the bright May sunlight.

Hawk did not answer but busied himself with the task. When he had finished stripping the deer hide off the carcass and tossed the bloody remnants to one side, he straightened up and said, "Maybe things will get better. The government makes a lot of mistakes."

Indeed, over the last couple of years the government had made many mistakes concerning the western lands. Still under the Articles of Confederation dating to the Revolutionary War, the federal government had held several meetings with the Cherokee without consulting the Franklin officials. They had met with many of the chiefs at Hopewell, South Carolina, on the Keowee River. Most of the upper Cherokee towns were represented. The Cherokee had been hopeful that the new United States was going to give them justice and fair treatment in this first federal-Indian conference. Here, for the first time, the Cherokee had acknowledged the supremacy of the United States, and the commission disavowed all previous treaties, such as Dumplin Creek, and promised the return of much of the disputed land—including most of Franklin—to the Cherokee.

The Hopewell meeting had adjourned, but not much of any practical consideration had been accomplished.

"But there's one consolation—the state of Franklin disregarded the Hopewell Treaty," Hawk said. He leaned down and sliced one rear quarter off of the doe, then the other. It took only a few seconds. He had become adept at dressing deer since coming to the frontier.

"There were promises made as there always are," Sequatchie sighed, "but they always come to nothing."

There had been what was called the "Tomahawk War" in 1786, a fight led by Dragging Canoe. Tense feelings were running high, both from the white settlers and the Cherokee, and the situation was likely to get worse.

When the two men had finished dressing the does, they hung the meat in the smokehouse and kindled a fire of green hickory. The process would preserve the animals until winter, when game might be more scarce.

"Come on. Let's go get some cider," Hawk said.

He led Sequatchie inside the house, and the two sat down as Elizabeth put two tumblers before them and filled them with an amber-colored liquid. The two men drank thirstily, and Hawk said, "This is the best cider we've ever gotten out of those apple trees. Do you remember when we planted them, Sequatchie?"

Sequatchie grinned faintly. "We were much younger then."

"Why, you don't look a day older!" Elizabeth exclaimed. "I'm getting to be an old woman and you just stay the same."

Sequatchie shook his head. "I feel old on the inside."

Something in Sequatchie's face caught Hawk's attention, and he asked quietly, "You're worried about Fox, aren't you?"

"Yes, and so is Awinita. He's beginning to ask more and more questions about all of this trouble, and he's becoming more resentful of the treatment of the Cherokee by the white men."

Hawk did not answer for a time but sipped the cider. Elizabeth sat down beside them and listened as the two men spoke. Sequatchie spoke mostly of Fox, of whom he had grown very fond. He had begun to pour his store of wisdom and woodlore into the youth, and the two had become very close. Indeed, Fox had become the son of Sequatchie in all but blood.

"We'd like to direct our children's lives," Hawk said slowly. He grinned suddenly and looked at Elizabeth, adding, "Elizabeth always said my spiritual gift was meddling."

"Well, you do like to meddle, Hawk."

"I just like to help people!"

"Sometimes you can't help people. They have to make their own way. I remember once," she said, "back home when I was just a little girl. Oh, I couldn't have been more than seven or eight. My parents let me take care of some of the chickens. A lot of them had laid eggs, and they all started hatching out at the same time." Her face grew gentle and her eyes thoughtful as she remembered that day long gone. "Well, you know how little chickens are. They start pecking at the shell, and it's a hard job for them to get out. Well, I thought I'd help, so when I saw one beginning to come out, I would take the shell off for him." She laughed and shook her head. "I spent most of the day peeling chickens!"

"What happened?" Hawk asked with curiosity.

"Most of the chickens didn't make it. My father told me later that the chickens needed the struggle of getting out of that shell to prepare them for life. I didn't do them any favor by trying to go through their struggles for them."

Sequatchie laughed aloud. "You are a wily woman indeed, Elizabeth Spencer! You're preaching me a sermon, aren't you?"

"No, I'm not," she protested. "I'm just saying that it's natural for parents or relatives to want to help young people through hard times."

"That is true," Sequatchie said. "But what is one to do? Just stand by and watch them go down and make foolish mistakes?"

Hawk suddenly laughed aloud. "Well, I made my own foolish mistakes. I wish someone had stopped me."

Elizabeth said, "You want to help Fox because you love him, and Awinita is the same. He's a good boy, and he will find his way. But he may have to stumble a few times."

"That's right," Hawk nodded. "Ultimately, you've got to let Fox choose his own course. You can lead him and guide him and teach him in the way you want him to go, but the final decision—well, that lies with him, Sequatchie."

Sequatchie dropped his head and fixed his eyes on the tumbler in front of him. He was quiet for a long time, and when his words finally came, they were soft as the summer breeze. "I hope that he will choose the only true Way."

Fox stood back from the stream watching his line. He loved to come here to fish, and his stringer was full of plump bass and sunfish. Now the line suddenly tightened, and with a convulsive jerk, he set the hook. His eyes glowed and he uttered a short cry of exultation as the line zipped to and fro throughout the water. This was a big fish! The pole bent almost double and Fox—afraid that it would break—stepped out into the water following the fish. Back and forth the line whipped. Once the fish broke the surface of the water, and Fox gasped, for he had never caught a fish this big.

The string he had was not all that strong, and the pole was just a thin sapling he had fashioned himself. He wished now that he had made a stronger one, but it was too late. Downstream he went, sometimes floundering as he stepped in potholes. Once he went completely under, but he held the pole up over his head.

Finally the fish began to tire, and Fox worked him to the bank. He drew him in cautiously, and although the huge bass gave a convulsive flurry and almost broke loose, Fox's hand shot out and his thumb went inside the fish's mouth. With a cry he flung the huge prize up on the bank and then scrambled up to make sure it didn't flop back in. He picked up a rock and struck the fish a sharp blow, and the fish's struggle ceased.

"Well, you've got the grandfather of all bass, I believe."

Fox whirled around startled and saw Sequatchie standing in the shadows of the hickory trees that lined the bank of the creek. "It's a big one, isn't it, Uncle?"

"I never caught one that large myself." Sequatchie came forward and squatted down. He touched the scales of the fish and said, "He must weigh ten pounds."

"Oh, fifteen at least!"

Sequatchie laughed. "You have a fisherman's tongue," he said. "Well, this will feed the whole family."

The two squatted there on their heels admiring the fish and talking about Sequatchie's own success as a fisherman. Finally they rose, and Sequatchie said, "You have enough. Let us go home and clean them."

Quickly Fox got the rest of his fish, which looked very small compared to the big bass. Sequatchie said, "I'll carry these and you can take the prize."

The two started home, following the trail that led from the small branch to the house. Sequatchie listened as the young man spoke with excitement of the battle with the fish and was pleased at the excitement he saw in Fox's eyes. He thought, *He's grown into a man and hardly anyone has recognized it.*

They were halfway home when a fox suddenly sprinted out of some bushes and ran for deeper cover.

"He doesn't like us coming this close to his home," Sequatchie murmured.

Fox traced the flight of the red animal and then said moodily, "Well, at least there's one fox that has a home."

Instantly Sequatchie's eyes fastened on the youth. He heard the sadness in Fox's voice and it grieved him. "You know, Jesus said the foxes have holes and birds have nests, but I don't have a place to lay my head."

Fox nodded. He was accustomed to Sequatchie quoting Scripture. He himself had heard that Scripture more than once. "But Jesus was different."

"Different? What do you mean *different*?"

"Well, He was just different from everyone else."

"Don't you think He would have liked to have had a home?"

"Why, I don't know. I never thought about it."

"Some of the most beautiful scenes in the New Testament are when Jesus was at the home of Mary and Martha and Lazarus in Bethany. That seemed to be the closest thing to home for Him. He was so comfortable there. I think that He longed to have a home like that for himself, but He had come to be the Savior, and that meant He could never have a real home on this earth. Not like you or I could have."

"That's sad, Uncle."

"It may have been a little bit sad for Jesus, but the Bible says He was anointed with the oil of joy above His brethren. So even though He didn't have a home, He had joy. I've always thought that Jesus died so that He could have a home in the hearts of men. And then later on we could all have a home in heaven with Him."

Fox kicked at a stick that lay in his way. It broke and went sailing away. The fish swung heavily from the string, its tail dragging the ground, and Fox did not answer for a time. He was not happy. He and his mother were still guests in the home of Sequatchie and Iris.

They had been hospitable ever since they had arrived in Watauga two and a half years earlier, and he loved them. His mother seemed more content than she had been back in Havenwood, but still Fox longed for a place he could call home.

"I guess all that's true, Uncle, but it doesn't seem to help me now. I don't know who I am. Am I white or am I Cherokee?"

Abruptly Sequatchie reached one of those decisions that seem to come almost instantly. For a long time he had seen the uncertainty and unhappiness that troubled Fox, and now he said almost abruptly, "I think it's time for you and your mother to go to our people."

"Do you mean it, Sequatchie? We can go live with the Cherokee?"

"Yes, you have been with your father's people all of your life, but now you need to spend time with your mother's people."

"When can we start?" Fox asked eagerly.

"One good thing about being a Cherokee—you don't have to make long-range plans. We can leave tomorrow."

Fox suddenly felt a glow of happiness, and he swung the fish around in a huge circle and uttered a hearty cry. Then he turned to face Sequatchie and said, "Why can't we leave today?"

Sequatchie laughed. "That may be too soon for your mother. Women require a little more time than men. Come. We will tell her the news."

A Summer With the Cherokee

Eighteen

Sequatchie, along with his wife, Iris, and Awinita and Fox made their way to the upper Cherokee villages. Awinita and Fox were excited but for different reasons. Awinita longed to see some of her friends from her girlhood of long ago. Fox was filled with high expectations. He had begun dreaming of becoming a mighty chief among the Cherokee, and the journey was far too slow for him.

They camped out along the way. At night around the campfire Sequatchie and Awinita would talk of the days of their youth. Fox sat back from the fire, listening avidly as the two recounted some of the ancient Cherokee legends. Fox had written down much of what Sequatchie and his mother had told him with a vague idea of writing a history of the Cherokee someday.

After Sequatchie and Iris had wrapped up in blankets and gone to bed underneath the open sky, Iris rolled on her side and whispered to her husband, "Fox is having a wonderful time, isn't he?"

"Yes, he is, but I fear he's in for a disappointment."

"Why, what do you mean? Surely you want him to get to know the Cherokee better."

Sequatchie was quiet for a time. He turned and took Iris's hand and held it in both of his. A deep love had blossomed between these two. It had been such an unlikely match, for Iris was a white widow, and Sequatchie a bronzed chief of the Cherokee. Many in the Watauga settlement had made prophecies of gloom concerning the marriage, but Sequatchie and Iris had ignored all their dire predictions and had formed a happy union. Now Iris, her hands held captive in Sequatchie's, waited until he chose to speak. She knew this man of hers thought things over profoundly before he passed any judgment.

"I fear," Sequatchie said quietly, "that Fox will not find all that he is looking for."

"In what way?"

"Many times when we look forward to something with great expectations, the waiting is better than the getting of the thing. I remember when I was just a boy, I looked forward to going on my first hunt. I could think of nothing else for days. I prepared my weapons ahead of time. I was practically leaping out of my skin with anxiety. And then the day came, and the hunt started."

"It didn't go well?"

"My expectations were too high. It was a good hunt, I suppose, but no hunt could be as wonderful as the way I had imagined it in my mind."

"And you think that's what Fox will discover?"

"He has some high ideals, and he's a very imaginative young man. He has a romantic idea of what life is like among our people. He has no idea of how hard it can be, Iris. I think he will be disappointed."

Two days later when the small party arrived at the Cherokee village, Fox got his first glimpse of how the Cherokee people lived. The village was not a large one. He found out later there were only thirty houses, with approximately two hundred Cherokee inhabiting them. As Sequatchie led the party through the center of the village, Fox did not know why he was filled with a sudden sense of depression. The village was nothing but a group of one-story log cabins. His mother had told him the village would be small, but somehow he had expected something grander. The logs were stripped of bark and notched at the ends, with grass mixed with smooth clay plastered over the walls. They were roofed with bark, long broad shingles, or some of them with thatch. Most had no windows, and when he went into the house that had been set aside for visitors where he would live with his mother, it was a dark, dank place with only an animal skin covering the small doorway.

When he saw a long structure that seemed to be sunk in the ground, Fox said, "What is that, Uncle?"

"That is the longhouse," Sequatchie said. "It's where families sleep during cold weather. Longhouses are warmer than the huts. The white men call them hothouses." He took Fox over to examine the longhouse and explained how the floor was dug four feet below ground level and was about twenty by thirty feet in size. Large upright logs formed the framework, which was covered with clay plaster. Cane couches were built around the walls, and a small scooped-out fireplace was located at one end. "The fire burns day and night in the winter."

"Why is there a fire in there now?" Fox inquired. "It's hot."

"The medicine men use this for treating diseases and for purification rights," Sequatchie informed him. "The shamans live here, too."

"What's a shaman?"

"Well, they're sort of medicine men. You might call them keepers of the myth. They know all the lore of the tribe and instruct the young men in the history of the people."

When they came out of the longhouse, Fox was wringing with sweat and wiped his face on his sleeve. He had not worn buckskins, nor had Sequatchie, although Fox wished that he had.

"Greetings, Sequatchie."

Fox looked up to see a tall, strongly built Cherokee approaching. He was deeply bronzed and wore a breechcloth with a tousled sash down over his thigh. His legs were covered with fringed leggings, and his chest was decorated with intricate gunpowder tattoos that had been carved into his skin, leaving raised welts. He wore moccasins, and ornaments of silver dangled from his earlobes, which had been stretched and cut ornamentally. His head was shaved except for one long braid at the crown of the scalp, which was heavily greased with oil. The hair had been plucked out by the roots. The warriors never flinched when this operation was performed, for pain apparently meant nothing to them.

"It has been a long time, Akando."

Suddenly Fox stiffened. He shot a quick glance at his mother, who was standing back, and wondered what she was thinking. Her face was expressionless, but Fox knew that she was afraid of this man. He remembered the story of how Akando had courted her and had lost her to his own father.

Akando took Sequatchie's curt greeting, then came to stand before Awinita. "It has been too long. You have not changed, Awinita."

"Yes, it has been a long time." Awinita's voice was even and low, and she did not lower her gaze but kept her eyes fixed on the tall Cherokee.

"I think often of the days of our youth and am glad that you have returned."

"Thank you, Akando."

Akando's dark eyes suddenly shifted. "Who is this?"

"This is my son, Fox."

Akando's obsidian eyes seemed to pierce Fox. He stood there enduring the stare almost as if it were a physical blow. A power seemed to flow from this man in a way Fox had never experienced before. He could see the strength in his arms, and the merciless gaze in his eyes made Fox shiver. Yet, still, he was a Cherokee war chief.

"Do you know the ways of our people, Fox?" Akando asked.

"No. Not really. Sequatchie has taught me much, but I have come to learn."

A pleased look lightened Akando's expression. "Perhaps I can help you, especially with weapons." He turned and said, "I would like to be a friend to your son."

Awinita did not answer for a moment, and then her permission came reluctantly. "He would have a good teacher. You were always a great warrior, Akando."

Akando smiled at her words, then nodded and turned to Fox. "Tomorrow I will take you on a hunt. You will be ready at dawn."

After Akando left, Fox said with excitement, "Is he the greatest war chief among the Cherokee?"

"He is a great fighter," Sequatchie nodded. "None of the young men can run as fast, and none are as strong to bend a bow so accurately."

"Then I will learn from him."

"Be careful, Fox," Awinita said. She saw that Fox was surprised and added, "He is a strong man, but his cruel heart knows no mercy. That is a terrible fault in a man. Your father was just as strong, but he was generous and kind to his enemies. Akando has no compassion."

"I will not learn that from him," Fox said. "But he can teach me much."

Awinita exchanged a quick glance with her brother. Both were apprehensive about Fox spending any time with Akando, for they felt he could not be trusted. Yet they knew they could not forbid Fox to see him. Akando was a prominent man in the Cherokee world, and his attention meant a great deal to Fox. Nevertheless, they were both concerned, and each of them purposed to keep a close eye on the situation.

The summer days flew by and then weeks. Fox rose early and his days were filled. He learned, to his surprise, that the Cherokee society was largely matriarchal, wherein women enjoyed a freedom not usually exercised by other tribes. In most cases they were in charge of the home, had control over the children, and had a full voice in council. Women were given titles such as Honored Woman or Beautiful Woman.

He learned also that old warriors who had distinguished themselves were greatly honored by the tribe. They were too old to fight, but they formed a group of elders and formed the council that aided the chief in making difficult decisions.

As he immersed himself in the way of life of the Cherokee, he discovered that clan organization was an integral part of the Cherokee Nation. Each clan had its own symbol, and the clan membership was indicated by the color of feathers that the individual wore. Marriage between clans was forbidden, and each person was expected to marry into their paternal or maternal grandfather's clan.

"These things are very important to the Cherokee," Sequatchie said. "I am not certain that they are good."

"But the white man's ways are the same," Fox protested. The two were sitting outside the cabin, and Fox was listening avidly as Sequatchie taught him the ways of the people. "There are rich people and poor people, and southerners don't marry northerners. White people are just as clannish as the Cherokee."

"I do not think that is entirely so, my nephew," Sequatchie said. "You do not understand how strong these beliefs are with our people. One who marries outside his clan is cast off. He never can have a place back in the life of his own clan."

Fox pondered all that he had learned from his uncle, but the most exciting part of this summer among the Cherokee was when he learned the skill of weapons and of the warrior code from Akando.

At first Fox had been cautious about Akando. His mother and uncle had warned him that the man was without true pity. This side of Akando, however, was not what Fox saw. What he found was a tall strong man who smiled often and who spent great care teaching him the skills of hunting and the art of fighting with the tomahawk, with the spear, and especially with the bow. Fox reveled in the affirmation he received and was adept at learning all the new skills. Akando had quickly discovered that Fox was a talented young man, stronger than any of the young Cherokee his own age. Fox could outrun any of them and throw any of them in a wrestling match, a sport in which the Cherokee delighted.

One summer afternoon, however, when Akando suddenly appeared at their cabin, Fox began to wonder about his teacher. Akando stayed all afternoon, and Awinita and Sequatchie reluctantly invited him to stay for the evening meal. It was obvious to both of them that Akando had come to see Awinita.

Akando said little, but he never took his eyes from Fox's mother, and when he left that night, Awinita was unusually subdued.

"Are you worried, my sister?" Sequatchie asked quietly.

"Yes, I am."

"Why are you worried, Mother?" Fox asked. He had been allowed to stay, and now he was puzzled.

Awinita did not answer at once, and then finally she said, "Akando wants me for his wife."

Fox was stunned. "But he didn't say a word about it."

"That is not his way, but that is why he came."

"How do you know that?"

"Because I know the man. He never gives up on anything," Awinita said in a desperate tone. "Back when your father was courting me, I was afraid of Akando, and so were my parents. He would have stolen me away if they hadn't kept me guarded carefully."

From that time on, the war chief of the Cherokee came often. Once Fox saw something that disturbed him greatly. Akando and his mother were sitting outside the cabin, and Fox was off to one side out of sight. He heard Akando talking.

"I have never forgotten you, Awinita." When he received no answer, his voice came clearly. "I still care for you."

Fox sat up straight until the silence was broken by his mother's voice. "Don't say that, Akando. I could never be your wife."

Fox stood then and moved around the corner and saw the two standing close together. Awinita's back was against the wall of the cabin, and Akando was standing in front of her. He wheeled quickly and, upon seeing Fox, smiled and said, "Oh, there you are. I think it's time for another lesson in tracking if you're ready."

"I'm ready, Akando."

Fox followed Akando, but he looked back and saw fear in his mother's eyes. He said nothing to Akando about the scene, and Akando did not mention it all day long.

By late July Sequatchie was ready to return to Watauga. He said as much to Fox early one morning, and Fox listened carefully.

"There are many things we must do back at the cabin. We have had a good visit. You have learned much, have you not?"

"Yes," Fox said.

"Well, it is almost time for you to go back to school."

The thought of returning to school, where he did not fit in, made Fox anxious. He was having a great deal of fun learning the skills of his people and would rather have stayed than return to Watauga. Later that day as he was shooting with Akando, both of them equipped with smooth-bore muskets, Fox said, "I've got to leave, Akando."

Akando took his shot and smiled with satisfaction. He was not a naturally good shot with a musket. As a matter of fact, Fox was a much better shot, but Akando never complained. Now he lowered the musket and turned to Fox. "That will be sad for me. I wish you would not go."

"I don't want to. I would like to stay here and learn more about my Cherokee brothers."

"Why do you not stay, then? You and I could go on a long hunt—for weeks, perhaps."

The thought excited Fox and his eyes lit up. "I don't like the way the white men are treating the Cherokee," he said. "Now that I see what the Cherokee are, I would like to help them."

"That is good that you see the injustice that we suffer at the white man's hand," Akando said. A fire seemed to burn in his eyes at the mention of the white man. "Anger alone will not help our people, but if you would join with us, we could drive the white settlers back out of our land."

"But the government has promised to give you the lands back."

"Empty words. They will never do it, Fox," Akando said. "They always make promises and they have not kept a single one of them. Come back and I will teach you more of the way of the warrior."

Fox kept this in his heart as they made their way back to their home in Watauga. Somehow he knew he could never fight against the white settlers in the region, but still he was determined to prove himself a Cherokee warrior.

Hannah's Birthday

Nineteen

August of 1787 found the western territories of North Carolina in the midst of a long and lush season. Hannah Spencer had spent the day before this, her birthday, making soap. Of all the chores she liked, it was her favorite. Something about the process of preparing the sweet-smelling item pleased her. She had collected lye water, which was simply water filtered through wood ashes, and grease from the time of hog killing. She had poured in two and a half pints of lye water and then added the grease to the large pot perched on stones out in the backyard. The lye dissolved the grease, and all day long she kept the fire burning. At first it looked dark, but as she kept adding more grease, the mixture got to the consistency of a thick gray jelly. She had saved some perfume her mother had given her on her fourteenth birthday. Carefully, she added it to the soap until the whole yard was filled with the sweet aroma.

The sun was barely up when Hannah took a mug full of the soft fragrant soap, grabbed a large towel made of coarse tow, and made her way down to the creek. She went far enough away from the house so that she could not even hear the dogs barking. The creek made a bend and deposited sand on the bottom of a pool about waist deep. It was one of her favorite places. Hannah placed the towel on the ground, slipped out of her dress and undergarments, and taking the soap, stepped out into the water. It was cool and she shivered, but as it curled around her body, she reveled in the luxury of bathing. During the winters when the creeks were frozen over it was too cold. Simple half baths had to do. But now that the weather was hot, she came to the creek almost every day.

She took some of the fresh perfumed soap that was of a soft gray texture and worked it over her body, then immersed herself in the smooth waters to rinse it off. When she had finished washing, she took another generous portion and began to lather her hair, luxuriating in the slight bite of the soap on her scalp.

After rinsing her hair, she came up on the bank, dried herself with the coarse towel, and threw on an old dress to help with preparing breakfast. Going back to the cabin, she went inside and met Elizabeth, who was already cooking.

"You been down at the creek bathing again?"

"It's my birthday, Mama," Hannah said. "I've got to be nice and clean when I put on my new dress for the party."

"You're going to wash all your hide away going down to the creek every day." Elizabeth smiled. "It is fun though, isn't it? Nothing feels better than a good bath."

Hawk stepped inside then with an armload of wood for the fireplace. He dumped it with a miniature thunder into the woodbox and turned to say, "Well, that's a pretty dress you've got on. It's your birthday dress, isn't it?"

Hannah was accustomed to his teasing. "This isn't my birthday dress, silly! You know better than that."

"It's not! Well, you've got so many dresses, I just can't keep up with all of them."

"I've got three, and two of them are too small!"

Hawk came over and suddenly put his arms around Hannah and squeezed her, lifting her feet up off the floor, saying, "That's because you're becoming a beautiful young lady, and I'm as proud as punch of you. Fifteen years old! Why, it seems like almost yesterday I was giving you your bath in a big iron pot right here on this table. You wouldn't fit in it now, though."

Hannah laughed. Birthdays were special for her, and today she was especially happy. Entering into young womanhood was a new adventure for her. Her honey brown hair was wet and lay plastered against her head. Her green eyes sparkled as she stood there enduring her father's teasing, which she loved.

"Well, your mother's cooking up enough food for a whole Cherokee village," Hawk said. Turning to Hannah, he winked and said, "At least I'll get something to eat out of it. Your mother's an awful cook, but that doesn't matter."

"I don't notice you turning down anything," Elizabeth said.

"I don't want to hurt your feelings," Hawk said. "Maybe I'll give you a few lessons. I've about decided to keep you on."

"Oh, you have!" Elizabeth said almost angrily. Seeing the twinkle in his eye, she laughed out loud and said, "Go along with you. You're underfoot all the time."

Hawk turned to say, "Which one of these young bucks are you favorin' now?"

"Oh, Papa, I'm not favoring any of them!"

"Well, seems to me like Ethan Cagle's been hanging around here quite a bit lately."

Hannah flushed, for indeed Ethan Cagle had grown up to be a very handsome young man, one whom all the girls in the settlement admired. "I'm not studying Ethan Cagle," she said and ran to her room to finish getting ready.

While there, Hannah put the soap away and pulled out the new dress she was going to wear. She had made it with her mother's help and now held it up. "I wish I had a mirror six feet tall," she said. "I can only see a part of myself."

Finally she laid the dress down carefully on the bed and went to the window, where the sun was streaming in. She sat with her back to it, letting the hot rays of the morning August sun dry her hair, and wondered what the day held for her.

The area surrounding the Spencer cabin was filled with the shouts and the laughter of young people. Life was hard on the frontier, and any special occasion for games or recreation was quickly seized by everyone in the community. A birthday party was fair game, and it seemed every young person in the immediate vicinity had come to join in the festivities. The rest of the family had come to celebrate with Hannah, also. Seth and Sarah brought little Joanna, who was almost two now. Andrew and Abigail brought little Susanna, along with her two older brothers. She had been born in July. Jacob and Amanda brought their two children and shared the news that they were expecting another baby the following year.

Hawk and Elizabeth stood on the porch watching their daughter and the other youngsters playing games such as tag, hide-and-seek, and hopscotch. Some of the younger children were singing "Here

We Go Round the Mulberry Bush" and "London Bridge Is Falling Down."

At the moment the older ones were playing blindman's bluff. Hannah was in the middle and Ethan Cagle was putting the blindfold on her.

"That's a beautiful dress she's got on, Elizabeth. You did a good job making it," Hawk said softly.

Indeed the dress was beautiful. It was made out of a light blue cotton, with sleeves that came to the elbow, ending in a large white lace ruffle. The neckline was square, edged with white lace, and the stomacher was overlaid with white lace. The dress itself was edged with ruching, worn open to reveal a petticoat of the same soft blue material.

"She made a lot of it herself," Elizabeth said. "She's a beautiful girl, isn't she?"

"Almost as pretty as her mother."

"Oh, you're always saying things like that."

"Maybe I ought to stop." Hawk grinned and put his arm around her.

"No. Don't stop," Elizabeth said quickly. "You keep your eye on the games while I go get the refreshments."

Hawk watched as Ethan Cagle finished tying the blindfold on Hannah and asked her, "How many horses has your father got?"

"Three," Hannah answered, knowing the game well.

"What color are they?"

"Black, white, and gray."

Ethan said, "Turn around . . . turn around . . . and turn around and catch whom you can."

Ethan spun Hannah around until she was dizzy, and then she put her hands out and began trying to catch someone. As part of the game, the youngsters would come as close as they could to the "blindman" and speak, teasing her with a chance to grab them.

Finally a voice in her ear said, "Here." She turned around and grabbed and caught someone. "I've got you!" she laughed, pulling her blindfold off.

"You've got me, all right," Ethan Cagle said.

"All right. I'll blindfold you now and you can be it."

Ethan suddenly reached out and gave Hannah a kiss on the cheek.

"Why, you awful thing!" Hannah said, flushing.

"No. It's a rule. When you get caught, you have to give the blind-man a kiss on the cheek."

"I never heard of that rule," Hannah said, aware that the others were laughing. She looked up and saw her father on the porch, his feet propped up against the post and grinning.

"I just made it up," Ethan smirked.

"Well, you're not going to catch me. Not unless you peek."

"I might do that." Cagle smiled broadly. He was a fine-looking young man with a shock of dark hair and sea green eyes. He was tall, and Hannah had to reach up to tie his blindfold.

"Now, see if you can go catch somebody else." Seeing her best friend close by, Hannah said, "Try to catch Eve!"

Eve colored and said, "Oh, Hannah."

"I'd rather catch you, Hannah," Ethan replied.

No one noticed the disappointed look that quickly flashed across Eve's face.

The game went on for some time, and finally Elizabeth came out and said, "Time for presents and then refreshments!"

Everyone came inside the cabin and crowded around and watched as Hannah began to open her gifts. She received a beautiful shawl made by Eve and Rachel Anderson, and her eyes sparkled as she unfolded it and put it on. "Just my color," she said.

"You look beautiful in it, Hannah," Rachel said.

"I wanted to give you an anvil, but your mother said it wouldn't be right," Hawk said.

"An anvil! What would I do with an anvil?" Hannah laughed.

"Make horseshoes. Here, your mother and I found this somewhere. It's probably no good, but you're welcome to it."

Opening the small package her father gave her, Hannah stood stock-still.

"What is it?" everyone cried, and she held up a gold locket with a dark green stone set in gold.

"Mama, Papa, it's beautiful! Put it on!"

"It's too little for me," Hawk quipped, "but I'll put it on you."

Hannah waited until he had fastened the delicate chain around her neck, then turned and gave both her parents a kiss. "Thank you. It's so beautiful. I'll keep it always."

"You're welcome, sweetheart. It looks very nice on you," Elizabeth replied with tears in her eyes.

Hannah opened several other presents, and then Ethan came forward to say, "Here. Hope you like this, Hannah."

Hannah smiled. "Why, thank you, Ethan. What is it?"

"Open it and see."

Hannah took the brown wrapping paper off and saw a beautifully carved wooden box. She lifted the lid and saw that it was lined with soft green material.

"A jewelry box. You can keep your new locket in there."

"Oh, it's beautiful, Ethan! Just beautiful! Did you make it yourself?"

"Sure did."

Impulsively Hannah reached out and hugged Ethan, who winked at her father. "She's very forward, isn't she, sir?"

"She gets it from her mother. All of us men are well behaved, but the Spencer women can be a mite flirtatious."

"Oh, Papa!" Hannah said.

"It's a beautiful gift, and I thank you for it. And for all the other gifts, too," she said to everyone else.

Fox had been standing on the outside, his back against the wall. He had only decided to come to Hannah's birthday party at the last minute, and now he was embarrassed that he had not brought her anything. While the others were looking at the presents, he turned and slipped out of the cabin. He had not gone far, however, before he heard Hannah call out, "Fox, wait a minute!"

Fox turned and saw Hannah coming to stand beside him. "Where are you going?" she asked.

"I . . . I don't know."

"Aren't you having a good time? We're about to have refreshments. Come on back in."

Fox was embarrassed. "I'm sorry I didn't get you a present," he said.

"Why, just having you here is good enough, Fox."

"I missed you while I was gone to be with the Cherokee."

"Well, I missed you, too."

Hannah's kind words made Fox feel better. He had grown very tall now, two inches over six feet, though he was only seventeen. He was wiry and strong and would gain in size and strength as he grew older. Now he looked down at Hannah Spencer and thought she was the prettiest girl he had ever seen. He wanted to do something to make up for not having brought a present, and he said with some embarrassment, "I did bring you kind of a present."

"Oh, what is it?"

"It's a little poem I made up."

"A poem for me?"

"Yes. I was thinking about you when I was out hunting with the Cherokee. It just came to me. I don't have it with me written down, but I can say it."

"Please. Let me hear it."

Fox cleared his throat with some embarrassment and said,

Her hair is soft as the fresh summer grass,
And her eyes are as deep as the blue waters of the big lake.
She moves gracefully like the deer,
And she has in her a kindness bigger than earth.

"What a beautiful poem! Was it really for me?"

"It's not much," Fox shrugged. "It doesn't rhyme or anything. It's just . . . well, I thought of it and that's how I always think of you, Hannah."

"It was wonderful! You'll have to write it down for me." Suddenly she reached forward and gave him a hug. "There," she said. "Now let's go inside and have refreshments."

Hannah was too excited to sleep, as Eve Martin and Rachel Anderson were spending the night with her. Eve, who was often quiet, was even quieter than usual, claiming tiredness. Hannah and Rachel were playing checkers while Eve watched.

They had played for some time when Rachel said, "You got some wonderful gifts today, Hannah! Especially the locket. May I see it again?"

"Of course." Hannah picked up the carved box and handed it to Rachel, who pulled the necklace out and admired it.

"It sure is pretty," Rachel said. "It looks good on you, too." She put it back in the box and held the box for a moment. "Ethan's a good carver. I didn't know he could make things like this."

Taking the box back, Hannah ran her hand over the carved surface. "It is beautiful, isn't it?"

"You know what? You just lost two men looking at that box." Rachel grinned and took two jumps, then said, "Your move."

The game went on for some time, and finally Rachel said, "One of these days Fox and Ethan are going to fight over you."

"Why, don't be silly. Fox is just a good friend and so is Ethan."

"Well, they're both giving you funny looks."

"What do you mean 'funny looks?' "

"Oh, I mean they cut their eyes around and study you. I've seen 'em."

"Don't be silly."

"I'm not being silly. Ask Eve. And you noticed it, too, Hannah. Don't try to put anything over on me."

Eve said quietly, "They do seem to favor you, Hannah."

Hannah was so flustered that she could not answer, and Rachel quickly snapped up her last three men.

"You're so busy thinking about romance you're not any good at checkers," she announced.

"I noticed David and Joshua paying you a lot of attention, too," Hannah protested. "It seems I'm not the only one being made over."

"We're all just friends, and you know it, Hannah Spencer."

Hannah and Eve giggled.

"What?" Rachel asked.

Hannah replied, "I have two men courting me, but you have two friends. Sounds the same to me."

Rachel finally laughed at their teasing, then asked innocently, "Who are you going to dream about? Ethan or Fox?"

Hannah laughed. "Oh you! Let's just go to bed."

Later in bed, lying awake and looking out the small window at the pale moon, which tossed its beams down on the cabin and lit up the room, Hannah thought about her friends' teasing.

They're just silly, she thought. *Ethan and Fox are not courting me.* But deep down she knew her friends had been right. She had caught the glimpses that the two young men had given her, and being a young woman just becoming aware of such things, she was pleased by their attentions.

She finally dropped off to sleep and dreamed of both young men—the pale, handsome face of Ethan Cagle and the dark, severe face of Fox Carter.

Another Fight

Twenty

Late September brought cold blasts throughout the Watauga area. The trees had turned to red and gold and scarlet, and almost overnight the grasses had lost their emerald green and now draped the earth with a gray dead carpet. All of this, the settlers knew, was a preamble to a winter that they suspected would be hard. Many of them studied the thickness of the fur on the caterpillars to determine the severity of the winter. Others gauged the months that lay ahead by the thickness of the shells of the acorns that had begun to fall. All the signs agreed that it would be a bitter winter.

School had proved to be harder than Fox Carter had imagined. His mind, perhaps, was still back with the Cherokee; and at times in class, while Samuel Doak drilled lessons into the students, he daydreamed of all he had learned with Akando. More than once he was punished for his inattentiveness, and the time came when he dreaded getting up in the morning for school.

"I don't see why I have to go to that old school, Mother."

"You're almost through. Another few months and you'll be finished, and then we'll see."

Fox had had this argument with Awinita every day, it seemed, and now on this chilly September morning, he rode his horse to the school and tied it up outside the door. He was late, and the other pupils were already in class.

He caught a quick glance from Hannah but turned his eye away from her. Ever since her birthday party, he had somehow been jealous of her attention to Ethan Cagle. He knew that Cagle was spending a great deal of time at the Spencer cabin, which made Fox even gloomier.

Just as he walked down the aisle, he heard Eli Harrison whisper loudly enough to be heard by everybody, "I smell something bad. It really stinks."

Isaiah Tompkins took up the refrain at once. "Yeah, it must be an Indian. I could smell one a mile off."

A blinding rage fell on Fox so quickly that he did not even pause to reason. He whirled suddenly, grabbed Eli Harrison by the shirt, and pulled him to his feet. As soon as the startled young man was upright, Fox drove a hard right blow into his nose. Harrison let out a yell and fell into the desks of Joshua and David. Isaiah Tompkins came roaring out of his chair and caught Fox half turned with a blow under his ear. Fox went careening across the room, crashing into Hannah's desk and turning it over. He scrambled to his feet just in time to catch the combined onslaught of the two boys.

"You boys stop that!" Samuel Doak cried out. But all three of the young men were too blind with fury to pay any attention to the schoolmaster. They fought all around the room, pummeling one another with blows. Finally Fox was driven out the door by Tompkins, who simply ran at him and tackled him. The two struck the ground, and Fox kicked and struck out like an angry bear. He got to his feet just in time to catch Harrison coming in with a punch right in the mouth.

All of the students piled out of the classroom and surrounded the trio. Hannah cried out, "You stop it! Stop it, Eli!"

But Eli Harrison was beyond reason, and when Mr. Doak tried to intervene, he got caught in the cheek with a wild fist that knocked him backward.

Both Harrison and Tompkins were big young men, muscular from hard work, but Fox had spent the past few months training with Akando, running through the woods under very hard conditions.

Joshua was only thirteen, but he saw his chance to jump into the melee. With a wild yell he leaped onto Eli Harrison's back and clung like a burr. Harrison tried to throw him off but couldn't. To make matters worse, David Martin ran straight into him and began hitting him around his face.

"Hey!" Eli yelled. "You two get off of me!"

Fox, now only having one adversary, quickly struck three hard blows that put Tompkins down with a bloody face. He lay there refusing to get up, and Fox ran over and grabbed Harrison by the collar.

"I give up! Leave me alone!" Harrison yelled.

Seeing that the two boys had surrendered, Doak came over at once and said, "All right! That's enough of this!" His cheek was red from the punch he had taken, and he was angry to the bone. "All three of you leave this school! You won't come back here until your parents have a talk with me."

"I don't care if I never come back," Fox said angrily. He ran over to the rail, untied his horse, and swung himself on. Kicking the horse's flanks he sped away.

"That was some fight, wasn't it?" Joshua said. He was grinning broadly.

"The best fight I ever had." David smiled back at his friend.

But Hannah was not happy. She said, "I'm going to go talk to Fox. Joshua, you tell Mr. Doak what I'm doing."

"He won't like it."

"I'll worry about that later."

Hannah ran to the mare she had ridden and quickly climbed on. It took her some time to catch up with Fox, for he was mounted on a faster animal. But finally she pulled within reach of him and cried out, "Fox, stop!"

Hearing Hannah's voice, Fox pulled his mount up and turned to face her. "What do you want, Hannah?"

"I want to talk to you."

"There's nothing to talk about."

"Yes, there is. Now, you get off that horse and listen to me."

Fox reluctantly slipped off the bay and stood there holding the reins tightly in his hand. Hannah came to stand beside him, also holding her own mount. "Are you hurt?" she asked.

"No."

"Yes, you are. You're bleeding." Hannah reached into the pocket of her apron and pulled out a handkerchief. She dabbed at his face, but he roughly shoved her away.

"There's nothing wrong with me!"

"Fox, I don't understand you. Some days you seem all right, and then you do something like this."

"Didn't you hear what they said?"

"What difference does it make what they say? You know what they're like."

"Yes, I do. They're like white men, and they never miss a chance to put an Indian down."

"You know all white men are not bad, just as all Indians aren't good."

Fox was irrational. He was still seething with anger, and he said flatly, "The Indians had the land first."

Ever since Fox had returned from his visit with the Cherokee, Hannah knew he was angry over the broken treaties. She said, "Your uncle and my father say that the Cherokee and the white people can share the land."

"Not with people like Eli and Isaiah."

The argument went on for some time, and Fox slowly calmed down. He looked at Hannah and suddenly realized that although he had been growing more and more aware of her as she had matured into young womanhood, still he was afraid to trust her. He was torn in two by the forces that had brought him from boyhood to manhood, and now as he looked into her face, he did not know what to say. He was too angry to talk anymore. "I'm going now. Good-bye, Hannah."

Hannah watched Fox as he rode away, and slowly she mounted her horse again and turned back toward the school. "What's going to become of him?" she wondered. "He can't keep on going like this." Her heart was still agitated, and as she moved slowly along the dusty trail, she began to pray that God would do something for Fox Carter that no human being seemed able to do.

Song of the Mockingbird

Twenty-One

Fox hardly spoke when he got home, but his mother saw the cuts and bruises the two young men had inflicted on his face. She waited for him to mention what had happened, but he was quiet during the evening meal. As soon as he finished, he excused himself and went outside to do some chores. Later on she got the story out of Joshua, who was thrilled about his part in the fight. "You should have seen Fox pound on them! He could have whipped them both by himself!" he boasted. "Of course, I jumped in and helped, and so did David."

Awinita was disturbed by all of this. She knew that young men fought sometimes, but she also knew that Fox was at a vulnerable point in his life. As soon as she could, she pulled her brother off to one side and said, "Sequatchie, Fox had a fight in school. Someone made a remark about his being an Indian."

"It's not the first time, and it probably won't be the last."

"Maybe the best thing will be for us to go stay with our people."

"I don't think so," Sequatchie said.

"Why not? At least it's peaceful there."

"It's not going to be peaceful for long."

Quickly Awinita looked up. "What do you mean?" she asked.

"I mean, sooner or later there will be other conflicts, and it can only have one end. I've seen it before. The white men will move into a part of the Cherokee land and settle there. The Cherokee will attack, and some of the white settlers will be killed." Sequatchie's face grew sad and at the same time stern. "Then the white men will raise an army and come and raid our people. They will push us farther back."

"We can always retreat."

"Do you think we haven't thought that? There is no end. Sooner or later we're going to be overrun by the white men. There is no way except to learn their ways. If we want land, we must settle on it and pay for it. It does not make me happy, but that is the way it is. It does have its good side, though. I feel this is the only way that all of the Indians will hear about Jesus from good men who will come west as well. Men who want to teach all of us about the love of Jesus."

Awinita said nothing, but shortly after, she found Fox. He was skinning several coons he had trapped. "Tell me about the fight, Fox."

"It was nothing." Fox looked very trim and fit as he stood beside the skinning tree where the animals were nailed. The skinning boards were beside him, and two of the coon hides were already stretched out. His hands were bloody, and he could not meet his mother's eyes.

"I've been talking to your uncle. I said that perhaps we ought to go live with the Cherokee."

"That would satisfy me."

Awinita studied her son's face. She saw the strong resemblance to Titus, his father, and wished desperately that he were still alive.

"Sequatchie says it will not work. Sooner or later our people will lose all their land, and then where will we be?"

"Not without a fight. Akando says—"

"Don't tell me what Akando says! He's a cruel man, and all he knows is killing!"

"You don't really know him!" Fox said sharply to his mother.

"I know him better than you could ever know him, Fox! I've known him for years. Don't put too much stock in the words of that man!"

Awinita walked away, and Fox was greatly disturbed by his mother's sharp reaction to Akando. He knew that Akando was a man of violence, but the Cherokee had always had to be fighters against other tribes. Against their own sometimes.

All day long Fox moped around the house. He had refused to go back to school, and his mother and Sequatchie had agreed that it would not be wise to send him for a time. "He's a man, Awinita,"

Sequatchie said. "Not a schoolboy. Now he's got to make his own way."

Hannah had gone out to the smokehouse to get a ham. The dawn had come early, it seemed, and as she came out, she stood and admired the red as the sun slowly crept over the horizon.

"Hello, Hannah."

The sound of a voice startled Hannah, and she dropped the ham and whirled quickly. "Oh, it's you, Fox! You scared me."

"I'm sorry. I wanted to talk to you."

"About what?"

Fox looked around nervously. He did not want anyone overhearing what he had to say. "Could we go for a little walk?"

Hannah hesitated, then nodded. "Let me put this ham back."

"I'll do it."

Fox put the ham back in the smokehouse, came outside, and nodded. "Let's walk down to the creek."

Hannah could not imagine what Fox had come for. She had listened as Joshua had told her parents, with great relish, of the fight, and she sensed that both of them were worried about Fox.

When they reached the creek, he turned suddenly and said, "I just wanted to say I'm sorry I lost my temper yesterday."

Hannah was caught off guard. She had not expected him to say such a thing. When she hesitated, he added, "I guess I need to apologize for what I did. I tried to apologize to Eli and Isaiah, but they just wanted to fight again, said I was a 'dirty Indian' and not worth anything."

Hannah felt a sudden compassion for her friend. She stepped forward and put her hand on his arm, saying, "You can't help what they do, Fox, but you did the right thing. And when you do the right thing, it's always best."

"I guess so. Do you want to walk along the creek?"

"All right, but not for long," Hannah said. "Mama will worry about me."

They followed the winding creek, which made a sibilant sound as it swept around a steep bend. Once a kingfisher swooped down and took a minnow, and Hannah cried out with delight, "Aren't they the prettiest things!"

"They are pretty."

Finally Hannah stopped and said, "I can't go any farther, Fox. I've got to get back."

Fox wanted to say more to Hannah. He was torn by a maelstrom of emotions he could not understand. He knew that he truly cared for this girl, but there was no way he could say such a thing to her—not in his confused state.

Over to their right a mockingbird began to sing.

Hannah turned with delight. "I love the song of the mockingbird, don't you?"

Fox smiled. "It goes like this, doesn't it?"

He pursed his lips, and to Hannah's shock, the perfect sound of a mockingbird song issued forth.

"Where did you learn to do that?"

"I learned it this summer. It was one of the Cherokee boys who taught me how to do it."

"Well, it's beautiful. I wish I could do it. Could you teach me?"

"I could try. It took me a long time, though."

Hannah was aware that the glade in which they stood was very quiet. Except for the muted sound of the mockingbird that flew on into the deep woods, she only heard the sound of the water. Finally she resolved to say something to Fox that she'd been wanting to tell him for some time.

"Fox, I'm glad that you learned something about your Cherokee heritage, but you can never forget that you have a European heritage, too. And both of those sides of you should belong to the Lord."

Fox suddenly felt uncomfortable. Indeed, he had recently been so confused that he did not know his true feelings about God. He had listened to the sermons at the church preached by Paul Anderson and Seth Donovan, and he had read the Bible from time to time, but there was such a turmoil inside him that he could not put together his thoughts about God in a way that made sense.

"I suppose you're right," he finally said. "But I'm so mixed-up I don't know what to think. How can I understand God when I don't even understand myself?"

Hannah felt a moment of confusion. She had been fascinated by Fox since he had first come to live at Watauga. They had become good friends, but now as she stood there, she was drawn to his tall, athletic figure and the smoothness of his bronzed cheeks. He had grown more handsome as he grew older. There was a cleanness in the sweep of his high cheekbones, and his hair was smooth and as black as coal. She suddenly felt a shyness come upon her, and Fox sensed it. He reached out and put his hand on her arm and would have pulled her forward, but Hannah suddenly broke away and cried, "I . . . I've got to go back, Fox!" She turned and almost ran down the pathway.

Fox did not follow her but watched her trim form and thought as she disappeared around the bend of the creek, *I have feelings for her, but she could never feel anything for me. And no matter how much I've come to hate some of the things white people do, I could never hate Hannah Spencer.*

Gifts for Hannah

Twenty-Two

As it did every year, Christmas came to Watauga differently than it did in more populous areas. In the East, no doubt, there would be decorations hung in the cities, and the store windows would be decked with holly. But in the Watauga valley, the men and women and young people were so engaged in the struggle to survive that they had little time for many of the fancy festivities east of the Misty Mountains.

True enough, most cabins managed to at least find room for a small tree on Christmas Eve, and the Christmas dinner included turkey, assuming one could be caught, and mincemeat pies. But it was primarily in the church that Christmas was observed most keenly.

The Spencers had gathered with others from the community, and Paul Anderson stood before them to preach as he had for years. After the singing of Christmas carols, Anderson stood and began his sermon. He was fifty-two now, and his hair was liberally sprinkled with gray. In front of him, his wife, Rhoda Anderson, sat with their daughter, Rachel.

Anderson read the Christmas story and then said, "On Christmas there is only one sermon in my heart. You've all heard it for many years. So if you don't want to hear it again, now is your first chance to escape."

Hawk spoke up and said, "It's the best sermon on Christmas I ever heard. So give it to us again, Pastor."

Paul Anderson grinned and said, "Very well. Since Mr. Spencer insists, you will have it again."

For some time Anderson preached on the background of the text. He stressed how the Jews had looked for a Messiah for centuries, but none had come. And then finally he said, "But one morning in Judea a child was born, and although almost no one knew it, the Savior of the world, who from time immemorial had lain on the Father's bosom, now lay in the arms of an earthly mother in a lowly stable."

He preached quietly, and everyone stayed absolutely still when Paul Anderson spoke about how God became man.

Finally Anderson's voice, which had grown very soft, raised like a trumpet. "And this same Jesus is coming again. He came first as a helpless child. He will come again as a conqueror, to whom all powers and dominions will answer. Every knee shall bow and every tongue shall confess that Jesus is Lord. This is the Savior that we worship this morning."

The crowd stood, and as always, Paul Anderson called for one verse of the popular hymn "Come, Thou Almighty King" to close the service.

During the special service, Joshua Spencer had not been doing what he was supposed to be doing—listening. He had been looking at Rachel Anderson instead. Lately he had begun to notice changes in his longtime "pal." Rachel was almost fourteen and was beginning to mature into a beautiful young lady. Her pale green "going-to-church" dress set off her light green eyes and sandy blond hair perfectly. Hawk had noticed that his son's mind was wandering and had nudged him to alertness, but this had only lasted momentarily as Joshua had returned to his careful watching of Rachel Anderson.

As everyone filed out of the service to head home for family gatherings, Joshua, reacting without truly thinking, hurried over to where Rachel stood. He was surprised to find himself arriving at the same time as his friend David Martin. Both of the young men looked at each other in shock for a moment and then turned to Rachel and said in almost perfect unison, "May I escort you, Rachel?"

Rachel smiled coyly at her two friends and replied, "Thank you both, but I already have an escort for today."

Before either could ask who, Paul Anderson walked up to his daughter and offered her his arm. As Rachel walked away with him to join her mother, she flung back over her shoulder, "I'll see you both later at your house, Josh."

Joshua and David stood staring after the young girl, dumfounded. When the Andersons had driven off in their wagon, the two looked at each other as if seeing his closest friend for the first time. Joshua finally muttered, "See you later, David."

David ran his hand through his blond hair and said, "Yeah, see you later." They turned and joined their families, knowing, but not fully understanding, that things between the three friends would never be the same again.

The usual crowd gathered at the Spencer cabin for Christmas dinner: Hawk, Elizabeth, Hannah, and Joshua; Jacob, Amanda, Jared, and Emily; Andrew, Abigail, Abel, Caleb, and Susanna; and Seth, Sarah, and Joanna. Eve and David Martin had come with their parents, Will and Rebekah. Sequatchie, Iris, Awinita, and Fox brought Ezekiel and Mercy. Abigail's parents, George and Deborah Stevens came. The Dentons—Thomas, Leah, Sherah, and, baby Micah, born earlier that year—and the Cagles—Ethan and his parents, Stephen and Dorcas—had also come. Stephen had moved to the frontier with his wife and son after the Revolution. A slight limp with his right leg attested to his bravery as a fighting patriot. Stephen and Dorcas were staunch Christians and had found a good home in the Watauga area.

Paul, Rhoda, and Rachel Anderson were the last to arrive. As they were all seated around various makeshift tables in the Spencers' cabin, Joshua and David tried to seat themselves beside Rachel, but away from the other. They managed to maneuver themselves on either side of her. As Rhoda Anderson observed Joshua and David hovering around Rachel and seeing to her slightest whim, she also noticed that her daughter seemed to enjoy the attention. Seeing that Paul had noticed all of this as well, she leaned toward him and whispered in his ear, "Maybe our child will really turn out to be our *daughter* after all."

Paul sighed and murmured back, "I think you're right about that. But suddenly I miss my little tomboy."

Rhoda chuckled and said, "I doubt she's gone for good just yet, but I'm afraid the day will come before we want it to."

After the dinner, the women began to gather the dishes while the men wandered outside to avoid the cleaning up. The young people decided to play games while waiting to open any presents. While Joshua was starting a game, Fox asked Hannah to step outside for a moment. They excused themselves, and after going outside, they headed for the barn.

As they entered the barn, Fox turned to Hannah and said quietly, "I brought you a present this time, but I wanted to give it to you in private. It reminds me of a time that meant a lot to me." Reaching into his pocket, Fox pulled out a small object.

Hannah took it and then blinked with surprise. "Why, it's beautiful, Fox!"

What she held was a perfectly carved bird, a mockingbird. It was colored in delicate shades of light gray on the breast and darker gray on the edges of the wings. The eyes were black and shiny. "Why, it is absolutely perfect!"

"I've been working on it a long time. Do you know why I'm giving it to you?"

"It's to remind me of the time we stood out by the creek and you imitated the mockingbird."

"That's right. It was a special morning for me. You ran away that day, Hannah. Do you remember?"

Suddenly Hannah felt sad. She reached out and put her hand on his chest. "I did. I was afraid of what might happen."

"Were you afraid I might kiss you?"

Hannah started to shake her head as she stared into Fox's dark eyes.

Suddenly the barn door opened and Ethan Cagle walked in. "There you are, Hannah. Everyone is looking for you. We're ready to open the gifts. I can't wait for you to see what I got you." Ethan waited for Hannah to join him before leaving the barn.

Fox watched her leave, then slowly followed.

Inside the cabin was a melee, with everyone talking and exclaiming over gifts at once. Ethan immediately got a package and handed it to Hannah. Hannah smiled as she opened the gift, then squealed with delight at the beautiful rabbit coat that was now hers. Hannah hugged Ethan tightly and said, "Oh, Ethan, it is beautiful! I truly love it!"

Ethan said, "I made it myself." Hearing Dorcas clear her throat, he quickly added, "With a little help from Ma." After everyone chuckled at this, Ethan, pleased at Hannah's obvious joy, said, "Well, try it on."

"Help me please, Ethan." After allowing Ethan to hold the coat while she slipped it on, Hannah replied, "It fits perfectly. Thank you so much."

"You're very welcome," Ethan said. "I'm glad you like it."

Elizabeth spoke up from the other side of the room. "Hannah, come over here and let us all see that beautiful coat."

As Hannah moved around the room so everyone could admire the fine garment, she failed to notice that Eve was not as enthusiastic as the others. Rachel noticed, however, and asked, "Is something wrong, Eve?"

Eve quickly put a smile on her face and answered, "No, everything is fine."

Rachel, still wondering about Eve, said, "Isn't the coat beautiful?"

Eve could not completely hide the wistful look that came to her face as she answered, "Yes, it is very pretty. And it looks great on Hannah." Eve then replied, "I think I'll get a drink of water."

Rachel watched Eve walk away and wondered how she truly felt about Hannah's gift and why.

Hannah, unaware of Rachel and Eve's conversation, turned and walked back toward Fox. "Do you like the coat, Fox?" She was surprised to see a sad and dejected look on his face.

"It is lovely," Fox answered, "which makes it perfect for you, Hannah."

Hannah smiled and said, "Thank you."

"Well, I think I will go home," Fox said. "I'm pretty tired."

"Do you have to leave now?" Hannah asked.

"Yeah." Fox turned to go. "I hope you have a good Christmas."

"Thanks, Fox. And thanks for the mockingbird. It really is beautiful." Hannah followed Fox to the door. As he walked outside she called, "Good night, Fox."

"Good-bye, Hannah."

As Hannah turned to join the others, she wondered why Fox's good-bye upset her so much.

As Fox got farther from the Spencer cabin, he muttered, "I don't know why I even try. She won't ever care for me. What can I offer her that someone else like Ethan can't give her?"

He continued on toward home and finally said aloud, "She

doesn't want a dirty half-breed anyway. No one does." Fox kicked at a rock in his path and tried to hold back the tears that sprang to his eyes. He ran the rest of the way to the cabin, his heart breaking with every step.

As Hannah prepared for bed later that evening, she wondered at the actions of Fox. Picking up the carved mockingbird from a bedside table, she stroked the smooth wood as she thought of the hands that had lovingly fashioned it just for her.

In Williamsburg, Julia Carter had, as usual, planned a big Christmas party. As she and her husband were dressing for it, Naaman suddenly said, "Do you realize, Julia, that Nathanael is eighteen years old now?"

"What does that mean?"

"Don't you understand?" He turned to her with his brow knitted. "It means that he could claim this place anytime he wants to."

"But he won't, will he? I mean, we haven't heard from him."

"But he can come back now. He's a full-grown man. He could hire lawyers. He could take Havenwood from us. I won't have it!"

"What can we do?"

"I'm going to do *something*, you can believe that."

Later in the evening, while the party was in full swing, Naaman met with his lawyer, Philemon Dodd. The two men were sequestered in the ornate office that Naaman used for his business, and he began the conversation by saying, "Nate Carter's eighteen years old now, and you know what that means."

Dodd nodded. "I've seen this coming. What are you going to do?"

"I don't know. What do you suggest?"

"Unless you can prove that he's dead, you can't do anything, Naaman."

"I haven't heard anything about his dying. Of course, we're not in touch with them. Tom Denton writes Annabelle occasionally, but he hasn't mentioned anything happening to Nathanael."

"Then you may as well get ready for it. You're going to lose Havenwood."

"I won't, I tell you! It's not fair! It's not just! He's an interloper. Havenwood belongs to me!"

"As a lawyer I can advise you what to do," Dodd said. "But I think you may as well accept the fact that according to law, Havenwood belongs to the boy."

Dodd's words did not seem to reach Naaman Carter. He was thinking rapidly. *I'll get Jasper Tatum and I'll go to the frontier. Tatum will take care of Fox and Awinita. We can leave in the spring as soon as the weather gets better.* He suddenly smiled and said, "Thanks for listening, Dodd."

Dodd could tell that Naaman was up to no good, and he quickly turned away. "You've got something in your head, Naaman. Don't tell me anything about it," he said firmly. "I don't want to know."

After the party was fully under way, Edward and Annabelle Denton arrived. Annabelle had had to make her usual grand entrance. Naaman pulled Edward aside quickly to tell him of his plans to go over the mountains. He did not go into detail, but Edward Denton was a quick thinker and saw plainly what was on Naaman Carter's mind. "You'd better look up my son, Thomas. He might have information that will assist you. But mind what you tell him. He has turned out to be a great disappointment, I'm afraid."

Naaman laughed loudly and said, "Well, next Christmas, Edward, we'll have a party at my plantation, Havenwood. It'll be all mine. You wait and see!"

PART IV

A Home With Christ

March 1788 – March 1789

"Hereby know we that we dwell in him, and he in us, because he hath given us of his Spirit. And we have seen and do testify that the Father sent the Son to be the Saviour of the world. Whosoever shall confess that Jesus is the Son of God, God dwelleth in him, and he in God."

1 John 4:13–15

Setting Traps and Playing Games

Twenty-Three

"I don't see what we're doing this for!" Joshua complained. He threw down a log that he had chopped and dragged to the clearing where Fox and Ezekiel were building a structure. It was built according to the same pattern as the cabins that all the settlers built on the frontier, except it was no more than ten feet square, and the logs were much smaller. Joshua wiped the sweat from his face and looked up at the sky. "It looks like there'd be an easier way to get turkeys than this."

Ezekiel winked at Fox, who was notching one of the small logs, and said, "Ain't no easy way to get a turkey. They's mighty shy creatures."

"I bet I could get one," Joshua maintained. He hefted the ax and said, "Let's just go hunt 'em."

Fox laughed at Joshua. He had taken off his shirt to do the heavy work, and now the smooth muscles of his torso reflected the strength he had gained. It was a strength not of a heavy draft horse, but of a lithe, muscular cougar. He moved easily and swiftly and never wasted a fraction of his strength. Now as he quickly made a notch on each end with a few strokes of the ax, he said, "It takes too long. Sometimes you have to sit for half a day and wait for one of those pesky critters."

"That's right, Joshua, and then you've got to be a good hunter to shoot one."

"I could get one, I bet!"

"Well, you went out and tried last week. How many did you get?" Fox teased.

"They wouldn't show up. If they had come, I would have hit one."

"They were probably all around you, but they don't show themselves."

"Well, I think it's dumb. All this work for turkeys. You can shoot one deer and have more meat than ten turkeys."

"Don't you ever get tired of deer meat?" Fox demanded.

"Well, sure I do, but—"

"Just go on and chop another tree down. We're going to need at least six or seven more of those logs," Fox said.

As Joshua went off grumbling, Ezekiel grinned at Fox. "That boy would argue with a stump, wouldn't he, Mas'r Nate?"

Ezekiel had never gotten accustomed to calling Fox anything but the name by which he had known him back at Havenwood. Now the burly slave lifted his ax and with a smooth, easy motion notched the end of the log. He lifted it up and set it on top of the two logs that were already at right angles, then went to pick up his ax again. The two men worked steadily, and within an hour, they had built a framework ten feet square and three feet high.

"Now all we got to do is put the top on it," Fox said with satisfaction.

"You mean we have to cut more trees?"

"We can use small ones. Just saplings to lay across and then put some brush on top of that."

They worked for another hour and before the top was on, Ezekiel grabbed a shovel and began digging a trench, starting about three feet away from the outside of the structure. "You dig the inside, Joshua," Fox said.

"Why don't you do it?"

"Because I'm bigger than you are, and I could make you do it," Fox grinned. "Would you rather have your nose rubbed in the dirt?"

"I ain't a-scared of you, Fox!"

"I know you're not. Come on. We'll both do it."

"No. That's all right. As long as you're not *making* me do it."

The trench that began outside soon extended under the logs and to the middle of the enclosure. "What do we do now?"

"We cover up all this inside trench with logs and brush," Fox said. They began chopping short pieces of saplings, creating, in effect, a tunnel with its opening in the center of the log structure.

"I don't see how it's supposed to work."

"Well, turkeys aren't very smart," Fox said. "We'll put some grain outside in that trench and continue it all the way under the wall and into the inside here."

"What good will that do?" Joshua demanded. "They'll just go right out again."

"No, they won't," Ezekiel laughed. "They ain't very smart, like Mas'r Nate says. They gets in here, and they walk all around the side trying to get out. It seems like they ain't none of 'em smart enough to figure out all they gots to do is go to the center and back out the tunnel."

"I don't think it'll work."

"It'll work, all right. I did it all last summer when I was living with the Cherokee," Fox said.

"Yes, and I done it back in Virginia when I was out in the deep woods huntin' with Mas'r Titus."

At the reference to his father, Fox shot Ezekiel a quick look but said nothing.

"Well, let's cover the top up good so they can't get out," he said.

It took little enough time to finish, and finally they stood surveying the turkey trap with satisfaction. "The good thing about this," Fox said, "is that all we have to do now is come back and bait the trap. Then the next day, or maybe two or three days, we come back and check it for turkeys."

Ezekiel nodded, adding, "Why, once I remember when we built a trap like this, Mas'r Nate, we went back the next day and we had six big fat hen turkeys in there. My, oh my, we did eat good off of them turkeys!"

"When was that, Ezekiel?"

"Oh, that was back when you wuz jist a nubbin', Mas'r Nate. Maybe one year old, somethin' like that." He suddenly turned and faced the young man, noting with satisfaction the strength and height he had gained in the past year. Shaking his head, he said, "You favors yo' pappy mightily, Mas'r Nate. You shorly do."

"He was bigger than I am, though."

"Maybe he was thicker, but by the time you get your full growth and get a few years on you, you'll be the spittin' image. And he was a handsome man! Everybody said that."

"I miss him, Ezekiel."

Ezekiel stared suddenly at Fox. It was the first time since his father's death that Ezekiel had ever heard Fox express such a sentiment, and now he said, "Well, it's natural you would."

"I hope I can be as good a man as he was."

"Ain't no reason why you couldn't. You've got the same blood. You've got a good ma and a good pa. They's strong blooded, both of 'em."

Fox did not answer for a time, and finally Ezekiel said, "Mas'r Nate?"

"Yes. What is it, Ezekiel?"

"Me and Mercy, we been wonderin' what you gonna do."

"Going to do? What do you mean?"

"Well, I mean you done turned eighteen now."

"That's right. What about it?"

"Well, maybe I didn't understand right, but it seems to me that I heard your mama say that when you was eighteen, the whole plantation would belong to you."

"I guess that's right enough."

"Well, ain't you never thought 'bout goin' back?"

Fox did not answer for a long moment, then shook his head and picked up his ax. Without a word he plunged into the thick woods and disappeared in the direction of the house.

Joshua stared after Fox with consternation. "What's wrong with him? Is he mad?"

"No. He ain't mad."

"Well, he just picked up his ax and run away, and he looked funny."

"I 'spect he feels a little bit funny."

"Why would he feel that, and what were you two talking about?"

For a moment Ezekiel hesitated. He did not like to talk about family business, but after all, Joshua was a growing young man. He assumed that most people already knew the story of Fox and Awinita. He picked up his ax, felt the edge of it for a moment, then said, "It done seem like Nate was left the whole place of Havenwood. At least his pappy was."

"But didn't Titus have a brother?"

"Yes, but he took his part of his inheritance a long time ago. Since Mas'r Titus is dead, the whole plantation belongs to Mas'r Nate."

"I wish I owned a whole plantation!" Joshua said with envy dripping from his voice. "I'd go back and just sit on the porch and let people wait on me all the time."

"I don't 'spect you'd be happy there."

"Why not?"

"Well, it ain't a happy place. At least not as long as Mas'r Naaman's there," Ezekiel said.

"That Fox's uncle? What's he got to do with it? He doesn't own it, does he?"

"He done been in charge since Mas'r Fox and Awinita run off with us. I don't know no law. Maybe he own it all now since Mas'r Nate walked off and leave it there."

Joshua stared at the bulky form of Ezekiel and suddenly blurted out, "Ezekiel, what's it like to be a slave?"

"What's it like? What do you mean?"

"I mean, what's it feel like to belong to somebody else?"

"What do you reckon it feels like?"

Joshua stopped and considered the ebony features of the tall, strong man before him. There were many slaves on the frontier but very few free black men. Some men were beginning to bring slaves out with them, trying to create the sort of plantations they had had back across the mountains. Joshua had never known any of these intimately, and now he stood there pondering the question. Finally he just shook his head. "I don't know what it would feel like. Not very good, I suppose."

"That's right. It don't feel very good."

"What about you and Mercy? You still belong to the plantation, don't you?"

"I 'spect we do."

"Will you ever go back there?"

"I hope not. Not as long as Mas'r Naaman is there."

"Is he a mean man?"

"He ain't so bad, but the overseer—his name is Tatum—he mighty bad."

"What did he do?"

"I seen him beat a man to death once just 'cause Mas'r Tatum thought he was talkin' smart to him. Just put him on the ground and beat him till he died. He's a mighty cruel man."

"Well, couldn't somebody arrest him?"

"Who'd want to do that? The sheriff? The slave's name was Billy.

He was a good man. A little high tempered, but he didn't deserve no beatin' like that."

"I don't like it," Joshua said abruptly. "And it ain't right."

"No, it ain't."

Joshua stared at Ezekiel. "If Fox ever went back and owned the plantation, would you and Mercy go back with him?"

" 'Spect we would. Wouldn't be bad at all with Mas'r Nate there. He seem to understand how colored folks feel."

"Maybe that's because he's part Indian."

"No. It ain't that. His pa, Mas'r Titus, he was the same way. He just as good a man as this earth ever made, I 'spect."

Suddenly Ezekiel seemed to shy away from the conversation. "Come on. We gonna go home now."

The two made their way home carrying their tools. Joshua went to the Spencer cabin, while Ezekiel went to the cabin Sequatchie and his wife, Iris, occupied. He found Mercy sitting on the cabin porch churning milk to make butter. He put the tools down and sat down on the porch beside her. "We been makin' a turkey trap. Gonna have fresh turkey, I bet."

"You and Mas'r Fox?"

"Yes, and that young Joshua, he go, too. Fox is just like his pa, you know."

"Well, then, he's like a mighty good man." Mercy churned the butter with a strong, regular motion, hardly conscious of the effort.

The two talked for a time, and finally Ezekiel said, "I asked Mas'r Nate if he ever goin' back to Havenwood."

"What did he say, Ezekiel?"

"He didn't say nothin'. It seemed like he couldn't answer. He's all mixed-up, I think."

"I don't want to go back to that place as long as Mas'r Naaman or his overseer is there." There was a calmness on her even features, but fear in her eyes as she questioned, "Do you think we ever have to go back?"

"Not without Mas'r Nate going with us. He own the place now."

"I don't trust Mas'r Naaman, and I don't want nothin' to do with that overseer."

Ezekiel saw that the talk had troubled Mercy, and he said quickly, "Why don't I sing you a tune and play you somethin' on my fiddle?"

"That would be right good."

Leaping up, Ezekiel went inside and came back with his fiddle in his hand. It looked very small in his massive hands, and it was a wonder he could place the fingers of his left hand on such small strings. Mercy watched as he fiddled, playing little tunes and humming. Finally he began to play and sing a tune she knew:

Sometimes I feel discouraged,
And think my work's in vain,
But then the Holy Spirit
Revives my soul again.

"I always like that tune," Mercy said. "Sing some more."

If you cannot preach like Peter,
If you cannot pray like Paul,
You can tell the love of Jesus,
And say, "He died for all."

Mercy lifted up her voice and joined in with Ezekiel as they sang the chorus several times:

There is a balm in Gilead
To make the wounded whole;
There is a balm in Gilead
To heal the sin-sick soul.

"That's a mighty good song, Ezekiel."

"It is, ain't it? We just gonna trust in Jesus, wife. He ain't gonna do nothin' bad, Jesus ain't."

"But Mas'r Nate and Miss Awinita, they got to go back. I don't want to live on that place with it like it was."

"I don't think we got to do that, but we just trust in Jesus."

Joshua Spencer and Rachel Anderson were playing at quoits. Joshua had made the quoits out of pieces of rope, and he had driven stakes in the ground. Each quoit had been stained a color with berry juices, some red and some blue. Joshua bit his lip and tossed the quoit, but it missed the stake completely.

"Oh no!" he said. "Give me another chance."

"No," Rachel laughed. "You had your chance. Now it's my turn."

Rachel, having just turned fourteen, was very graceful. She had already developed a figure that had attracted the eyes of many of the younger men, and although her parents still considered her a child, there were girls at her age already married.

Pausing for a moment, Rachel tossed the quoit. It sailed through the air and settled neatly on the peg. "Ha!" she said. "That's a point for me!" She sent two more quoits, both of them settling on the peg, and then said, "I win!"

"Come on. Let's play again."

"No. I'm tired of that," Rachel said. "You're not very good at it."

"Well, that's a girl's game."

Rachel stared at him. "It's your game. You're the one that made it up. Now don't get mad just because I won."

"I'm not mad."

"Are too."

"Am not!"

Rachel suddenly laughed. "Joshua Spencer, you are a caution!"

"What's that mean?"

"It means that you're funny."

"What do you mean funny?"

"I mean you make up a game and practice until you can beat most people, and then when a girl beats you at it you feel insulted."

"Well, let's play another game."

"No. Let's not."

The two were standing outside the Spencer cabin. Paul Anderson and his wife, Rhoda, had gone off on a short missionary trip to the Cherokee and planned to be gone for several nights. They had left Rachel with Hawk and Elizabeth, which was always a pleasure for Rachel. She enjoyed the Spencers, and she especially enjoyed spending time with Hannah. The two girls were very close friends, and although Hannah was almost two years older, that made little difference.

"Let's go pop some popcorn," Rachel said.

"All right. That sounds good to me."

"You're always ready to eat. I declare, you're a bottomless pit, Joshua!"

At that moment Ezekiel came by and shouted, "I's goin' down to check the turkey traps. You two wants to come?"

"Come on, Rachel."

"Where's he goin'?"

"To check the turkey traps we built the day before yesterday. Come on."

Rachel nodded. "All right. We can pop the corn later."

The two raced down the path and joined Ezekiel, who waited for them. They made their way through the deep woods, and when they got to the turkey trap, Joshua fell on his knees and looked inside through the cracks. "Look! It's full of turkeys!"

"It sho 'nuff is," Ezekiel said. "Now the hard part begins."

"The hard part? What's that?"

"We got to catch 'em and dress 'em. I don't mind trappin' turkeys, but I sho' do hate pullin' them feathers out."

Rachel stood watching as Ezekiel pulled off a small section of the roof. "Now," he said, "one of you has to get in there and hand them turkeys out. I's too big."

"I don't want to do that. It's probably nasty in there," Joshua said.

"Don't make no difference. One of you gots to go."

"Why don't you go, Rachel?" Joshua said. "You're smaller than I am."

"I'm not going to do that. They're your old turkeys, and I think it's mean."

Joshua and Ezekiel stared at the young woman. "What do you mean it's mean?" Joshua demanded.

"You're gonna kill them, aren't you?"

"Well, you don't want to eat 'em alive," Joshua said as he grinned at Ezekiel. "Now, *that* would be a nasty mess, eatin' a live turkey."

Rachel did not answer, and she watched as Joshua eased himself down into the trap. There was a sound of wild movement underneath, the turkeys gobbling frantically, and finally she heard Joshua's mumbling voice, "I got one!" He handed it up and Ezekiel grabbed it. He had his sheath knife there, and as soon as he got the bird, he expertly sliced its head off, then threw the body over to the side.

Rachel made a face and backed away. She watched as the two emptied the turkey trap of the five birds that had wandered into it. When Joshua came out, she saw that he was filthy from head to foot. She laughed aloud and said, "You're going to have to take two baths! Look at you!"

Joshua did not like to be teased. He started toward her, holding his hands up. "I'll just wipe them off on you."

"Don't you dare!" Rachel screamed and turned to run.

"Let her alone, Joshua. We got to get these birds plucked. But not here. We carry 'em back to the cabin. We do it there. Why don't you put some corn in and bait up the trap again?"

But Joshua did not pay any attention. He pursued Rachel until he caught her and then wiped his hands on her dress. She began to cry, and he was shocked. He stepped back and saw that he had spoiled her clothing.

"Now, what did you do that for, Mas'r Joshua?" Ezekiel said sadly. "That ain't no way for a young man to treat a young lady."

Rachel jerked away from Joshua and ran away sobbing.

"Hey, Rachel, I was just teasing!" Joshua called out. "Don't be mad at me."

"Mas'r Joshua, ain't you got no sense at all?"

Joshua turned and stared at the big slave, who was shaking his head in dismay. "I thought you had a little more judgment than to spoil her dress like that."

"I didn't mean to make her cry."

"Well, you did."

Joshua stood there watching Rachel as she ran down the trail. Now he felt terrible. His face grew long, and he muttered, "Well, I didn't mean nothin' wrong."

They baited up the trap, and then Ezekiel said, "Come on. Grab these turkeys. We tie their legs together and haul 'em home. You carry two and I'll take three."

They made their way back down the path and soon found Rachel waiting for them. Her face was stained with tears, and she had tried to clean her dress off with her handkerchief.

Joshua dropped his turkeys and moved closer. "I'm sorry, Rachel. I don't know what's the matter with me, doing a thing like that. I'm just stupid."

Suddenly Rachel smiled and said, "It's all right. You can make it up to me."

"Anything you say, Rachel."

"I'm going to hold you to that. You heard him, Ezekiel." Rachel laughed and turned and ran away, saying, "You're going to have to do a lot to make up for this, Joshua Spencer."

Ezekiel stared at the young woman and said, "That young'un gonna break some hearts soon."

"She's not old enough for romance, Ezekiel."

"She's fourteen! She ain't no child. Girls grow up quick out here on the frontier." He suddenly grinned at Joshua, who was sprouting up like a weed himself, and added, "And young fellows, they grows up fast, too."

Enter Andrew Jackson

Twenty-Four

Usually Joshua Spencer had to be practically dragged out of bed by one of his parents, but on Christmas Day and one other occasion, he was always up before dawn and agitating for the rest of the family to get up. This occasion was called the Spring Meeting, which took place in Watauga the first week in March. After the grim winter, the settlers along the rivers and the dwellers in the far-flung cabins were ready to begin planting and come together in Watauga to celebrate.

"Sit down and eat your breakfast, Joshua," Elizabeth Spencer commanded. "You're like a worm in hot ashes."

Hawk cut a piece of flannel cake, dipped it in the syrup, and stuck it in his mouth as he watched his son. "I've been thinking maybe we ought to skip the Spring Meeting this year," he said with a sly wink at Hannah. "After all, there's lots of work to be done around here."

Joshua gave his father a shocked look. "Miss the Spring Meeting! Why, Pa, we can't do that!"

"Oh, you go to one of those, you've been to all of them," Hawk said. "I thought we might stay home and work on curing those deer hides that have been stacking up out in the barn."

Joshua's face was such a picture of disappointment and grief that Elizabeth had to laugh. She went over to Joshua, put her arms around him, and hugged him. "Don't torment the boy, Hawk. You know you enjoy the Spring Meeting as well as anybody."

"Well, if you insist, I guess we might go for a little while."

The family ate breakfast quickly and an hour later were all in the wagon headed for Watauga. As they moved along the trail, Hawk began speaking to Elizabeth about the year to come. "I'm going to clear that other fifteen acres this year."

"That's so much work," Elizabeth protested. "You've got to cut down all those trees and then burn the stumps, and I hate to see you let yourself in for that much work."

"Well, I'm going to hire Ezekiel to help me. He's a good hand. He wants to save up enough to buy his freedom, his and Mercy's."

"You know, I think if Fox ever takes over that plantation back in Virginia, he'll give Ezekiel and Mercy their freedom. He's awfully fond of those two."

Hawk slowed the horses as the wagon lumbered through a patch of thick spring mud. "I don't know how that's going to turn out. I don't understand why he's so reluctant to go back and take over."

"Well, he's afraid of his uncle Naaman."

"The place is legally his. I'd be glad to go back with him and see that he got it. In a court of law, Naaman Carter wouldn't have a chance."

"I don't think Awinita was very happy there without Titus, and neither was Fox."

Hawk flicked the reins as the road evened out once again. He turned to Elizabeth and said, "Well, they could sell it and then buy a place out here."

They continued to speak and were joined by several other groups all headed straight for the Spring Meeting. Finally the settlement rose up in the distance, and soon Hawk was placing the wagon alongside of others. He unhitched the horses and staked them out. They would stay all day visiting, and it seemed cruel to have the team standing in place. Most of the other settlers did the same, keeping all the horses in a corral made of ropes.

"Come on. We're going to miss everything," Joshua said impatiently.

They made their way toward the center of town, which was filled with people milling around. The smell of smoked meat was already in the air, for an entire ox was being barbecued, and the women had brought vegetables, cakes, and other dishes to go with it.

Joshua spotted David Martin there and greeted him.

David said, "Hey, Josh, they're about to have a gander pull."

"Oh boy, I love those things! I wonder if I could enter," Joshua said.

"I doubt it. Just grown men," David said. "But we can go watch."

"I don't think you two ought to watch such a thing," Elizabeth said. She had overheard the conversation and was frowning.

"Why, Ma, everybody's going!" Joshua protested.

The argument went on for some time, and finally Hawk laid his hands on Elizabeth's shoulders. "It's a rough country, Elizabeth. If a gander pull's the worst thing Joshua and David ever have to see, I guess they'll be pretty lucky. Let 'em go."

That was all the permission needed. Joshua and David hurried off until they got to an open field where all the races would be held.

The gander pull was always an exciting event, and men had gathered around to place their bets. A circular path had been laid out, a hundred and fifty feet in diameter. Two sapling posts were set about twelve feet apart on either side of the path and a slack rope hung from pole to pole. A live gander with all its feathers plucked off its head and neck was produced. Joshua and David laughed with the crowd as the goose squawked loudly while a man put goose grease over the bird's neck until it was impossibly slippery. Then he tied the bird up by his heels and hung it from the slack rope, directly over the middle of the path. The bird began to flop around, swinging wildly in an arch just low enough so that a rider standing in the stirrups could barely reach the gander's neck.

David, growing bored with the gander pull, said, "Let's go see somethin' else, Josh."

Josh remained mesmerized by the event. "You go ahead. Maybe I'll catch you later."

Shrugging in resignation, David muttered, "Okay," and moved away to look for Ethan Cagle and other friends, leaving Joshua to watch the barbaric sport on his own.

Shortly after David left, a voice interruped Joshua, "Think you'd like to have a try at that someday, young fellow?"

Joshua turned quickly to see a tall, lanky man in his early twenties with an extremely lean face smiling at him. His hair was fixed in a peculiar way, pushed up like a rooster's comb in front, and though he had a rather serious visage, his eyes twinkled with humor.

"I bet I could grab that old goose if I had a chance."

"What's your name, son?"

"Joshua Spencer. My father's name is Hawk Spencer."

A light flickered in the man's eyes, and he obviously recognized the name. "My name's Andrew Jackson." He put out a lean hand,

and his grip was very strong. He treated Joshua exactly as a man, which pleased the boy.

"Do you live around here, Mr. Jackson?" Joshua asked.

"Not yet. I'm planning on settling in Jonesborough. I'm a lawyer."

"A lawyer!" Joshua was impressed. "I bet that's a lot of fun."

Jackson laughed shortly. "Not as much fun as a gander pull. Look, they're starting up."

The two watched as a gun was fired off and a group of riders all sped around the circle. It was amusing to see rider after rider swiping at the goose and missing. Some of the riders were too short, and one squatted on his saddle and then sprang up when he came close. He succeeded in falling off his horse and had to scramble to avoid being trampled.

Joshua and Jackson laughed at the sight, and Joshua said, "I can do better than that."

"I'll bet you could, son. How old are you?"

"Fourteen years old."

"Why, I would have taken you for sixteen at least."

Jackson knew how to please a boy, and Joshua swelled up under the comment.

A large crowd had gathered, and there was much cheering and laughter until finally one of the riders managed to pull the head off the gander.

"Well, maybe next year you'll be able to enter. Do you have a horse?"

"Yes, sir, a fine one, too."

"I'd like to see him sometime. Are you entered in any of the races?"

"I'm going to enter the footrace."

"Well, I'm always ready to make a bet on a winner. Do you think you'll win, Joshua?"

"I know I'll win, Mr. Jackson. You just come and watch me."

"I'll be sure and do that." Jackson suddenly straightened up. "Look. It's about time for the shooting contest. I wouldn't want to miss that."

"Me, either, and my pa will win, I'll bet."

"Your father's a good shot?"

"He's the best I ever saw," Joshua said loyally.

The two made their way along to where the crowd had shifted away from the gander-pull track and found that the shooters and judges had all gathered together.

"That's my pa. You see the tall one in buckskins."

"I've heard of your father. He's a fine man. You're very fortunate to have such a father."

Joshua felt proud. He ordinarily was somewhat shy, but something about Andrew Jackson drew him out, and he said, "You just watch now and you'll see what a good shot my pa is."

The rifle was the very center of frontier life, and most boys learned to shoot before they were ten. Joshua himself had been knocking squirrels out of trees for years now. "You know what my pa taught me to do, Mr. Jackson?"

"What's that?"

"He taught me how to bark a squirrel."

"Bark a squirrel! What's that?"

"Well, a musket ball tears up a squirrel pretty bad. Tears up the meat and the hide, so Pa taught me how to shoot at the tree just below the animal. It'll stun 'em, and they'll fall out of the tree. Then you get 'em and kill 'em before they wake up."

"Why, that's quite a trick! I'd like to see you do that sometime, young fellow." Actually Jackson had performed the same feat himself many times, but he did not want to spoil the boy's pleasure in the telling of it.

Before the actual shooting match started, there was some candle snuffing. Candles were lit and men would take shots trying to snuff out the candle without knocking it down. Hawk did not enter this, nor did Sequatchie, but the crowd cheered all those who did.

The first real shooting event had to do with driving a nail. A common-sized nail was driven two-thirds of the way into the target, and the shooters backed off forty paces. The shooting began, and there were hoots as some of the shooters missed the nail altogether.

Joshua explained it all to his new friend. "You see, bending the nail don't count for nothin'."

"It doesn't?"

"No. You got to hit it square on the head and drive it into the target."

"Oh, I see! Well, that takes quite a marksman."

"My pa can do it. You watch him."

Indeed, Hawk Spencer seemed to drive home every nail he aimed at, and he and Sequatchie got into quite a contest. The two were noted as the best marksmen in Watauga, and they matched each other shot for shot for over fifteen minutes. But it was Sequatchie who finally won.

"That's all right. Sequatchie taught my pa everything he knows. He's gettin' old now, but he's still one of the best shots. You watch when they shoot for beef. Pa says he only gets serious when he's shootin' for the beef."

"Shooting for the beef" was the heart of the shooting contest. A beef was divided into six sections. The sixth section was actually where all of the lead was fired in the match since musket balls were worth money. The fifth section consisted of the hide and the tail. The other sections were the four quarters of the beef.

"You look there. Every shooter fixes their own target. You see?"

"Yes. I see."

Jackson watched as pieces of white paper were placed on a board that had been burned black. The distance was sixty yards, and the square was about two and a half inches. In the center was cut a diamond-shaped figure one inch wide called the bull's-eye or the diamond.

At once the men began making bets. Jackson bent forward and whispered, "You think it's safe to bet on your pa?"

"Sure. You can't lose, Mr. Jackson."

Jackson immediately made several bets with the men standing around.

Two judges were selected, and during the match that followed, the contestants kept up a running conversation. They ribbed the poor shots and bragged on their own gun. Most of them had named their guns—names such as Old Hair Splitter or Old Blood Letter—and one man remarked, "Old Panther Cooler's going to strike plumb center."

The match went on for some time, and the judges measured the shots with a thread.

Sequatchie apparently had lost his touch, for he did not shoot as well this time. Joshua grew excited and yelled at his father, "Come on, Pa. You got to win!"

Spencer turned and looked at his son standing beside the tall stranger and nodded his head. "Do the best I can, Joshua."

Finally the contest came down to two shots, one by Hawk Spencer and another by a lean frontiersman named Luke Sewell.

The two men fought it out, and finally on the last shot Hawk won by a thread. He turned to Sewell and said, "Luke, it's too close. What do you say we split that critter right down the middle?"

Sewell grinned. "That's just like you, Hawk. I'd call that mighty fair."

Joshua ran over, his eyes shining. "Pa, you done good! Real good!"

"Thanks, Joshua."

Joshua turned and said, "This is my friend, Mr. Andrew Jackson."

"I'm glad to know you, Mr. Jackson."

"I've heard a great deal about you, Mr. Spencer. I'm going to set up a law office in town, so I'm out meeting people today."

"Well, I don't need much lawyerin', but you'll get my business when I have some."

"Well, I've already collected the fee," Jackson smiled. "I won on your shooting. Josh here tipped me off."

"And now he's going to bet on me in the footrace. Come on, Pa."

Joshua raced away, and Hawk said, "I'd like for you to meet the rest of my family, Mr. Jackson."

Jackson met the family, and afterward, as they made their way back toward the race field, Elizabeth questioned him about his accommodations for the night.

"Well, I haven't found a place yet. I suppose I might just move on."

"Oh, don't do that! We've got plenty of room at our place. Be glad to have you."

"Why, that's gracious of you, Mrs. Spencer. I'll take you up on that offer."

The group all moved over to the field, where they found Joshua lining up with at least twenty other boys.

"Competition's pretty keen. Do you think your boy can win?"

"He's never lost a footrace yet," Hawk said. "Don't mean to boast, but for his age he's the fastest thing in these parts."

Joshua was crouching down, and when the gun sounded for the race to begin, he shot out. Within twenty yards he was well in the lead of the pack. He never slowed down but flew along the track.

When he crossed the finish line, his closest competitor was ten yards back.

"Well done, Joshua!"

Jackson was collecting money from others, for he had wisely bet on Joshua. When Joshua came over, his eyes shining, to take the congratulations of his family, Jackson waited. Finally when Joshua turned to him, he said, "I don't feel justified in keeping all this. Won enough on your pa, so this is yours." He handed Joshua the fifty cents he had won, a substantial sum of money for the boy, saying, "Joshua, you run like a deer." Jackson smiled. "You do the running, and I'll do the lawyering."

The group got back to the house well after dark, and Elizabeth showed Jackson to the spare bedroom. "We call that the prophet's room, Mr. Jackson," Hawk said. "Anytime a preacher comes along during a meeting, or at other times, we try to keep him here."

"Well, I've never been accused of being a minister, but I did make a good 'profit' today, so to speak. I appreciate the room."

They had all eaten well at the meeting, but Elizabeth insisted on fixing a late supper. While Hawk and Mr. Jackson talked, Elizabeth scurried around and warmed up slices of beef, baked potatoes, and bread she had baked the day before.

As they gathered at the table, Hawk, as usual, asked the blessing and ended by saying, "Bless our guest and be with him in his new career. Amen."

"I'm glad to be included in your prayer, sir."

"We could use a good lawyer here."

"A *good* lawyer? Well, some people say there is no such animal. There's some prejudice against lawyers."

"Why is that?" Joshua demanded. "I think it's great to be a lawyer. You can help people."

Andrew Jackson laughed and said, "I wish everyone looked at it that way, son, but they don't."

"What about your family, Mr. Jackson?" Hannah asked.

Jackson hesitated, then said, "Well, it hasn't been a happy time. Most of my family died when I was young. My father died a few months before I was born, so I never knew him. I had one brother, Hugh, die from injuries he sustained fighting the British. My other brother, Robert, and I contracted smallpox while we were prisoners of the British in Camden, South Carolina. I recovered, but unfortunately Robert didn't. He died in 1781. My mother succombed to cholera later on that year. I was left alone in the world except for some distant cousins. They helped me to finish my studies, and here I am, ready to make a fresh start in this great land."

Joshua had leaned forward and listened intently as Jackson told of the struggles he had had as a youth and during his training as a lawyer. He did not miss a word as the tall, bushy-haired attorney spoke, and his mother whispered to Hawk, "I never saw Joshua so taken with a man."

"Well, he is a charismatic fellow, and I think he's going to be an asset to the community."

"I just can't get over how much suffering and loss he has gone through at his young age," Elizabeth said with sympathy filling her voice. "We must remember to pray for him often."

Jackson went to bed after the late supper. As soon as the door to the spare bedroom closed, Joshua turned to his father before going to his own room and said, "Pa, I'm going to be a lawyer when I grow up."

"Well, that would be a mighty fine thing, I think. You like Mr. Jackson a great deal, don't you son?"

"I ain't never met anybody quite like him, Pa. Of course he can't shoot like you can or skin a deer."

"Well, I couldn't try a case in a court of law."

"Do you think I could do it, Pa?"

"Be a lawyer? I don't see why not. Mr. Jackson, he's got big plans for this frontier area. Why, he even talked about going into politics—becoming governor or even a senator. He'll need some sharp young lawyers."

"I'd sure like to be a part of that, Pa."

"Well, you can be, Joshua. If that's what God has in mind for you, then you can do it. You know it says in the Scripture that the steps of a good man are ordered by the Lord—"

Joshua finished, " 'And he delighteth in his way.' I know that one, Pa. You quote it all the time."

"You just pray that God will open doors. One of these days I'll be sitting in a courtroom, and there'll be my son, a lawyer, pleading a case and winning it."

Hawk leaned over and gave Joshua a hug. "You're getting so tall I can't do that much anymore. I'll have to do all the hugging on Hannah."

"Aw, you can hug me if you want to," Joshua said. "As long as no one's around."

Hawk Spencer laughed and struck his son a good-natured blow on the shoulder. "Get to bed with you, now! No more nonsense!"

The following day, Joshua went to see Rachel Anderson. He was so excited about having met Andrew Jackson and about wanting to be a lawyer that he just had to tell someone. As he and Rachel were sitting outside the Andersons' cabin, Joshua told her all about Jackson.

"And I want to be a lawyer just like him. Maybe go into politics and become governor. Then I would have enough money to do whatever I wanted."

"Money won't get you everything, Josh," Rachel said, concern on her face.

"It will sure get a lot!"

Joshua continued talking about his big plans as Rachel grew more and more concerned for her friend and the direction he seemed to be taking for his life.

Warpath!

Twenty-Five

Hawk was sitting on the front porch discussing planting with Sequatchie. Both men had decided to expand their tillable ground and had worked diligently at clearing it. The ground was hard, and clearing new ground was, perhaps, the hardest task the settlers had to contend with. Some girdled their trees and let them die, but most chopped them down and then hauled the logs off for various purposes: firewood, building cabins, and other structures. Then all the brush had to be piled and burned. As for the stumps, they had to rot, which took as long as five years, and then they were pulled out with great effort by multiple teams of oxen. Until that happened, the only solution was to work around the stumps, which meant that a man trying to plow was continually being thrown down and the team jerked to a dead standstill when the plowshare caught the roots.

Sequatchie suddenly laughed softly. "Do you suppose there's new ground to be broken in heaven?"

"I hope not," Hawk said. "It's not one of my favorite things to do." He turned to look at his friend. The sun was settling down in the west, and the strong features of Sequatchie caught the reflections of the red glow. Hawk knew that Sequatchie was in his mid-fifties, but the years had worn him down. And now for the first time, he could see the toll that time had taken on his friend. "I think a lot about heaven. Maybe it's only natural when we get closer to it."

"I don't believe that's so. I've always thought about heaven ever since I first heard about it." He studied the distant hills, lit now by the golden rays, and asked, "Do you remember when we first met? How you read the Bible to me even when you didn't believe it yourself."

"I think about those days a lot," Hawk said.

"So do I. They were good times, although there were occasions when I wondered if you would make it."

"You had a hard time getting me through, didn't you? I was a real prodigal."

"No more than some of the rest of us. I think your boys' Spencer blood has been tempered by that of their mothers."

"I don't know about Joshua. He's a lot like I was. Headstrong and ready to jump into anything."

"It's hard to believe he's growing up so fast. I can remember when Andrew and Jacob were his age. We had a time with them, too, especially Jacob."

"All boys are the same, I guess," said Hawk. "Just takes a little cooling off. A few good fights help to settle a fellow down."

Hawk laughed quietly. Sequatchie turned to Hawk and studied the profile of the slightly younger man. "God has been good to give me a friend like you, Hawk Spencer."

The words took Hawk off guard. He did not turn to meet Sequatchie's gaze for a moment, but when he did, he saw the affection in the Cherokee's dark eyes. "That goes for me, too," he said softly.

The two men had a tremendous regard for each other, but were embarrassed at expressing their feelings.

Finally Sequatchie said, "Someone's coming."

"Who could that be at this time of night?"

Hawk rose and Sequatchie followed him as they stepped down off the porch in the dusk. The May twilight was soft and mild, and all the settlers were looking for a mild summer and abundant crops.

"Why, that's Governor John Sevier!" Hawk said with surprise. "What's he doing here?"

Sequatchie did not answer for a moment, and then as the rider dismounted and came forward, he said so quietly that only Hawk caught his words, "Every time he comes it's to get us to do some fighting."

Sevier took off his hat and slapped it against his leg. "Dusty out tonight. Getting hot. How are you, Hawk—Sequatchie?"

"Fine, John. What brings you out in this part of the world?"

"Bad news." Sevier's face twisted into a grimace. "I suppose you can guess what it is."

"I would guess that you came to get us to do something we don't want to do," Hawk grinned.

"We've got a real problem on our hands, and we've got to do something quickly," Sevier said.

"What's the trouble?" Hawk demanded.

"Well, do you know the John Kirk family? They live down on the Little River."

"I've met them."

"Well, you may not know it, but Kirk and his family had befriended that Indian Slim Tom."

"Slim Tom is a corrupt man," Sequatchie said.

"Yes he is, but nobody could convince Kirk of that. Anyway, he's paid for it now."

"What has happened?" Sequatchie asked quietly.

"Slim Tom went to the Kirk cabin and asked for food, and they gave it to him. After he left there he met up with Chief Red Bird. You know about him."

"A renegade. Even his own people won't put up with him," Sequatchie answered.

"That's right. Well, Slim Tom told Red Bird about the Kirks, I guess they were all drunk when they rode to the cabin. Killed eleven of them, the whole family . . . and then took their scalps."

Hawk and Sequatchie were silent for a moment. From far off a bird began singing as it settled down for the night. From inside the cabin came the sounds of the Spencer family, soft gentle voices and laughter. As Hawk thought of the senseless massacre, he grew angry and said, "Those two were never any good. We'll have to run them down."

"Well, that's not all, I'm afraid. You remember Colonel James Brown? He served in the campaign with us back in '83."

"I remember the colonel," Hawk said. "What about him?"

"Well, Dragging Canoe always hated the man. The Browns were traveling by riverboat, and when Dragging Canoe heard about it, he took his band and captured them. He killed the colonel, two of his sons, and five other men."

"What about Mrs. Brown and the children?"

"They took them captive. I'm hoping to get them back. That's why I've come to see you."

"You're taking a party out?"

"I've got a hundred and seventy-five men. Colonel James Hubbard's with me."

"I don't know him," Hawk said.

"Good soldier. A little bit hot-blooded and seems to have a fixed hatred of Indians"—he glanced apprehensively at Sequatchie—"but we have to take everyone we can get. What about you two?"

Sequatchie spoke up instantly. "I will not go. You do not need this many men. Send someone to talk to Dragging Canoe. He'll be glad to turn Mrs. Brown over for ransom."

"Well, who's going to pay it?" Sevier demanded. "I'm tired of this killing! Dragging Canoe and Akando think they can strike whenever they please, but they're not going to get away with it this time. I'm going to run them to the ground, and I'd like to have you two there with me. Especially you, Sequatchie."

"No. I will not do it."

His reply angered Sevier, and he said, "Hawk, what about you?"

Hawk hesitated for a moment, then said slowly, "I'll go with you, but I want you to promise me we'll try peaceful means first."

"Oh yes, of course! We always try that, but you know Dragging Canoe and Akando. They are both firebrands and they're on the warpath. I'm afraid the only argument they may listen to is a musket ball in the head. We'll be leaving early in the morning," Sevier said. "You can join us at the fork down by the river."

"I'll be there, Colonel," Hawk said.

"Any more of your men you could get would help."

"Jacob and Andrew will come."

"Fine—fine! Maybe we can settle this once and for all. Good night. I'll see you in the morning. Sequatchie, I'm sorry, but it has to be done."

Sequatchie watched silently as Sevier mounted and rode away, then said, "No good will come of it. I wish you hadn't agreed to go."

"Well, John listens to me sometimes. I thought there might be a chance to avoid bloodshed. I'll do my best."

Sequatchie did not answer as he turned and made his way to his cabin. When he stepped inside, everyone looked up.

"What is the matter, brother?" Awinita said.

Sequatchie's eyes met those of Iris, then he glanced at Fox and explained the reason for Sevier's visit.

"You're not going, are you, husband?" Iris said.

"Not this time."

Fox listened while Sequatchie explained his objections, and then finally he slipped out of the cabin. He was angry and had not gone far before he heard Sequatchie call him. He turned and waited as Sequatchie came up to him.

"You must try to be patient, nephew."

"How can I be patient? You see what's happening. You know better than I do that just because there are a few bad Cherokee, the white men want to take it out on everyone."

"I know, but there's nothing we can do. I thought of going to see if I could stop some of the violence. But if Akando and Dragging Canoe knew I was with the force, it would just make them harder to deal with. Both of them hate me." He moved closer and Sequatchie said, "You are like your father—tall and strong—but I hope you have some of your mother's gentleness and wisdom."

"I hope so, too, Uncle. But it breaks my heart to see what's happening. I know it must tear you all to pieces."

Sequatchie nodded. "I have endured for many years, and my people now are not what they used to be in the old days. And I fear that there is worse to come."

"But we've got to do something."

"God is good. His hands are in all things. Do you remember what we have been studying in the book of Jeremiah?"

"Yes, Uncle."

"Do you remember that God had sent Jeremiah to tell his people they were going to be made captive by their enemies?"

"I remember."

"God's promise was that He would bless those that would give themselves to what He had planned. This meant losing their homes and being under the hands of those who had been their enemies."

"That doesn't seem fair."

"God's judgment was upon them. And we cannot question His ways, Fox. That is what I do now. It seems hard to me at times, but I believe that God's hand is on those who love Him. That is why, for years, I have tried to preach to my people, as have Reverend Anderson and others. The only hope for the Cherokee is in Jesus, as it is for all men. Do you understand?"

"No. I can't accept that," Fox said abruptly.

"I could not have accepted it, either, when I was your age."

Sequatchie put his hands on Fox's tall, strong shoulders. "But I will pray that you will not become bitter. Nothing destroys a man or a woman quicker than bitterness. It is worse than a tomahawk in the head. Come, now. Back to the cabin."

Hawk, along with Jacob and Andrew, met with Sevier and his men the next morning. When they arrived they were surprised to find that General Martin, the Indian agent for North Carolina, was also there.

"I wonder what Martin's doing here?" Hawk said.

"Looks like there's an argument going on," Andrew said.

The three men listened and soon discovered that Martin had come to persuade Sevier to give up the expedition.

"Governor Samuel Johnston doesn't want you to make this foray against the Cherokee, Sevier," General Martin said. "He wants us to be more lenient, take a broader view of the situation."

John Sevier was ordinarily a very reasonable man, but he was also stubborn. "My mind's made up. I'm going to get Mrs. Brown and her children back peaceably if I can. But if not, by force."

The argument went on for some time and finally General Martin grew angry. "Do you understand you're going against the governor of your state and against my authority?"

"As you well know," Sevier spat back, "I am the elected governor of the state of Franklin and do not answer to anyone in North Carolina, especially you and Governor Johnston."

"You're making a grave mistake, Sevier," said General Martin. "Congress refused to recognize Franklin, and besides, your term as governor is almost up. The 'state' of Franklin will soon be nothing but a historical footnote. And you may well end up in a North Carolina jail."

"I'm not going to wait for you and your governor to go get Mrs. Brown and her children," Sevier said. "Come on, men! We can argue about this after we get the Browns back."

"Looks like it's not going to be a very pleasant trip," Jacob said with a worried frown.

Andrew nodded. "Liable to be more unpleasant when we get back. John Sevier's a strong man, but Governor Johnston is, too. I think Sevier has bitten off more than he can chew."

Hawk said nothing at the time, but later that night when they had broken for camp, he found an opportunity to draw John Sevier off to one side. "John, I think we ought to listen to the governor and to General Martin."

"I'm surprised at you, Hawk. Don't you care about Mrs. Brown and her children?"

"Yes, I do, but suppose we get into a pitched battle with Dragging Canoe. We're going to lose men. There are going to be good men killed. That means widows and orphans."

"That's always the case when you go to war. We've got to protect ourselves. If Dragging Canoe and Akando think they can get away with murder, no settler on the frontier will be safe."

They argued for a long time, and both men lost their tempers. They had become fast friends over the years, but now they were firmly opposed to each other. Finally Hawk said, "I'll go with you, John, but you're wrong. The whole thing has gotten out of hand."

Sevier listened but said shortly, "I don't want to argue about this anymore, Hawk. I admire you greatly, but this must be done."

The next morning Sevier divided his forces. He sent James Hubbard with half of the party to a Cherokee village called Chilhowee. "You can destroy that village if you have to," he ordered, "but if they surrender, just simply take them prisoner."

"Yes, Governor Sevier. I'll see to it."

As the force rode out, among the men was John Kirk, Jr., whose family's massacre had brought on this military action on the part of the settlers. He said, "Colonel Hubbard, my family is all dead, and all we're going to do is burn a few houses?"

Hubbard said, "They'll never surrender peaceably. Don't worry. You'll get your revenge."

Hubbard drove the force hard, and all the while Kirk was growing more and more angry, for he was a fiery young man. On their way there the force picked up Chief Old Tassel, who had been helpful at other times in settling disputes. Kirk said in private to the commander, "We don't need this old Indian."

"He may be of some help," Hubbard replied tersely.

Chief Old Tassel gathered some of his men to come along, and the combined force was ferried across the river under a flag of truce. When they reached Chilhowee, Hubbard had all the Cherokee leaders gather in a single house, the largest in the village. The chiefs and the elders had come and were seated for a council talk. Hubbard commanded his forces, "Surround the house! Don't let anybody in!" Then he walked back inside and looked around at the Cherokee who had gathered. He hated them violently and felt that Sevier was acting too mercifully. Now he did something that would have effects for many years. He pulled a hatchet from his belt, handed it to John Kirk, Jr., and nodded at the seated leaders. "Now take vengeance for the massacre of your family."

Young Kirk needed no urging. He fell upon the Cherokee and slew Old Tassel, the chief of the Overhill towns; Abram, who owned the house; his son, Hanging Maw; and his brother.

It was a cold-blooded slaughter for which there was no excuse, and it forever changed relations with the Cherokee in the lands over the Misty Mountains.

When John Sevier's force reached Chilhowee two days later, they discovered at once what Colonel Hubbard had done.

Hawk was appalled. His lips grew into a tight line, and he turned to face Sevier. "That's your man that did this!"

Sevier could not answer. A wave of guilt swept through him, and he immediately sent for Hubbard and Kirk. The sound of his voice could be heard over the whole camp, and he called the two men by every insult he could think of. He threatened to have them shot and even challenged them both to a duel, which both men refused.

There was nothing to be done now, but Sevier saw that he had overstepped himself. He knew that when news of this massacre reached Governor Johnston, he would be in serious trouble.

"You're not going to get much sympathy from me when the governor raps your knuckles," Hawk said.

"I know. I was wrong, Hawk. I should have listened to you."

"You made the worst mistake of your career," Hawk said sternly. "A lot of Cherokee have been waiting to see if they were going to get fair treatment and if the white man could be trusted. And now they know that we cannot be trusted."

Sevier hung his head and chewed on his lip. "I'll have to go to the Cherokee villages and explain."

"You can't explain this to warriors like Dragging Canoe and Akando. The frontier is going to be on fire. The Cherokee will take the warpath, and many of their brothers, the Chickasaw, will join them. John, you've allowed a terrible thing to happen. And there is no turning back."

Hawk returned to Watauga and went at once to give the bad news to Sequatchie. He was aware that Fox was watching him with burning eyes, and finally he said, "It was all wrong, Sequatchie. Sevier is crushed over it, but that doesn't help, does it?"

"No, it does not. There will be war now for certain."

Fox said nothing, but, filled with fury, he left the cabin. He walked through the woods for a time, and when he emerged, he found Hannah waiting for him.

"Fox," she said, "Pa told me what happened. I'm so sorry."

Fox looked at Hannah, his features tense. His mouth was a pale line, and he said, "Now I despise my white blood."

"Don't say that! Your father was a wonderful man. Everyone says so."

"John Sevier's not a wonderful man! He thinks no more of killing Cherokee than he thinks of stepping on ants."

"It wasn't Mr. Sevier. It was Hubbard and that young man Kirk."

But Fox was past listening to reason. He turned to her and said furiously, "Don't talk to me anymore about this, Hannah. I'm not a white man. I'm a Cherokee!"

Race at Greasy Cove

Twenty-Six

"I don't see that we have any business over at Greasy Cove, Joshua." Hawk was molding bullets for his musket but looked up briefly at Joshua. "What do you want to go for, anyway?"

"Well, Mr. Jackson's going to be there, and I thought I could talk to him more about how to become a lawyer."

Hawk had been shaving lead into a cast-iron pot and had put it among the hot coals. When he saw that the lead was melted, he picked up an iron bullet mold and said, "Grease this for me, will you, so these bullets won't stick."

Joshua obeyed, but he continued to argue. "Pa, the crops are all taken care of for now, and you were going to take me hunting anyhow. Why can't we just do both? Go over to Greasy Cove and see Mr. Jackson and watch the horse race, and then we could go hunting."

"What horse race is this?"

"You didn't hear about that?"

"I don't reckon I did. Wait a minute. Let me get this metal poured."

Hawk picked up a heavy iron ladle and dipped it down into the molten lead. With a steady ease and motion, he poured a slithering, shining stream of liquid into the molds. "This always fascinates me, Joshua," he murmured. "It looks like you could just reach out and touch it. It doesn't look hot at all."

"Did you ever try it?"

"I sure did, and it raised a blister on my palm. It's hot enough, all right."

Carefully he put the mold down and then picked up another one he had poured the day before. Pulling one of the bullets out, he began trimming the roughness off with a knife. He listened as Josh pleaded to go, and then he began rubbing the balls with an old piece of deerskin that was very worn and slick. As he finished each one, he dropped them into a deerskin pouch. Finally he leaned back and said, "It's hot in here. Let's get outside."

The two walked outside, and Hawk said, "What's this now about a horse race?"

"Well, you know Colonel Robert Love?"

"Yes. I know him. What about him?"

"Colonel Love loves horse racing, and he's got a private track laid out near his home. It's over in the lowlands by the Nolichucky River."

"I know about Colonel Love's racetrack. I've even been there and raced once."

"You did! You never told me about that."

Hawk grinned. "A few things I haven't told you about. What's this about Mr. Jackson?"

"Mr. Love has got a horse that he says is the champion, and everybody's talking about it."

"What's the horse's name?"

"Victor of All, I think."

"Nothin' modest about that. Mr. Jackson has a horse, I take it?"

"Yes, he's got a fine one. He told me that horse of his could beat any other horse in the country. Everybody's going, Pa. Couldn't we go?"

"I suppose so. That is, if your mother agrees."

"I'll go ask her."

Dashing into the house, Joshua ran at once to the bedroom, where his mother was putting a counterpane on the featherbed. "Ma, Pa says we can go to the horse race over in Greasy Cove."

"What horse race?" Elizabeth smoothed the counterpane down. It was a quilt she had made herself at one of the quilting bees. She remembered almost every bit of the pattern she had sewn into it. She enjoyed the time when the women had all gathered and spent some happy hours quilting. "Sounds like foolishness to me."

"It's not foolishness! Mr. Jackson's going to race his horse against Colonel Love's."

"I don't hold with horse racing, son."

"But, Ma, everybody's going!"

"No, they're not. *I'm* not going. I'm going to see Amanda and my newest grandson today." Amanda had had Jonah Spencer toward the end of February. "Jonah's been a little under the weather, and I told Amanda I would come help her do a few things, as she has been busy with tending to him. So everyone is not going."

"I mean all the men. All of them that can go."

"Let's go out and talk to your father."

Elizabeth stepped out on the front porch and said to Hawk, "I heard you're going to leave all your work and go out watching horse races."

Hawk made a grimace. "I thought you and I could talk about it."

"That's not what you said, Pa. You said we'd go."

"Wait a minute! I said if it was all right with your mother."

Elizabeth had no intention of arguing. Indeed, she was glad to see Joshua spend time with his father. But she loved to tease her two men. "What do I get out of it?"

"I'll take you into town, and you can buy some satin and make yourself a pretty dress."

"Oh, you get to watch horse races, and I get to make dresses."

"What do you want? Most women would be glad to get a pretty dress."

"Why don't you make it, then?"

Hawk started to argue, and then he saw the humorous light in Elizabeth's eyes. He grinned and said, "You do persecute me, but I hear the righteous are always persecuted by worldly people."

"I'll teach you worldly people!" Elizabeth ran over and grabbed a big handful of Hawk's hair and yanked at it.

Joshua laughed as his father struggled to free himself, lifting his mother clear off the ground. Finally he grabbed her around the waist and squeezed her, saying, "Now, you be nice."

"Hawk, you're squeezing me to death!"

"All right." He kissed her and then set her down. "Are you going to be good now?"

"I haven't decided yet, and after the way you've acted, I'm not sure you can go to that horse race."

Hawk winked at Joshua. "Oh, you don't think so!" Without a word he scooped Elizabeth up. She began pummeling him with her fists, but he fended them off and carried her straight into the house. Walking over to the fireplace, he suddenly set her on her feet, then put his hands on her waist. With one smooth motion, he lifted her up and set her on the mantel. Stepping back, he said, "Now, you can come down when you agree to everything I say."

"Hawk Spencer, you let me off of this mantel right now!"

"Go on and jump. You'll probably break both ankles."

Actually the mantelpiece was rather high, and the floor was covered with stones so that sparks would not jump out and catch a fire. Hawk stood there, his eyes dancing with fun, and Joshua grinned and said, "What do you say, Mama? Will it be all right?"

Elizabeth suddenly burst out laughing. "All right. Go on to your old horse race! Now, get me down from here."

"That's a good wife." Hawk reached up and plucked Elizabeth down and set her on her feet. He kissed her and said, "Now I know how to get what I want. Just set you up on the mantel until you give it to me."

"I'm going to start carrying a stick to hit you with when you try it."

"Well, Joshua, we got our way," Hawk said.

Joshua grinned and said as he dashed out of the cabin, "I'm going to get my stuff ready, Pa."

"He's really serious about becoming a lawyer, Elizabeth. You know, I wouldn't be surprised if he followed through with it."

"That's fine if that's what he wants to do. We'll have to see he gets a good education."

"Perhaps he could study under Andrew Jackson. I was very impressed by that young fellow. I daresay if he went into politics, he'd be elected. Smart as a whip, but he's also a real man's man—loves horse racing, hunting, target shooting, and he's got a fine pack of hounds."

"Don't you let him give you any of them. It's all we can do to feed the pack you've got."

"Why, we've only got six, Elizabeth."

"I know it. And they eat more than the rest of us put together. Now, you go on to your horse race and don't you bet."

"Do I ever?"

"No, but I'm always thinking you might start. On with you, now."

Colonel Robert Love's plantation was packed. Everybody from miles around had lined the half-circle, half-mile track that meandered near the lowland by the Nolichucky River.

Jackson was speaking to Hawk, and Joshua was brimming with confidence. "Why, that poor Colonel Love hasn't got a chance. I hope you got some good bets down, Spencer."

"Nope. My wife says no betting. It's good advice, too."

"Well, let's walk around. Maybe we can get something to eat before the race."

People had gathered since early morning, and barbecue pits were now sending their pungent, spicy aroma through the air. The tangy smell of cooked beef and venison was mouth-watering. Everywhere men were trading guns, horses, dogs, and even homesteads. It was a gala occasion, and Joshua stuck close to Andrew Jackson. He did not pester him with questions, but Jackson would often stop and offer his comment to the boy. He had developed a real fondness for Joshua. Having had such a hard time getting a start himself, Jackson went out of his way to encourage Joshua.

Joshua happened to notice John Sevier walking toward them with a young couple. The young woman was carrying a toddler. Sevier walked up to Jackson and shook his hand. "I just wanted to wish you luck on the race, Mr. Jackson."

"Luck is not necessary, Governor Sevier." Jackson grinned and added, "A good horse is what's most important."

"You're quite right there." Sevier then turned to his companions and said, "Let me introduce you to John and Rebecca Crockett. They have settled over in Greene County."

Jackson shook Crockett's hand and tipped his hat to Rebecca. He then introduced them to Joshua.

"It is very nice to meet you," Joshua said. He noticed that the child Mrs. Crockett held had squirmed the entire time they were talking. "Your son seems to have a lot of spirit."

"That's putting it mildly," John Crockett said. "He is certainly a handful, but we expect he'll do great things with all of this energy one day. At least we hope so."

Joshua then asked, "What's his name?"

Rebecca Crockett answered this time. "His name is David, but we call him Davy."

Joshua shook the young lad's hand and said, "Well, Mr. Davy Crockett, I hope to meet you again one day." Joshua was rewarded with a big grin from the two-year-old as everyone chuckled.

"Well, if you'll excuse me," Jackson said, "I must get ready for the race."

"Certainly," Crockett replied. "It was great meeting you. And you, too, Joshua."

Finally the hour came for the big race, and an impatient crowd was yelling for the main event to start. The big roar went up when two groups of horsemen were seen approaching the starting point. Jackson was accompanied by a group of his friends, and when he met with Colonel Love, Love said, "Where is your jockey, Jackson?"

"He got sick with fever. I'm going to ride my own horse, if you're agreeable."

Love was certainly agreeable because Jackson weighed considerably more than his jockey. "All right. Let's select the judges and get this race over with."

The judges were selected with a maximum amount of argument, and finally both parties took their places at the starting point. The riders maneuvered the horses into position and waited.

Joshua had joined Rachel Anderson and David Martin to watch the race. Joshua was wild with excitement, a fact that was not lost on Rachel.

"You're gonna bust, Joshua," she grinned.

"Look, they're starting!"

The signal had been given, and spurred by their jockeys, the horses charged down the track, sending up a plume of dust. The riders stayed close in a tight pack, no one horse gaining a visible lead. Frenzied yells echoed from hill to hill, and even the competing horses seemed to realize the importance of the race. Finally Colonel Love's horse began to inch ahead and crossed the rope just a length ahead of Jackson's horse.

"Whoa! Your Mr. Jackson lost," David said.

"Ah, it wasn't a long enough race. If it had been longer, he would have won," Joshua insisted.

Joshua, Rachel, and David made their way through the crowd, and by the time they reached Love and Jackson, they saw that an argument had started. Andrew Jackson was not an easy loser, and he had begun to hurl insults at Colonel Love. Love was not a gentle man, either, and at that moment, he said, "Why, you long, gangly sorrel-topped soak stick!"

Jackson's face flushed with anger, and he stepped forward to challenge Love to a duel. Both men were quick on the trigger, and one or both of them would certainly have died. It was only when they were separated by their friends that David said, "Well, that was a close one."

"Come on, Mr. Jackson. Don't pay any attention to that old Mr. Love," Joshua said.

Jackson looked down, flustered, and managed a wry smile. "You can't win every race you're in, I suppose, but I surely hated to lose that one."

"You'll win the next time," Joshua said loyally.

As Joshua walked on with Jackson, Rachel turned to David and said, "I'm worried about Josh. He seems to be getting too caught up in all of these things."

"Oh, he'll be all right. He'll settle down after the excitement wears off."

Rachel answered with a pensive look on her face, "I hope you're right, but I'm just not so sure myself."

Sequatchie and Fox had decided belatedly to attend the race, and they had found plenty of company. Hannah, who had begged to go with her father and Joshua and had been refused, managed to elicit an invitation with her mother's reluctant approval. Several others from the surrounding territory were going and arrived just in time to witness the horse race.

In the milling crowd, Hannah, who had been joined by Ethan Cagle and Eve Martin, said, "Come on. Let's go find Pa and tell him we're here."

"All right," Ethan said.

"And you come on, too, Fox."

Fox said nothing, for he had looked forward to making the trip alone with Hannah. He accompanied the trio, however, and once Hannah had greeted her father, who was most surprised to see her, Ethan said, "Let's go watch some of the other stuff."

This was agreeable to everyone, and they spent the next hour wandering around watching various contests.

Finally they reached a group of younger men who were participating in fisticuffs, sparring bareknuckled and laughing and carrying on.

"Hey, Fox, come on and take a try," said James Burleson, a schoolmate of the group.

Fox at once said, "You're too small for me, James."

"Well," Burleson said, "take on Ethan. You two are of a size."

Instantly Fox thought this was the perfect chance to show up Ethan Cagle. "That'll be all right with me. What about you, Cagle?"

Ethan knew he was no match for Fox. He was, indeed, somewhat lighter—as tall as Fox but very slender. He had not endured the hard training Fox had had with the Cherokee, but he knew he could not turn him down in front of the other young men. "Well, I'm not much good, but I'll give it a try."

The two boys stripped off their shirts, and it was obvious to everyone that Cagle would be no match for Fox.

Hannah said, "Come on, Ethan, you and Fox don't need to do this."

"He can quit if he wants to," Fox said coolly.

"I won't quit!" Ethan snapped.

The two squared off, and it did not take long. Ethan tried valiantly, but Fox had sparred with the strongest Cherokee braves many times. He had achieved the strength of a full-grown man, whereas Ethan, a couple of years younger than Fox, had not.

Fox knew he had the advantage and tried to go easy on Ethan. But as he stood there easily avoiding Ethan's punches, his thoughts turned to Hannah and his jealousy flared. Fox pulled back his right arm and released a fast, rock-hard blow to Cagle's face, sending him sprawling.

Everyone cheered, except for Hannah and Eve, and Ethan finally managed to prop himself up on his elbows, dazed and with a bloody nose.

Eve was concerned about Ethan. She went to him and handed him a handkerchief. "Here, Ethan. Are you all right?"

Fox came over and said coolly, "Sorry about that nose."

"I hope you're satisfied, Fox!" Hannah said angrily.

"Me! What do you mean? It was just a friendly fisticuffs contest."

"I don't care. You shouldn't have done it."

Fox grew angry at once. Somehow Hannah had the ability to

provoke him. He was carrying his rifle, intending to join some of the younger men in a shooting match, and he stormed off without another word.

"Are you all right, Ethan?" Eve asked again.

"Why, sure. It's just a bloody nose. I don't think it's broken." He turned to Hannah. "You shouldn't have jumped on Fox like that."

"He's bigger than you are, Ethan. He should know better."

"Well, he's tougher than me. That's for sure," Ethan said wryly. "Come on. Let's go watch the shooting contest."

"Are you going to enter?" Eve asked.

"No. I think I've had enough battles for one day."

The three wandered over and found that Fox had made a wager with Isaiah Tompkins, betting the beautiful hand-carved hunting knife that Sequatchie had given him last Christmas.

Eve immediately said, "Fox, you can't do that. You know how much that knife means to you."

"I won't lose it," Fox said airily. "I can beat old Isaiah anytime."

Ordinarily that might have been true, but Fox was still angry. Perhaps that's why his shots were off. And at the end of the match, Isaiah grinned and said, "I always wanted a Cherokee hunting knife, Fox. Thanks a lot."

Fox handed over the knife, his face a mask as he turned away.

"Maybe you could buy it back from Isaiah," Eve suggested.

"I can get me another knife. Don't worry about it."

As they watched Fox stalk away, Hannah decided she needed to immediately tell Awinita and Sequatchie what had happened.

Awinita said, "He is a man. He must stand beside his action."

Sequatchie said nothing. He had spent hours making the traditional knife, but he knew that Fox was going through a very difficult time. His eyes followed the tall, bronze-skinned young man as he left the crowd and mounted his horse. "He's going home, it looks like. I wish he wouldn't do that. It's not good for him to be alone."

"He feels cut off," Awinita said. "As I always did back in Virginia."

The two watched Fox as he rode away. Neither of them spoke, but both feared for the future of this young man.

Twenty-Seven

Attack!

Akando, war chief of the Cherokee, had always been a brooding individual. Even as a child he had been set apart by the isolation that he imposed upon himself. As he progressed from boyhood into manhood, he had walked alone, sharing his thoughts with few and his heart with no one.

From the beginning of the struggle between the white settlers and the Cherokee, Akando had fought alongside Dragging Canoe, the most vicious and fierce of all the Cherokee war chiefs. Time and again they had raided colonial settlements, and had spared no one, showing no mercy, regardless of age or sex.

For some time now the fighting had died down, but hot coals of anger and revenge still burned in the hearts of many warriors. Akando was certain that the Cherokee would be forced into a pitched battle against the settlers, who more and more encroached on their lands and stole their heritage. Akando kept his own counsel, for the most part, conferring primarily with those other kindred spirits who would never surrender to the white man's advances into their territory. Sooner or later, Akando knew, the war would come—and he was ready.

Although he had never spoken of it, his close friends knew that one event in his life fed his fierce anger even more than the white settlers. When Titus Carter had won Awinita's heart and taken her for his wife, Akando had been filled with rage. Most men would have been able to forget a lost love, or at least put it behind them, but as the years had passed, the victory of this white man had grown even more hateful to Akando. Very few days passed that he did not fuel his hatred for Carter, and even after he had finally learned of Carter's death, the rage Akando had felt for him now burned toward Awinita. He could not forgive her for choosing a white man over himself, and when she had suddenly arrived back in the territory of the Cherokee, old angers had been stirred afresh.

Perhaps if Awinita had accepted his courtship, he might have been able to put the past behind him. But she had shown her distaste and even disdain for him, and now Akando spent his days and nights plotting his revenge. Finally one raw September morning Akando took one man into his confidence. His second-in-command, Adahy, was almost as ruthless as Akando himself. He was a tried-and-tested warrior with an innate hatred of anyone with white skin. It was only to this man that Akando had decided to divulge his plan for revenge.

Adahy had risen earlier and was surprised to see Akando suddenly appear at the door of his house. The intensity on Akando's face alarmed the burly warrior, but he knew better than to speak. Akando was not one to take suggestions but demanded that his orders be followed.

"Adahy, I have need of you."

"Yes. What is it? I will do what I can."

"Come. Walk with me."

The two men walked around outside the village, and when they were beyond the sight of the sleepy houses, Akando turned to face Adahy, his ebony eyes burning fiercely. His presence was electrifying, and Adahy listened alertly.

"It is time to take our revenge on the white men for what they have done to our people."

"Yes. I am with you there. I say we will fight."

"Yes. We will fight. And the time to strike is now. Some may be timid, but we will gather the bravest of our warriors and we will have blood."

For a moment Akando hesitated, the years of bitterness reflected in the cruel planes of his face. He gave a mirthless smile, and his eyes glittered. "You alone, Adahy, know what grief I have suffered because of the sister of Sequatchie."

Adahy nodded briefly, although it was no secret that Carter's taking Awinita away from Akando had dealt the war chief a severe blow. He said nothing, however, but waited until Akando spoke again.

"I'm going to take my revenge on Carter through Awinita. She is a traitor to the Cherokee, leaving to marry a white man. And her brother, Sequatchie, is the same. Our women were not good enough for him. He had to marry a white woman. They are not fit to be called Cherokee, and they must die."

Adahy spoke reluctantly. "I agree with you, but many among our people will not. Many still admire Sequatchie and Awinita. They will not like it if we kill them."

"I have thought on this and I have a plan." Again the cruel smile touched the lips of the Cherokee warrior, and he said, "Listen carefully. There will be a raid on the settlers in the northern part of Watauga. It will only be a feint. Not a real raid. And those who are in that raid will quickly retreat, but it will draw out the fighting men."

"You want me to lead that raid?"

"No. Bainto will do that. You and I have another job—and we will have allies."

"Allies? Other Cherokee or some of the Chickasaws?"

"No. They will be Dorch and Miller."

The eyes of the thickset Adahy flew open. "They are our enemies! They sold the scalps of children to the English general called Hair Buyer."

Indeed there had been an English general who had bought the scalps from white renegades who attacked villages mercilessly and scalped old men, women, and children. The scalp buyer had not questioned the age or sex: the only thing he asked was that there be dead Indians.

"Yes. They are our enemy, but they are fools! They now come to our elders and say they want all of the furs that we trap."

"They will never get them!"

"No, they will not, for I have a plan for them. But first we will use them, Adahy."

"I do not understand."

The two had paused now and were standing beneath a towering chestnut tree. The sun was rising slowly, and though the air was still cold, neither man seemed to notice, both of them wearing merely breechcloths and leggings, their torsos bare.

"Here is what we will do. When Bainto and his warriors draw the fighting men out of the villages in the area to defend Watauga, these two men will attack Sequatchie and Awinita."

"They will kill them?"

"Yes."

"And the boy, the son of Awinita?"

"No. He must be kept alive, and he must see that it is white men who are killing his mother and his uncle."

Adahy pondered Akando's plan in silence for a time, and then he straightened up. "You want the boy to think that white men are his enemy so that he will join us."

"You are shrewd, Adahy. That is exactly what I want. Awinita's son will make a mighty warrior."

"It may be difficult. Perhaps not all the men will go to fight."

"I think they will if word gets out. But not Sequatchie. He will never go to fight the Cherokee, so he will remain at home to defend the women. But he will not be able to. He will die."

"Sequatchie is a fierce warrior. He will fight."

"He will die. We will see to it. Dorch and Miller are fools, but we will go with them. We will take them by the hand and put them in a spot where they will be able to kill Sequatchie and Awinita without doubt. Then they will take the boy."

Adahy shifted uneasily. "What about Dorch and Miller? They will get the furs?"

Akando smiled then, and there was a vicious humor in his expression. "We will pay them off for their services—with a tomahawk in their brains or a bullet in their hearts, whichever would give us the most pleasure."

Adahy suddenly laughed aloud. "When do we begin?"

"At once. Dorch and Miller are dealing with the elders now. They are not getting very far. We will tell them that if they help us, we will speak to the elders on their behalf. They will believe us, and their greed will lead them straight to death."

"May their spirits wander in darkness forever!" Adahy exclaimed.

"Come. We will begin."

Saul Dorch was a short, stocky man with bulging muscles and black hair and eyes. His companion, Otis Miller, was the complete opposite—tall, thin, and lanky with dirty yellow hair and cruel hazel eyes. The two men stood outside in the deep woods close to the cabin of Sequatchie and Awinita, and they drank frequently from a bottle they had brought with them. The raw whiskey burned their throats as they spoke excitedly of their good fortune.

"I never thought I'd have anything good to say about that devil Akando," Dorch said, his tongue thickened by the raw alcohol. "But he's got a lot of influence with the elders."

Miller took another pull on the bottle. "I don't know what's in it for him."

"I heard he fell pretty hard for that Indian woman, Sequatchie's sister, who turned him down flat and married up with a white man. That was over twenty years ago, but I guess it still really burns in him. So he wants her dead, and he uses us for the job."

The two had met with Akando and had listened suspiciously at first. Finally Akando's intensity had convinced them. He had promised to help them gain a monopoly over all the furs trapped by the Cherokee people.

"We're gonna be rich men! I can see us now, going into New York with all the money in the world in our pockets. All of the whiskey and all of the women we could ever want," Miller laughed.

The two went on boasting about what they would do when suddenly Akando and Adahy stood before them. Neither man had heard the Cherokee warriors approach, and both were startled.

"You would be dead men if we were your enemies," Akando said.

"Well, we're not enemies!" Dorch snapped. He was embarrassed at being caught unawares and knew that he had had too much to drink. "Well, let's get this thing over with!"

"All right. Come. Get your rifles. Are they loaded?"

" 'Course they are! You think we're fools?"

"Come, then. Sequatchie and the woman and the boy are outside dressing a hog. We will not be seen, but I want the boy to clearly see you so he will know that white men have killed his mother and his uncle."

"Whatever you say, Akando," Miller said. He started to take another drink, but Akando reached out, plucked it from him, and threw it far away. "You're drunk enough now!"

Dorch and Miller followed the two Indians through the woods until finally they came to the edge of the clearing. Akando whispered, "There. It will not be a difficult shot."

"You want us to shoot 'em from here?"

"Get as close as you have to. Just be sure that they're dead, and be sure that the boy sees you."

"Look at him. He ain't even got a gun. It'll be easy," Miller boasted.

"Then, do it!" Akando said harshly. He shoved them out of the thickest part of the cover, and he and Adahy stood watching as the two made their way from tree to tree through the cleared land. There were still enough trees to hide behind.

"They're so drunk I'm not sure they can do it," Adahy said.

"If they don't, we will shoot from here. The boy will think it is more white settlers. Come. We will move closer. . . ."

The hog had been lifted by his hind legs and now dangled as Sequatchie took his knife and began the work. He slit the belly open, and the intestines spilled out onto the ground. Turning to Awinita, he said, "This is a fine hog. Fed on corn. He will feed us throughout much of the winter."

Awinita smiled wanly and joined in as the three worked on the hog. Iris was visiting Dorcas Cagle with Elizabeth, leaving Sequatchie, Awinita, and Fox to deal with the hog.

Fox was puzzled. He had noted that his mother, for some reason, was very silent that day. She was never a talkative woman but always quick to respond to him. Finally he said, "Is something wrong, Mother?"

Awinita and Fox were now washing the entrails in the small creek that wound around the cabin, some thirty feet away from Sequatchie, who continued dressing the hog. They could use the intestines to make sausage, something that Hawk and Elizabeth had taught them.

Awinita looked up and then stood to her feet.

Surprised at her movement, Fox joined her. Suddenly she seemed very small. He had grown tall now. Smoothly muscled and fully developed, he was aware for the first time that his mother was showing signs of age. He had never thought of her as growing old, and for some reason it troubled him. Even now she was only fifty-one years old, but suddenly for the first time he noticed the fine lines around her eyes.

"I had a dream last night, son."

"A dream? What about, Mother?"

"It was a strange dream, but one I can understand."

"Tell me about it."

"Many of my dreams," Awinita said slowly, "are difficult, but this one was very simple. I don't know where I was exactly. I was aware that it was a vision."

The Cherokee believed strongly in visions, and Fox grew alert. "A vision? Tell me!"

"I saw one that I had never seen on earth, and I knew that it was an angel, or perhaps the Lord Jesus himself."

Fox stared at his mother. "You saw Jesus?"

"I cannot be sure, but I knew that I was in the presence of the Lord. Perhaps He sent His angel."

"What did he say?"

"He said only one thing." Awinita hesitated. "I was not sure whether to tell you, but now it seems I should. He spoke of you."

"Of me!" Fox was astounded. "What did he say?"

"He simply said, 'Your son will be a great man of God.' "

"Me, a man of God!" Fox was even more astounded. "I can't believe it! Maybe you misunderstood."

"I did not misunderstand. The words were clearer than any I have ever heard while waking," Awinita said. Suddenly she smiled and put her hand up on his shoulder. She had to reach up to do so. "I know you long to be a great warrior, but that is not what the messenger said. He said you would be a great man of God."

Fox loved his mother, and though he would not contradict her, doubt filled his spirit. He reached out in a rare gesture of physical expression, stroked her hair, and said, "You've always been the best mother in the world to me. I do not know about this dream. But if you say it is so, I will think on it."

Awinita's face lit up with joy. She had been afraid that in his present state of despair and doubt and anger, Fox would reject it outright. Now she said, "I believe God has His hand on you."

"If you say so, Mother," Fox repeated gently.

At that moment a shot rang out, and Fox reacted sharply. He threw himself to one side, reaching automatically for his musket, which he ordinarily carried. But both he and Sequatchie had left their weapons at the cabin, bringing instead the implements and tools for cleaning the hog, and now they were at least two hundred feet from the cabin.

Fox looked up to see his uncle Sequatchie fall to the ground. At the same instant that he saw this, one of the two men who had suddenly emerged stopped and raised his rifle. Fox tried to throw himself in front of his mother, but he was too slow. The bullet struck Awinita in the chest, and even as she fell, he saw crimson blood stain the front of her deerskin dress.

It's a raid! But it's white men, he thought. It was too late to run for the cabin, for the other man had stopped and reloaded and aimed straight at Fox. He gave himself up to death at that moment, leaned over, and lifted his mother. Her eyes fluttered, and she opened them for an instant. The shot had struck her directly in the heart, and she was dying as she whispered, "My son, be a man of God. Don't follow hate. Love the Lord Jesus. . . ."

Her eyes fluttered and her body went limp.

Fox held her for a moment, and then suddenly he knew that life was over for him. His uncle and his beloved mother were both dead.

He had time to place his mother gently on the ground, then stood and faced the approaching white men. The one still had his rifle trained on Fox, and the other had a long, wicked-looking knife in his hand, his rifle slung across his back.

"Well, Injun, ain't you scared?" the tall one with the knife jeered.

Fox did not answer. He knew he was as good as dead, and he determined to show no fear whatsoever. "I'm not afraid of death. Especially not from cowards like you who shoot men and women from ambush."

Dorch raised his rifle and pointed it directly at Fox's head. Fox turned and looked down the looming muzzle, a dirty black tunnel still faintly smoking from the bullet it had delivered. But Fox was cold and unmoved. He had nothing now to lose. He simply, without expression, stared into the eyes of Dorch and said, "Go ahead. Shoot."

Dorch hesitated, then lowered the rifle. He cursed and said, "Well, we'll make him beg. Tie his hands. We'll take him with us."

Fox stood still while the lanky man tied his hands behind him with a rawhide thong. Then Dorch said, "Now tie this around his neck. We'll get something out of him! He won't be so sassy if we put the fire to him."

Fox was sad that he had not been killed instantly. He knew that torture lay ahead of him, but he was determined to show no fear.

The noose tightened around his neck as Miller tugged him along. He looked back one time at the still bodies of Sequatchie and Awinita, knowing he would never look upon them on this earth again. He was taken deep into the woods, and Dorch said, "We'll drag him behind our horses—that'll take some of the sap out of him!"

These were the last words that Saul Dorch ever spoke, for suddenly from out of the shadows Akando stepped. He had a tomahawk in his hand. Dorch stopped quickly and turned to face him. He opened his mouth to say something else, but before he could speak Akando's arm swung upward and down with a mighty force. The keen edge of the weapon split Dorch's skull. He stood there for one instant, his eyes glazed over, his mouth opened as if to speak, and then he collapsed in a heap.

Miller yelled, "Hey—" But his sentence was cut short as Adahy, who had appeared beside him from out of nowhere, reached out, yanked the man's head back, and drew a knife across his throat.

Miller fell to the ground. He tried to speak, but his mouth was filled with blood. Adahy watched as he writhed on the ground, then slowly grew still. "So much for these vermin," he said.

Fox was stunned. He could not speak for a moment, so great was his surprise. Akando stepped toward him and slit the rawhide that tied his wrists. He then lifted the noose off of his neck.

"We heard that these white men would be coming to kill all of the Cherokee who had joined their white settlements," Akando said.

Fox was baffled. "The white settlers are behind this?"

"Not all of them." Akando was too shrewd for that. "But enough of them that you will have to leave. Your life will not be safe here."

"They killed my mother and my uncle."

"And they have paid for it," Akando said. "Now you must decide. The war is here. You must take your stand. Will you fight with those who killed your mother and your uncle, or will you avenge them?"

Fox had never known such a moment. The tragedy had come so quickly that he could not think clearly. But now as he stood there his mind was filled with the image of his mother and beloved uncle. "The whites killed them," he said, "and they would have killed me, too. I will go with you, Akando," he said, anger giving his voice a hard edge.

Akando's eyes glowed as he exchanged glances with Adahy. "Come," he said. "You will be a great warrior."

"We must go bury my mother."

"No. There are others on the way like these two. You will die, and then you will have no revenge for your mother and your uncle. Come quickly."

And so Fox Carter left the world he had known and joined himself to Akando of the Cherokee.

Naaman Arrives in Franklin

Twenty-Eight

"Well, wife, God has given us a good harvest."

Thomas Denton put his arm around Leah and hugged her. The two were standing out in front of their cabin looking over the fields that had dominated the last four years of their lives.

"It's been hard, Tom. You've done wonderfully well."

"Well, I didn't know much about farming when I got here," Thomas smiled, "but I've had to learn. If it hadn't been for Hawk and Sequatchie and others, I don't think we would have made it."

It was a difficult matter for settlers who came across the Appalachians to make a home for themselves. Just clearing the land was a monumental task. The trees had to be cut and split into logs. Some were made into clapboards or shakes for a roof, and then there was a house-raising. As soon as possible a barn had to be built and then a rail pen to keep the cattle in. The larger trees had to be girdled with a circular cut through the back around the perimeter of the tree, which eventually killed it. This was called "deadening." The area between these trees was farmed until they finally fell, but the dead trees often dropped their limbs on top of people. A speaker once said, "Well, men, love God, hate the devil, and keep out of a deadening in time of a thunderstorm." Indeed, after a thunderstorm came the tedious, backbreaking business on the part of boys, women, and girls picking up the chunks. The shrubs and brush then had to be dug out with a heavy grubbing hoe.

Both Leah and Thomas thought back over the past four years and the sweat and labor that they had poured into their place. The garden, which was now large and well fenced, had originally consisted of one small plot for garden truck and another for a patch of corn. Corn was the ideal first crop. No special preparation was necessary, and even without a plow, one could take a sharp, flattened hickory stick, jab a hole in the ground, drop grains into it, and then trample on it. There were no special tools necessary for harvesting, and corn made excellent food for man or beast.

After the first season, of course, it was necessary to furrow the ground, which was usually done with a wooden plow with a fifteen-inch-long sharpened prong. It was primitive, hard, grinding labor, much as it had been done two thousand years before.

"I remember the first crop we put in," Thomas mused. "It was right over there, and I didn't have the least idea of how to go about it."

"Well, you learned, dear."

They had indeed learned that harvesting corn came in four operations. Just before the leaves began to turn yellow, the settlers stripped off the green leaves from the ears. These were gathered in bunches and dried, to be used as fodder for the cattle. A few days later a man would drive a sleigh through the patch to haul in the fodder, and each bunch was bound and hauled to a shed. A while later the tops of the stalks were cut off, and finally, in the days of autumn as now, it was time to pull the ears, shuck and all, leaving the bare stalks standing in the field.

"We'll get to pulling the corn tomorrow, and then there'll be corn shucking."

"I'm glad you raised some wheat this year. It'll be good to have biscuits and gravy and pastries. Wheat's the best for that."

"Well, I think we've won. We'll have a place here, and we know that God has given it to us."

"Oh yes! We've got cows and even sheep, and I'll get my first harvest of wool soon," Leah said. "Then you'll see some spinning."

The two stood there for a long time watching Sherah as she ran around. She was four years old now and the joy of their lives. She was a beautiful girl with pale blond hair and bright blue eyes, inquisitive, intelligent, and full of imagination.

"Let's walk down the corn rows," Thomas said. "It gives me a good feeling just to know we've done this—with the help of God, of course."

"All right. But we can't go far. I just put Micah down for a nap, and I can't leave him for too long." Micah had been a blessed surprise to their lives. His father had doted on him since his arrival last April.

Sherah followed them through the mazelike rows, chattering all the time, and finally as they emerged from the field, Thomas suddenly looked up. "Who's that?"

Leah put her eyes on the two men who had ridden down the narrow trail and were stopping in front of the cabin. "I don't know them."

"Maybe they're lost," Thomas said. "Come on. We can offer them a drink of water at least."

The two hurried on with Sherah following close behind. When they got closer, Thomas exclaimed, "Why, that's Naaman Carter!"

As Carter stepped out of the saddle, he handed the lines to the other man, who had also dismounted, and came forward to say, "Well, Thomas, I suppose you're surprised to see me."

"I certainly am, Naaman. Is Julia with you?"

"No. It was too hard a trip for her. I left Linus at home to take care of her and Lydia. Had quite a time finding you."

"Well, it's good to see you."

"You remember Jasper Tatum, the overseer from Havenwood?"

"Of course. How are you, Tatum?"

Tatum held the lines and said nothing but nodded. He looked no better to Thomas Denton than he had before, a brutal man with a surly expression. Thomas wondered why in the world Carter would make a long journey with such an unpleasant companion.

"Well, come into the house. We'll fix up something for you to eat. We can do that, can't we, Leah?"

"Of course," Leah said. "Come along, Sherah, you can help Mommy. We need to check on your brother, too."

The two went into the house, and Thomas said, "Let me show you about the place. Of course, it's not much compared to Havenwood, but we started from nothing. When we got here, all this was just bare forest."

With pride Thomas Denton took the two around the farm, pointing out all the different aspects of it.

"Well, you've done a fine job. I'd hate to tackle the wilderness like this," Naaman said.

"It's not worth the effort, I reckon," Tatum said grumpily. "Give me a plantation."

"Well, I like it," Thomas said, ignoring Tatum's comment. He turned and faced Naaman, saying, "Did you have a good trip?"

"No, we didn't," Tatum answered instead. "We had to stop a hundred times, it seemed like."

Naaman Carter laughed ruefully. "It's a lot harder trip than I thought, Tom, and I don't like roughing it."

"Well, it's a rough trip but not as bad as it was a few years ago. The roads are a little better now."

"Roads! You call those things roads!" Carter exclaimed. "Why, they're terrible!"

It had been a difficult trip for Naaman Carter. He was a pampered individual and wished many times he had never started out over the Misty Mountains, but now that he was here, he knew he had a mission to accomplish.

"You may be wondering why we've come out all this way, Tom."

"Well, I suppose I am. It has something to do with the plantation?"

"Yes, it does. It seems that Fox and Awinita will never come back, so I was wondering if we could make some sort of an arrangement. Perhaps we could lease the place, maybe buy it eventually."

A painful look crossed Thomas Denton's face, and he shook his head as he said sadly, "You haven't heard the news, then?"

"What news?"

"About Awinita and Fox?"

Hope leaped in Naaman's eyes, but he quickly forced a look of concern on his face. "What's the news? Is it bad?"

"It couldn't be much worse, I don't think."

"Are they dead? Did something happen?"

"Awinita's dead. She was killed, and her brother, Sequatchie, was badly wounded. We didn't think he'd live for a while, but he pulled through."

"What about Nathanael?"

"That's a sad story, too. White men killed his mother, and very badly wounded his uncle, so he's resentful of all white people right now. He's gone to live with the Cherokee."

"Why, this is terrible!" Naaman exclaimed. Inwardly he was exultant. *If he's with the Cherokee, it won't be hard to hire someone to take care of him. The mother's gone, and now I can take care of the son.* He thought for a moment longer, then said, "I'll need to make some kind of arrangements for Havenwood. I'll have to talk to Nathanael."

"That may be hard to do. It's not safe for a white man to venture into Cherokee territory. Except maybe for Hawk Spencer."

"So this Spencer could go, you say?"

"He might be able to, and of course Sequatchie can go anytime."

"Well, I'll have to talk to him. Can you tell me how to get to his place?"

"Oh yes. It isn't difficult."

He gave clear instructions, and then Naaman said, "Well, one thing's for certain—those slaves they took will have to go back to the plantation."

"You mean Ezekiel and Mercy?"

"Yes."

"They have a good life now, you know."

"Well," Naaman said, "I'm happy for them, but they belong to the plantation. They'll have to go back."

The thought of Carter forcing them to return to Havenwood made Thomas Denton angry. Ezekiel and Mercy had proved to be diligent workers. Ezekiel had become a good man with a rifle, and everyone who could shoot was welcome in Watauga, for it took a strong man to survive out here in the wilderness.

"I don't think they'll want to go back," he said.

"They have no choice," Tatum said roughly. "They belong to the place."

"We can discuss it with Sequatchie," Naaman said quickly. "We'll be seeing you later."

"Wait. I want to know all about my family."

"Why, of course. I'll tell you all the news later, but really I need to get this matter of business concerning Havenwood settled."

"I understand," said Thomas. "You can't miss it if you stay on the road. Come back as soon as you can. We're always glad of visitors, Naaman."

Naaman mounted and rode out, closely followed by Tatum. When they were out of sight of the Denton property, he laughed. "Well, the woman is dead. That's good news."

"But the boy is still alive, and he's a man now. About eighteen or nineteen, isn't he?"

"Yes. But he's living with the Cherokee. It'll be no problem. All we have to do is find a renegade who'll take care of him. It'll never get reported."

"You'll have to have proof of his death," Tatum said.

"I know that. I'm not a fool! Come on, let's hurry."

Hawk had made it a point to stay very close to Sequatchie after his terrible wounding. Hardly anyone expected the Cherokee to live, but Elizabeth and Iris had nursed him day and night until finally he had survived. Hawk himself had pulled the bullet out of Sequatchie's back. It had come close to touching the heart, and removing it had been a terribly difficult thing. For days he had lain in a stupor from the fever that blazed in his body.

But Sequatchie had slowly recovered. He still moved with difficulty, and the incident seemed to have aged him. The tragic loss of Awinita had saddened him deeply, and the decision of Fox to follow Akando disappointed him. Even when Fox had learned that his uncle was still alive, he refused to return to Watauga. When Awinita and Fox had arrived in Watauga four years ago, their presence had been a source of great joy to Sequatchie. But now his sister was dead and his nephew was gone, and the sadness lurked in his eyes.

Hawk Spencer had come down to bring some fresh meat to Sequatchie and Iris. He'd given it to Iris to prepare and then had sat on the porch of the cabin with Sequatchie. They spent some time discussing the raid of John Sevier into the Chickamauga area against Dragging Canoe. It was a futile expedition in the opinion of both men, and Hawk finally had said, "I wish John would show a little bit more sense. He's a smart man, but he's listening to some bad advice."

They had sat there for some forty minutes when, as usual, Sequatchie heard the approaching horsemen before Hawk. "Someone's coming," he said.

Both men were cautious and watched closely as the two horsemen pulled up and dismounted. Hawk rose, as did Sequatchie, and stepped off the porch.

The first man said, "I'm looking for Sequatchie."

"I am Sequatchie."

"Oh, we didn't get lost, then. Mr. Denton, down the road, gave us directions. My name is Naaman Carter. I believe your sister was married to my brother. This is my employee, Mr. Jasper Tatum."

"This is Hawk Spencer," Sequatchie said. He had heard a great deal about this man from Fox and Awinita. He knew that Carter despised Fox and his mother and had done all he could to take their heritage from them. He did not invite the two to sit down but said, "What can I do for you?"

"I've come out to see if we could make some arrangement regarding the property back in Virginia. I understand your sister was killed and that Nathanael has taken up with the Cherokee. I'm sorry for your loss," he lied.

Sequatchie nodded slowly. "That is true," he said shortly.

"Things can't go on like this. Ownership needs to be settled."

Hawk Spencer stood there, taking all this in. He, too, had talked considerably with Fox and Awinita, and knew exactly what the legal status was about Fox's inheritance. "I don't know what you think there is to be settled. The property, as I understand it, was left to Titus Carter. And on his death it went to his only son, Nathanael, whom we call Fox."

Anger swept across Naaman's face, but he quickly covered it, saying smoothly, "Well, it's obvious that Nathanael will never come back to Virginia. It seems he's renounced his father's ways. I want to speak to him to arrange some method of transferring the property."

"You want to buy it?"

"Yes, or lease it. Whichever we can work out."

"You would not be wise to venture into Cherokee country at this time," Sequatchie said.

"So Mr. Denton told me. I was hoping that you could send for the boy."

"He's not a boy anymore. He's a man," Sequatchie said quickly. "I can do nothing to help you."

"Well, I'm disappointed to hear that. There is one thing that we can settle right here. The slaves, Ezekiel and Mercy, they must go back with us."

"They may not choose to do that," Sequatchie said.

"They don't have any choice," Jasper Tatum spoke up. "They're slaves. They belong to Havenwood."

"They belong to Nathanael Carter, who owns the place," Hawk corrected him.

"Legally I've been in charge of the plantation acting on Nathanael's behalf, and I have the papers here from the judge in Virginia ordering the slaves back to Havenwood."

"Let me see those papers." Hawk took them and read them and then looked up at Sequatchie. "They're exactly what he says."

"We're going to take them back when we return to Virginia," Naaman said.

"Fox may not choose to let them go. He's very fond of them."

"That's another reason why I should be talking to him. We can work all these things out. But if I can't see the boy, then according to these papers, these two slaves must be returned to Virginia."

"Come back tomorrow," Sequatchie said. "I will think of these things."

"It'd be best if we could talk to Nathanael. I would appreciate it if you could arrange it. Come along, Tatum."

The two mounted and rode away.

"This is bad news," Hawk said.

"Very bad. Especially for Ezekiel and Mercy."

"Fox will never let anything happen to them. He thinks a lot of the family."

"They may act without ever seeing him," Sequatchie said. "If they leave before they meet him, they have the legal right to take them."

"We'll have to get in touch with Fox."

"Yes. I think we must. Those two are evil men. It doesn't take a lot of discernment to see the greed in Naaman Carter's eyes. Fox has always said his uncle lusted after that plantation."

"So he said. Well, we'll have to pray about it, Sequatchie."

Sequatchie nodded, and then the two went back and sat on the porch. "I miss Awinita," Sequatchie said. "She was a lovely woman."

"Indeed she was."

"And Fox, he's in terrible trouble and doesn't seem to know it."

"The more reason to pray."

So the two men prayed right there on the porch, and they prayed for days afterward for the young man.

Fox did not know of their prayers, of course. He had joined himself to Akando but could not bring himself to join in the fighting.

For days Fox wandered by himself among the Cherokee but felt more than ever like a man without a home. Fox tried to convince himself that he was doing the right thing, but the longer he stayed, the more the loneliness in his heart seemed to grow.

To Hunt a Fox

Twenty-Nine

The latter part of the year of 1788 proved to be the death knell of the state of Franklin. John Sevier had run into political and legal problems and was arrested by North Carolina officials on a charge of treason, though he was eventually pardoned. With no leader and with no official recognition from Congress, the dream was over for those who had envisioned Franklin as the fourteenth state of the Union. It was a time of sorrow for many in the Watauga area.

When Christmas came, Hawk Spencer threw open the doors of his house, and, as always, it was filled with visitors. One problem that Hawk had was that Thomas Denton, still not aware of the true nature of Naaman Carter, had invited him to the celebration. Carter and Tatum had set up camp for the winter and were as determined as ever not to return empty-handed to Virginia in the spring. Sequatchie and Hawk had decided not to bring Fox into the settlement, for they did not trust Naaman Carter. It would have been impossible in any case, since they had discovered that Akando had taken the young man on westward journeys to meet with other tribes. Sequatchie had said, "Perhaps it's God's will for him to be gone at this time."

After discussing it and praying over it, finally Hawk had agreed. "He will come back one day, but I don't want Naaman Carter coming in contact with him."

"Neither do I," Sequatchie had agreed. So the two had simply told Carter that it was impossible at this time for them to bring Fox into Watauga.

As the men met outside the cabin during the celebration, Hawk spoke up, saying, "Have you heard that John Sevier is going to raise a force to fight the Cherokee?"

"I'm surprised at that," Thomas Denton said. "After his arrest I would have thought he was out of the picture."

Hawk grinned. "John Sevier's just getting started. You mark my words. Franklin may be history, but John Sevier will be right at the top of things in no time. He's the kind of man you can never get down."

Naaman Carter spoke up. "Which Cherokee will he fight against?"

"Probably against Akando's warriors," Sequatchie answered.

"Do you think Fox will be involved in that? It could be dangerous," Naaman said.

No one answered him, for none of the men took to the newcomer. Finally he got up and left, and Jacob said, "There's something I don't like about that man."

"Well, I wish he hadn't come," Hawk said. He turned to Sequatchie and said, "I think we did the right thing in not bringing Fox in. The farther he stays away from Naaman Carter, the better off he'll be."

Joshua Spencer was not having the best Christmas in the world. He was sitting at the table with Hannah, Eve, David, Rachel, and Ethan. It was Eve who finally said, "You look glum. What's the matter, Joshua?"

"I'll tell you what it is," Hannah said. "He's sad that Andrew Jackson's moved away to the Cumberland area around Nashville."

"Well, I don't think that's the worst thing that could happen," Ethan Cagle said. He had been courting Hannah steadily, and now he looked fondly at Joshua. "You don't want to be a lawyer."

"Why not? I think it would be great to be a lawyer."

"Why, you're a frontiersman," Cagle grinned. "You need to be out growing corn and doing things like that."

"No. Not for me. I'm gonna join Mr. Jackson one day and become a lawyer. He said he'd help me."

Hannah suddenly said, "You know, I forgot to feed the calf we've got penned up! I'll be right back."

Ethan volunteered to do it, saying, "Why don't you help the ladies with Christmas dinner. I'll take care of the calf."

After Ethan had left, the three girls got out a large mixing bowl and began to prepare biscuits for dinner. Hannah was surprised when Eve said, "Everyone's talking about how Ethan is courting you."

"Oh, that's nothing!"

"You don't care for him, then?"

"I don't know right now. Everything's so up in the air. There's not going to be any state of Franklin, Awinita was murdered, and Fox has gone away to live with the Cherokee. I just don't feel like talking about anything."

"Well, I think Ethan would make any woman a wonderful husband."

For the first time Hannah noticed a tone of deep affection in her cousin's voice for Ethan Cagle. She realized that Eve might truly care for Ethan. She determined to be more sensitive to the feelings of Eve, who had always been a true friend.

While the girls were fixing the food, Ethan entered the barn, put a pail full of crushed feed in front of the calf, and watched as the animal ate it. He sat there stroking it. He loved young animals of every kind. Suddenly he heard voices. They grew louder, and he realized they had come to stand right outside the barn door. He did not recognize the voices, but then they shifted so that they were standing directly in front of the gap between the two doors. He could see Naaman Carter and the burly man that followed him everywhere, Jasper Tatum. Ethan did not like either of them and continued to stroke the calf, ignoring the men, until he suddenly realized what they were talking about. A shiver raced up his spine as he listened closely.

". . . got to see that Fox gets put out of the way in this raid," Naaman was saying.

"Did you talk to those Indians?"

"Yes. It was hard to get in touch with them." Naaman's voice came clearly now. "But they've agreed to take care of him."

"The Cherokee? Why would they want to kill one of their own?"

"Well, in the first place, Tatum, they're not Cherokee. They're Chickasaws, and renegades at that, and they'll do it for money."

"When is all this going to take place?"

"It won't be long. Fox will be fighting beside Akando, and these Chickasaw know him by sight."

"Who? Akando?"

"Of course! And they know Nathanael, too."

"How much did you have to give them?"

"Ten dollars in silver."

"That's cheap enough. You'll get the whole place out of it."

Ethan Cagle sat stock-still until finally the voices seemed to move farther off. He got to his feet and went outside, watching the two men as they disappeared into the woods. They had come to get their horses, apparently, and had not been aware that anyone could overhear them inside the barn.

Slowly Ethan moved back toward the house. He was troubled by what he had heard, and now a complicated struggle stirred within him. He had come to care for Hannah Spencer, and he was well aware that she had feelings for Fox. He had thrown himself into the pursuit of Hannah with all of his might and felt that if he had time enough and if Fox stayed away, he would have a chance to win her. Still, Fox was a friend of his, and he was concerned about his well-being.

When Ethan went inside he was silent, unusually so, and finally Eve came to him and said, "What's wrong, Ethan?"

"Wrong? Nothing's wrong. What do you mean?"

"Well, you were having fun and laughing when you went out to feed the calf, and now you're all solemn. Is something wrong with the calf?"

"No. The calf's all right."

"Well, what is it, then?"

Ethan Cagle came very close to telling the girl what he had heard, but the thought of losing Hannah was devastating to him. He thought, *I'll take care of this myself, but I can't let Hannah know about it.* He knew he was doing something wrong, but a young man in love will do foolish things, and Ethan Cagle said nothing at all to anyone about what he had overheard in the barn.

Ethan's Dilemma

Thirty

Early in January 1789, Hawk, his two sons, Jacob and Andrew, and his son-in-law, Seth Donovan, found themselves joined to John Sevier's forces. They had all four dreaded the expedition, but the Cherokee, led in part by Dragging Canoe and in part by Akando, were creating a swath of destruction throughout the lands west of the Appalachians. The settlers felt they had little choice but to fight, as the very survival of their homesteads was in jeopardy.

"I always hate to see you go on these raids, Hawk," Elizabeth said. She was standing beside him as he got all his equipment together. He was looking down the barrel of his musket, and a grim look dominated his face as she told him, "I'm afraid for you."

Quickly Hawk lowered the rifle and placed it against the wall of the cabin. Going to her, he took her in his arms and said gently, "I don't want to go. You know that."

"Do you have to?"

"Somebody has to. I couldn't count myself as any kind of a man if I let others do my fighting."

Elizabeth put her face against his chest. He was wearing his buckskins, and she could smell the traces of old woodsmoke in them. As she had grown older, Elizabeth had learned that a woman had to accept these things, especially a woman living on the frontier. Fighting such battles was as much a part of a man's life on the frontier as going to work was back in Boston.

"How long will you be gone?"

"No way of telling. Depends on how soon we find 'em, and that may take a while."

"I'll pray for all of you."

"I knew you'd do that." Hawk held her firmly, and the two did not speak for a long time.

As she felt secure in his arms, she rejoiced now that the love she had for this man was the same as when they first fell in love. *No. That is not true,* she thought quickly. *It's greater than it ever was.* Then the thought came, *I can't send him away like this.*

Pushing her fears aside, she smiled and reached up to stroke his hair. "I'm glad you're not getting bald."

"Would you love me if I were bald?"

"I don't know. I'll have to wait and see," she teased him.

He laughed, then kissed her and said, "Well, I have to go. The party will be gathering. You take care of things until I get back. Watch out for Hannah and Joshua."

"I will. You know I'll do that."

The horses were all gathered at the hitching post, and Jacob, Andrew, and Seth were standing around idly talking. The gear was already loaded on the pack horses as Hawk turned to Joshua. "It looks like you're the man of the house again."

"I wish you'd take me with you, Pa."

"Maybe next time."

"No. I hope there won't ever be a next time," Elizabeth said. "I hope this will settle it for good."

Hawk had little faith that this expedition would put an end to the fighting, but he said nothing to his wife. He squeezed Joshua's arm and said, "I'm serious, son. We don't know what could happen here. You and Sequatchie have got to protect the womenfolk until then."

"I'll do it, Pa. You take care of yourself."

Hawk put his arm around Joshua and the two hugged. "You'll be as tall as I am soon," Hawk said.

"Taller," Joshua grinned. "I've decided to be even taller than you are."

Hawk laughed and turned to Hannah, who was hanging back. He went to her and said, "Well, you've got on a new dress."

Hannah flushed. "It is not, Pa. It's the same old dress you've seen a hundred times."

"Well, it must be because you're so pretty," he said. "You make a dress look good. How old are you now, Hannah? You must be at least fifteen."

"Oh, Pa, you're always teasing me! You know I'll be seventeen this summer."

"Well, I didn't realize you were such an old lady," Hawk said. He was holding her loosely in his arms and pretended to see something. "Well, look at that!" he exclaimed, amazement in his voice.

"What is it, Pa? What is it you see?"

"A gray hair. You are getting to be an old lady."

"A gray hair! Where? Pull it out!"

Hawk laughed. "I don't see any gray hairs. I was just teasing you. He held her more tightly and put his head down. Her hair was fragrant, and he said, "Don't tell your mother I said this, but you're just about as pretty as she is."

"Oh, Pa! Be careful."

"I will. You take care of your mother now."

"I will, Pa."

Hawk went to his horse and nodded. "Everybody ready?"

He received a chorus of grunts, and all the men swung up into their saddles. There were cries of good-bye from friends and family, and all stood watching as the men rode down the road, disappearing finally behind a tall stand of hackberry trees.

"Well, they're gone."

Hannah was feeling sad, and she turned and walked away. Ethan Cagle, who had come over to see her, followed along. "I wish I were going," he said.

"You're too young to go, Ethan."

"Well, I'm old enough to pull a trigger, but my folks wouldn't let me go." The two walked on for some time, and finally Ethan said, "You're real sad, aren't you?"

"Yes, I am. I always worry when the men go off to fight." Suddenly she added, "I'm worried about Fox, too."

Of all the things that she might have said, mentioning her concern for Fox disturbed Ethan more than the rest. He had had little peace of mind since he had overheard the plot of Naaman Carter and Jasper Tatum, and now he was in a particularly bad mood. "I knew you'd be thinking about him."

Hannah turned to look at him with surprise. Her eyes were large and expressive, and she exclaimed, "Well, of course I'm worried about him! Aren't you?"

"It's not the same thing." He turned and quickly left, leaving

Hannah to stare after him in bewilderment.

The next day passed in a most miserable fashion for Ethan Cagle. It seemed that the secret he bore within him was growing larger and more painful to his conscience every passing hour. He had slept hardly at all the night after he had left Hannah. All night long he tossed and turned, going over in his mind what he could do to win her. He finally thought, *Eve is Hannah's best friend. She is always so thoughtful of everyone. I'll talk to her.* Feeling somewhat better, he fell into a fitful sleep.

Early the next morning, Ethan rose and, after having breakfast with his parents, made his way to the Martins' cabin. He knocked on the door and was greeted by Rebekah Martin.

"Hello, Ethan. It is good to see you. Have you had breakfast? We just finished, but there is plenty left."

"Thank you, Mrs. Martin, but I ate at home." Twisting his hands nervously, Ethan finally asked, "Could I speak to Eve, please?"

"Sure. She was just helping me clean up after breakfast. I'll get her for you." Rebekah went inside the cabin, and Eve came out moments later, pulling on her coat.

"Hello, Eve."

"Hello, Ethan. Ma said you wanted to see me."

"Yes." Ethan hesitated. "I know it's a little cold, but would you walk with me for a little while?"

"Of course."

The couple walked away from the cabin and toward the barn. Finally Ethan stopped and turned to Eve and blurted out, "I think I've done something terrible, Eve, and I don't know how to fix it."

"I'm sure whatever it is isn't all that awful. Just tell me about it."

The true concern and kindness that Ethan saw in Eve's gentle brown eyes encouraged him to continue. "I heard Naaman Carter discuss a plot with that Mr. Tatum to kill Fox in the upcoming fighting."

Eve put her hand to her mouth in shock. "Oh, Ethan."

"See, it is horrible, and what's even worse is that I heard it at Christmas and haven't told anybody because . . . well, because . . ."

Eve knew the reason, but she encouraged Ethan. "Yes, go on."

"Because I'm jealous of Fox and Hannah." Ethan hung his head as tears sprang to his eyes. "I feel so terrible. If Fox is killed, it will be my fault. Oh, Eve, what should I do? I'm so miserable."

Eve Martin put her hand on Ethan's back and stroked it lightly as he silently wept. "First of all, Ethan, you have to tell someone. I think God allowed you to hear those awful men in order to help Fox."

"But I've failed."

"Not yet you haven't. You must tell Hannah. She'll help you tell Sequatchie and he'll know what to do."

"But she'll hate me. And I'll lose her."

"Oh, Ethan, she's not yours to lose. She belongs to God, as we all do. God may help bring the two of you together one day, but He cannot be where there is deception and deceit. I'm not sure how Hannah feels about you or Fox. I'm not sure she knows herself yet, but you wouldn't want to try to win her this way. You would always have to live a lie."

"You're right, Eve. I have to tell her and Sequatchie."

Eve put her hand on his arm. "Before you go, let's pray that God will help you and protect Fox."

"I don't think God hears me anymore, Eve."

"He will always hear the prayer of a repentant heart. Ask for forgiveness and then pray for Fox."

Ethan dropped to his knees and cried out to God for forgiveness. Eve knelt beside him and prayed earnestly for him and for Fox.

Ethan rose, pulling up Eve with him. A new peace and determination were evident on his face. "Oh, Eve, I finally feel clean again. I never realized what the jealousy was doing to me. Thank you so much for talking to me."

"It was nothing, Ethan." In a moment of uncharacteristic boldness that shocked Eve herself, she reached up and planted a quick kiss on Ethan's cheek. "Go with God, Ethan Cagle."

Ethan looked with surprise at the young lady and, pushing her dark hair over her shoulder, kissed her gently on the lips. "I must hurry now, Eve. Thanks again."

Eve, her eyes shining, yelled after him, "I'll be praying for you and for Fox."

Ethan arrived at the Spencer cabin out of breath. He found Hannah down by the stream drawing water and, dismounting, went to her at once. "I've got to tell you something, Hannah."

Instantly Hannah feared that he had come with bad news about the battle. She put the bucket down and said quickly, "What is it, Ethan?"

"You remember when I went to feed the calf on Christmas Day?"

"Yes. I remember."

"Well, you remember you asked me if something had happened out there and I told you it hadn't?"

"Yes. I remember that."

"Well . . . I wasn't telling you the truth. While I was there I heard something. I should have told you before, but I just didn't do it."

"You heard something? What did you hear, Ethan?"

"I heard Naaman Carter and that fellow that runs around with him—Tatum's his name—talking outside the door."

"What were they saying?"

"They were talking about Fox. Hannah, they're going to try to kill him."

"Ethan, you don't mean it!"

"I do mean it."

"I knew he was an evil man. Fox told me that much. What did they say?"

"They hired some renegade Chickasaw Indians to kill Fox in the next battle. He won't expect it coming from an Indian, but that's what they plan to do."

"Ethan, we've got to get word to him."

"How do we do that, Hannah?"

"Sequatchie," Hannah cried at once. "We have to tell Sequatchie right now."

Hannah turned and fled and ran quickly toward Sequatchie's cabin. She saw Sequatchie outside chopping wood and went to him at once. "Sequatchie, I've got to talk to you."

"What is it, Hannah?"

"Ethan overheard something that you've got to know about."

Sequatchie turned. "What is it, Ethan?"

Ethan repeated his story and said miserably, "I should have told somebody, but I didn't."

"Yes, you should have, but it's not too late."

"Sequatchie, we've got to get word to Fox," Hannah said.

"You're right." Sequatchie laid the ax down and stood up. "I will go at once."

"Do you think you can find him?"

Sequatchie smiled at her question. "Yes. I know the ways of the Cherokee warriors. I can find my nephew."

"When will you go?"

"Within the hour. The fighting may have started, and Fox may already be in danger."

Sequatchie went in to tell Iris, and when he stepped back outside, he was wearing his buckskins. His powder horn was strung over his shoulder, his bullet pouch at his side, and his musket in his hands. Ethan saddled his horse for him, and when he swung into the saddle, he said, "You two pray to the great God. I will need His help."

Ethan gave Hannah a cautious glance, then picked up his musket, leaped astride his horse, and said to Sequatchie, "I'm going with you."

Hannah gasped, "Ethan, you can't! You don't have to do this for me. I know why you did it. I'm partly to blame, too. I forgive you. Please, don't do this."

"I can't do anything else, Hannah. Go tell my folks—and pray for us."

"I will. May God go with you."

Sequatchie and Ethan rode out of the yard and spurred their horses to a gallop.

"They've got to find him," Hannah whispered. "They've just got to! God, please help them."

The Battle of Flint Creek

Thirty-One

Ethan Cagle had always considered himself a fine horseman. Most young men living on the frontier could ride as well as the finest trained cavalry men, and Ethan was no exception.

But as the race to Flint Creek began, Ethan soon discovered that Sequatchie was an even finer rider than himself. Perhaps his horse was somewhat better, too, for after a hard four-hour ride, Ethan found his mare faltering, while Sequatchie's stallion forged steadily ahead.

"Sequatchie, we're going to break these horses down!" Ethan protested.

"Then we'll break them down," the Cherokee yelled over his shoulder.

"What good will that do? We can't run the rest of the way."

"We must press on."

Ethan was properly rebuked. He clamped his jaw together and whispered to his mare, "Come on, girl, you can do it."

They rode on, following trails that were often little more than pig paths where Ethan had to duck his head to get through cane fifteen feet high on each side. They raced their horses across creeks that were almost the size of rivers, and Ethan struggled to maintain the tremendous pace set by the aging Cherokee.

Finally Sequatchie pulled up and his face was set. "Flint Creek is right over there. We will go slowly from here on."

Ethan did not speak, but he thought, *We'll have to. These horses are almost done in.* He looked down and saw his own mare lathered, her side heaving for breath. "Do you think we'll be in time?"

"Haven't you heard the sounds of battle?"

Ethan closed his eyes and listened hard. "I don't hear anything except the wind," he said.

Sequatchie gave a snort of disgust. "Come on," he said. "We'll hobble the horses."

Quickly the two lashed their horses' legs, checked the loads in their muskets, and plunged into the forest. Sequatchie ran at a swift gait, and young and strong as he was, Ethan was hard pressed to keep up with him.

Finally Ethan whispered, "I hear it now."

"I should think so! They're right over that rise, but we don't know who we'll run into."

"We've got to find Fox and warn him about what's going on."

"You'll have to be quieter than you have been, Ethan," Sequatchie said. "You sound like a bull stomping through a house. Come on."

Now the firing was even more pronounced, and soon Ethan recognized it was coming from a thick part of the forest that spread out before them. He followed closely behind Sequatchie, trying desperately to be as quiet as possible. He noticed how Sequatchie's feet seemed to find just the places to avoid sticks and other objects that would cause noise, and he tried to do so himself. He winced every time he stepped on a twig or kicked a rock. "I'm sorry, Sequatchie. I'm just not a woodsman."

"You're young. You will learn."

"They must be close," Ethan whispered as musket fire rattled off to their right.

"We will go toward it," Sequatchie said.

"What if it's the enemy?"

"Then we'll have to back out and try again. I will not lift a gun against my Cherokee brothers. They are misled, and they must be brought to the truth. Come."

The two made their way silently through the thick woods. Finally the forest began to open up, and Sequatchie said, "Wait."

"What is it?"

"Over there. You see the smoke?"

Ethan looked to where Sequatchie gestured and said eagerly, "I see it, but I can't tell who it is."

"Follow me."

Sequatchie led the way as they maneuvered through undergrowth and half-grown saplings until finally they came up behind a group of armed white men. Sequatchie said, "We are fortunate."

"Why? Who is it?"

"Don't you see? It's Hawk." He cried out, "Hawk!"

Ethan saw a form disengage itself from a small group of trees and come running back. Hawk's face was blackened by the powder, and he came to stand before them, obviously surprised.

"What are you two doing here?" he demanded.

"We've got to find Fox, Hawk," Ethan said quickly.

"What are you talking about?"

Ethan hesitated. "I heard his uncle Naaman talking to that fellow Tatum that works for him. They've hired some renegade Chickasaws to see that Fox dies in the battle."

Instantly Hawk understood it all. "So that's what Naaman's got on his mind."

"Yes. You see it all, my brother," Sequatchie said. "If Fox dies, then the plantation will all belong to him."

"I never did trust that fellow," Hawk said. A musket ball came winging through the trees and cut the air above Hawk's head. It snapped a branch, which fell to the forest floor. Hawk ducked slightly and shook his head. "The main body's right ahead of us. I imagine Fox is there with Akando."

"We can't go straight into their fire," Sequatchie said. "We'll have to go around and take them on the flank."

"All right. I'll take the left and you take the right. If you find Fox, get him out of here."

"How is the battle going?"

"It's been pretty bad," Hawk said. "We've lost some good men and so have the Cherokee. I hate this sort of thing. But go now—we've got to find that boy."

Sequatchie nodded to Ethan. "Come." And immediately he set out at a trot. He circled the edge of the battle and moved until the firing grew somewhat fainter and more spasmodic. "This is the flank," he whispered. "We will go until we can come up behind them. It's not likely that we'll find Fox. We're more likely to run into Akando or some of his men. If we do and are outnumbered, we'll have to run."

Ethan swallowed. He had never been in a battle before but was determined to do his best.

Naaman and Jasper had come to see that the murder of young Fox Carter was accomplished. Naaman ordinarily would have stayed as far away as possible from a battle, but he had whispered to Jasper, "He's got to die. It's the only way that Havenwood will finally be mine."

The two had at first stayed in the rear of the battle, but Naaman had discovered that the Chickasaws had fled. One of the Cherokee had told him this with a sneer. "They were never good warriors," he said.

As the Cherokee threw himself back into the battle, Naaman turned to Jasper Tatum, his face twisted with anger. "We'll have to do the job ourselves, Jasper."

"Well, come on. We'll find him somewhere. The last time I heard, he and Akando were side by side."

The two made their way along the back of the fighting. Bullets were whistling through the air, and both the white settlers and the Cherokee were keeping well behind cover.

"Do you see him?" Naaman whispered hoarsely. He was out of breath, and his face was scratched by the vines and brambles.

"Look. There he is—over there."

Naaman saw Fox and said, "We'll settle this right now. Kill him, Tatum."

Jasper Tatum ran forward and saw Fox turn to face him. The young man's eyes flew open in recognition, and without a word, Tatum threw up his musket and pulled the trigger.

Tatum was no marksman, but at this range he could hardly miss. He saw the bullet strike Fox, and the young man fell. Fox moved to get up, holding on to his side, wincing, and reaching for his musket.

With a shout Naaman ran forward. "You're not stealing what's mine!" he screamed. "Finish him, Tatum!"

Tatum jumped on Fox and prepared to plunge his knife into him. Beneath the crazed white man, Fox was dazed by the force of the wound he had suffered. He saw the knife plunging downward and managed to put up his hand. He caught Tatum's wrist, and the two struggled. With Fox's recently acquired strength and skill, it should not have been difficult for him to overcome Tatum, but the bullet had momentarily numbed his entire side, and he saw the keen blade still descending toward his throat. A thought then came to Fox: *I'm going to die!*

"Uncle!" he gasped. "Don't allow this!"

"I'll kill you, you Indian whelp!" Tatum yelled.

Fox knew that death was only a few inches away. He felt Tatum wrench his arm free and watched as he raised the knife with a primal yell. There was nothing Fox could do. But the knife did not touch him! Suddenly, Tatum was knocked from Fox by a flying body. Tatum's head struck the ground hard and he lay still.

Fox raised himself up and saw Ethan Cagle standing over Tatum. Fox then saw his uncle Naaman go for Tatum's gun and aim for Ethan. Fox shouted, "Ethan! Look out!"

Fox quickly grabbed his own gun and fired. Naaman Carter looked in shock at his nephew and then fell dead.

Ethan ran over and knelt down. "Are you all right, Fox?"

"I've been shot, but it isn't bad, I don't think." He looked at the dead body of his uncle. "What's wrong with him? Why did he try to kill me? I didn't want to hurt him!"

"I think you know, Fox. He wanted all your land back in Virginia. He was possessed by greed and jealousy." Ethan then grinned sheepishly. "And I know what jealousy can do to a person."

Fox smiled back, and an understanding passed between the two as a new bond formed.

Akando suddenly appeared and saw Ethan kneeling beside Fox. His warriors were losing the battle. Many of them had fallen, and he knew he would never be able to rally them for another battle. He determined to kill Fox and the young man who was with him. He lifted his musket and pulled the trigger, but just as he did something struck the long barrel and knocked it up in the air so the ball cut through the trees above.

Akando whirled to see Sequatchie standing before him, a tomahawk in his hand and the light of battle in his eyes.

Akando pulled his own tomahawk from his belt. "I will kill you, Sequatchie! I've always wanted to. Then I will kill your half-breed nephew."

Sequatchie said, "All of your life you have turned away from those who would help you, Akando."

"It is you who needs help, Sequatchie. You have been blinded by the white men and their Jesus God. You have betrayed your people, and what good has it done? Still the white men take our land and unjustly steal our heritage. You are an old fool, Sequatchie."

"It is true, Akando, that the white men are taking our land. And, no, it is not just. But someday you will see that hatred is not the answer. Jesus is not simply the God of the white men. He is the one true God for all mankind, and that includes the Cherokee." Sequatchie paused, and the sound of muskets firing filled the forest. He looked deep into the mighty warrior's bitter eyes and said simply, "He loves you, Akando."

At this Akando leaped forward, screaming, "I will kill you, you traitor!" With one swift blow, his tomahawk sliced through the air. It would certainly have killed Sequatchie had it struck directly, but Sequatchie ducked and deftly swung his own tomahawk. The clash of metal on metal rang out as both weapons collided and flew from each man's hand. Akando then lunged at Sequatchie, and the two fell to the ground wrestling.

Sequatchie was stronger than most men, but Akando was the best of Cherokee warriors and soon had the advantage. He pummeled Sequatchie until his face was bruised and bloody, pinned him to the ground, and wrapped his powerful hands around his throat. "Where is your Jesus now?" Akando mocked as he strangled the older man.

"Get off of him!"

Akando suddenly turned around to see Fox standing above him, his father's pistol aimed squarely at Akando's chest.

Akando lifted his hands slowly and said, "Fox, don't do this. I am a Cherokee, just like you."

"We may both be Cherokee," Fox replied, "but your ways are not my ways. Now, get off of my uncle and get out of here!"

Suddenly Akando sprang up and ran toward Fox. A loud crack penetrated the air and Akando fell lifeless to the forest floor. A curl of blue smoke came from the barrel of Sequatchie's gun.

After a brief silence, Sequatchie said, "It is over." He then turned to Fox. "You are hurt, nephew."

"Not badly. The ball grazed me." Fox surveyed the beaten body of his uncle and shook his head. "I'm so sorry, Uncle," he said.

"It would be a lot worse if not for you. Come. We must get away," Sequatchie said.

Ethan had now joined them, and he and Sequatchie roused

Tatum and tied him up. They then helped to get Fox away from the battle, where they stopped and stripped off his shirt, stanched the blood, and bound the wound tightly with a makeshift bandage.

Sequatchie left them to go back to the battle, and the two young men sat silently for a time. Finally Ethan said, "I have to ask your forgiveness, Fox."

"Forgiveness for what?"

"I knew about your uncle Naaman's plan to kill you. I overheard him telling Tatum, and I didn't tell anyone right away."

Fox turned his eyes on the young man. "But you did come, Ethan. You saved my life. I'll never forget that."

At that moment Sequatchie came back, and Hawk was with him. "The battle is over," he said. "I hope it's the last one."

"The Cherokee are defeated?" Ethan asked eagerly.

"For now," Hawk said. "We'll have to work out an agreement, but it'll need to be more fair than anything we've given them so far."

"I found out one thing, Hawk," Sequatchie said. "Akando's second-in-command was a man named Adahy. He was captured in battle and was very bitter. But he did tell me one thing." Sequatchie studied the face of his nephew. "He said that it was Akando who hired those two renegade whites to kill me and your mother. It wasn't a white plan at all."

Suddenly Fox understood. "He planned it so that I would come with him and hate white people."

"That's right."

Fox took a deep breath and for a long time seemed to be searching for the right words. "That makes more sense. I was so confused about the whole thing. Now I feel better."

"I think things will indeed be much better for you, nephew," Sequatchie said.

Despite the settlers' victory, a sadness lingered in the air, for many brave men had been lost on both sides and now had to be buried. After this had been done and the wounded had been cared for, the party finally made its way homeward.

Fox spoke a while later to Sequatchie. "What will happen now, Uncle? I mean about Havenwood."

"That's something you will have to decide. You could go back there and have an easy life."

"I'm not sure I want to. The only thing I'm sure of now is I want to go home with you."

As they rode along, Fox thought often of Hannah and wondered how she felt about him now. Finally, after much doubt swept over him, he came to a conclusion. *If she really cares for me, I'll find out about it,* he thought. *And then I'll know what to do.*

Fox's True Home

Thirty-Two

Fox Carter lay in the main room of Sequatchie and Iris's cabin. He straightened up and took a deep breath. It was March now, and the pain was completely gone from his side. The bullet had torn some muscles and cracked a rib, and it had taken several weeks to regain his strength. Ezekiel and Mercy, who were living with Sequatchie and Iris again, had helped nurse him back to health. He felt a surge of gratitude as he looked over toward Sequatchie, who was watching him carefully.

"The pain is gone, Uncle," he said.

"God has been good to you."

"Yes, He has." Fox surprised himself by agreeing to this, but he had been thinking about God more frequently of late. Fox stood and said, "I think I'll take a short walk. I'm tired of lying around."

"Take it easy and don't go too far this time. You are still not fully well."

"All right, Uncle."

Fox thrilled to be outside again. He reveled in the sights and sounds of spring beginning to find its way into the Appalachian Mountains. Fox chose a well-worn path and slowly walked along. He began to think of all that had happened to him over the past years since he had come to Franklin. With sadness, he remembered all of those he had lost: his mother, his father, his grandfather, and even his uncle Naaman. He was glad he felt no hatred for his uncle, only pity. He had had Thomas Denton send word of Naaman's death to his aunt Julia, his grandmother Naomi, and Linus and Lydia. He wasn't sure what they would do without Naaman. He then wondered about Jasper Tatum, who had escaped from the jail after he had been escorted back from the battle at Flint Creek. Tatum had long since disappeared from the area. Fox hoped he wouldn't cause any more trouble for him or his family. As Fox continued reflecting on his life, he realized he was more at peace now about his mixed heritage, but he also realized he still did not have a place to call home.

As Fox walked by a grove of maple trees, he heard the song of a mockingbird. He immediately thought of Hannah Spencer and the special day they had shared together in the woods. He began to think of all the things she had told him about God and how anyone could have a home with Him. Fox suddenly knew what he needed to do. Without ceremony, he simply lifted his face to the sky and prayed, "Father in heaven, please forgive me for all my sins. I am sorry for not trusting in you and for doing things that have hurt you. Please come into my heart and make it your home." Fox lowered his face and whispered, "Thank you," as a peace that passes all understanding washed over his soul. Fox slowly returned to Sequatchie's cabin, knowing he would never be without a home again as long as he trusted in God.

Hannah had been in the smokehouse adding green wood to the fire. She stepped outside and saw a shadow to her left. Turning around quickly, her hand flew to her mouth. "Fox, you startled me."

"I'm sorry." Coming closer, he studied her face and said, "Do you have time? I'd like to talk to you."

"Certainly. You want to come inside? Pa's there. He'll be glad to see you, and so will Ma and Josh."

"Not right now. Could we take a walk out through the fields?"

"If you like."

The sun was high overhead, and the March breeze cut through the woods. Their feet rustled the dead leaves of the year gone by, and neither of them spoke for a time. Finally they reached an open field, and stopping abruptly, Fox said, "I've got to tell you something, Hannah. Something happened to me last week." He began at once to speak of his newfound faith, and he ended by saying, "I've made such a mess out of everything. I've been so mixed-up."

"Well, of course you have. Who wouldn't have been mixed-up? I know losing your mother was terrible. And I think I understand a little bit how hard it must be for someone to have two vastly different heritages."

"I think you do understand, Hannah," Fox said quietly. "You have always seemed to understand me better than anyone else."

Hannah blushed and quickly asked, "What will you do now? Will you go back to Virginia to your plantation?"

"I'm not sure. I don't have very many good memories back there, and now that Mother's gone, I just don't know. I've thought of maybe allowing my cousins to live there while I stay out here."

Hannah's eyes sparkled. "I wish you would, Fox."

"Do you really, Hannah?"

"Why, of course I do!"

Fox took a deep breath and plunged onward. "I'm glad to hear that, because I want you to know that I've come to care for you a great deal, Hannah Spencer. I'm not sure of what my future holds, but I am sure that I want you in it somewhere."

"Oh, Fox, I feel the same way. I am coming to care for you more and more every day."

"What about Ethan?"

"I think Ethan may be spending more time with Eve, from what I understand."

"How do you feel about that?"

Hannah smiled. "If they fall in love, I will be very happy for them both. I do care for Ethan, but I don't think I care for him as I do for you."

Fox could not resist any longer. He took Hannah by the shoulders and kissed her tenderly on the lips. Pulling back, he said, "I still have to come to terms with both of my heritages, but with God in my heart and you supporting me, I know I'll make it just fine."

Hannah smiled back at Fox and said, "I know you'll be fine, too."

That evening Hawk and Elizabeth sat on their front porch enjoying the beginning of warmer weather. Hawk put his arm around his wife and said, "Well, old woman, we may be losing another daughter in the not-so-distant future."

Elizabeth poked Hawk and said, "Watch who you're calling old. You're not so young yourself." She kissed him and then said, "I think Hannah would do well to get Fox as a husband. But they're still a little ways away from that yet. We just need to pray that God will work His will in their lives. Besides, it's Joshua I think we should be more concerned about. I don't like this notion of his traipsing off to Nashville to join Andrew Jackson. He is much too young."

Hawk sighed. "I'm afraid he won't be too young too much longer. I don't really like the idea either, but we have to give him room to make some of his own decisions."

"I know, but that doesn't mean I have to like them. What do you think the future holds for our children?"

"Well, North Carolina has finally ratified the Constitution. We're going to have one central government now. I'm glad that George Washington is going to be the first president. He is a fair and honest man. And now that North Carolina has also ceded these lands to the government, we can try again to form us a state so that we can be represented in the new government."

"When we do become a state, it will make this area a better place to live for our children and grandchildren. They'll have a voice in the government and in the shaping of this new country. I'm sure that Andrew Jackson will have a say in the future of this land, too. Whether that is good or not remains to be seen, but Josh sure thinks it's wonderful. He's ready to tag along with him anywhere." Hawk paused a moment and then continued. "I hope everthing turns out all right for Hannah and Fox. I'm afraid he may still be facing some tough times with his heritage. With this area becoming a state, it could mean more trouble for the Cherokee.

"What do you mean more trouble for the Cherokee?" Elizabeth asked.

"A new state will mean more people coming across the mountains to settle here. This means less room for the Cherokee. I'm afraid their way of life may be coming to an end. I know it pains Sequatchie greatly, but he prays that despite their suffering—or maybe because of it—his people will come to know the love of Jesus."

Elizabeth snuggled closer to her husband. "I'm just glad Sequatchie still has Iris. Like I know you're glad you have me."

Hawk looked at his wife with affection in his eyes. "God couldn't have been any better to me than when He allowed you to fall in love with me."

With tears in her eyes, Elizabeth kissed her husband. "You do have your moments, Hawk Spencer. You do have your moments."

Epilogue

April 1789

Julia Carter sat in the parlor of her Williamsburg home in stunned silence. She had just heard from Jasper Tatum that her husband was dead at the hands of his nephew. Linus and Lydia had also been completely caught off guard by the news. Linus had listened the most carefully as Tatum told them his version of what had happened at the Battle of Flint Creek. He then went into a long discourse of his escape and subsequent journey to Williamsburg.

Julia cut him off, numbly thanking him and telling him he could return to his old job at Havenwood.

Linus rose and escorted Tatum to the door. "Don't you tell anyone the truth of what happened, or I'll make sure you hang."

Tatum nodded and hurried away.

Returning to his mother and sister, Linus put his arm around his mother's shoulders. Julia wept silently for a time. Lydia also wept as her mother tried to comfort her.

Finally Julia dried her eyes and said, "I must go upstairs and tell your grandmother."

"What are you going to tell her?" Linus asked. "You can't tell her what really happened."

"I know that, Linus. She thinks Naaman went to search for Nathanael to bring him and Awinita home. I will simply tell her that he died in an Indian attack while searching for them." Julia held her head erect as she ascended the staircase. She was not sure what would happen to her and Linus and Lydia now, but she knew she must be strong for all of them.

Linus moved to his father's study and Lydia followed. She watched as Linus slowly walked behind the desk and sat in his father's chair. He steepled his fingers in front of his mouth and said, "At least the squaw is dead, too."

Lydia cried out, “Linus!”

“Well, Father never cared for her and I didn’t either. If she had never married Titus, none of this would have happened.”

Lydia feared for her brother as she watched the bitterness creep into his face and seemingly even his very soul.

“Now we just have to make sure that Cousin Nate pays for what he has done. I think it is time to go hunting for a Fox. Don’t you agree, Lydia?”

Blood pounded in Lydia Carter’s temples as a dread for what the future held settled heavily on her.

Notes to Our Readers

Another chapter in THE SPIRIT OF APPALACHIA has now come to an end. We hope you have enjoyed the book. Thanks again to all of our readers for your kind words and wonderful support. You are a true gift from God!

We always pray that our books will minister to those who read them. We pray that all of our readers who have not found their home in Christ will turn to Him as Fox did and find that peaceful place to dwell forever.

The history of these first western settlers has always fascinated us. The story of "The Lost State of Franklin," as it is now called, is accurate. Politics kept this area from becoming a state until 1796. John Sevier was the governor of this short-lived state, and the meeting at Dumplin Creek and the Battle of Flint Creek were true historic events. Sadly, so was the massacre at John Kirk's place.

Andrew Jackson did live in the state of Franklin for a short period of time before moving west to Nashville. He did ride in the race at Greasy Cove and lose to the horse of Robert Love. We don't know if he really stood with John Sevier and young Davy Crockett at one place, but they were all living in the area at the time, so who knows? We found it an exciting idea that three people who played such important roles in the history of Tennessee, as well as the history of the whole nation, could have met on such an occasion.

The Reverend Samuel Doak did establish Martin's Academy in 1783. This was the first educational institution between the Appalachian Mountains and the Mississippi River. It was then chartered by the state of North Carolina. It received a charter from the state of Franklin in 1785. In 1795 it was chartered by the legislature of the "Territory of the United States South of the River Ohio" and renamed Washington College.

There will be at least one more journey over the Misty Mountains. Joshua Spencer will have more adventures with the enigmatic Andrew Jackson as the state of Tennessee struggles to be born. We hope you will join us!

Gilbert Morris &
Aaron McCarver